RECKLESS TO LOVE YOU

J. SAMAN

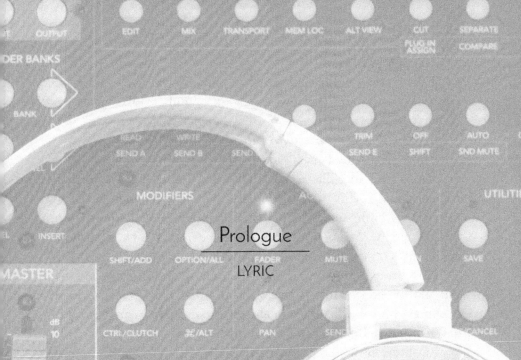

Prologue

LYRIC

I can't stop staring at it. Reading the two short words over and over again ad nauseam. They're simple. Essentially unimpressive if you think about it. But those two words mean everything. Those two words dive deep into the darkest depths of my soul, the part I've methodically shut off over the years, and awaken the dormant volcano. How can two simple words make this well of emotions erupt so quickly?

Come home.

I don't recognize the number the text came from. It shows up as Unknown. But I don't have to recognize it. I know who it's from. Instinctively, I know. At least, my body does, because my heart rate is through the roof. My stomach is clenched tight with violent, poorly concealed, sickly butterflies. My forehead is clammy with a sheen of sweat and my hands tremble as they clutch my phone.

It's early here in California. Not even dawn, but I'm awake. I'm always awake, even when I'm not, and since my phone has, unfortunately, become another appendage, it's consistently with me.

It's a New York area code.

Goddammit! I suck in a deep, shuddering breath of air that does absolutely nothing to calm me, then I respond in the only way I can.

Me: **Who is this?**

The message bubble appears instantly, like he was waiting for me. Like there is no way this is a wrong number. Like his fingers couldn't respond fast enough.

Unknown: **You know who this is. Come home.**

I don't respond. I can't. I'm frozen. It's been four years. Four fucking years. And this is how he reaches out? This is how he contacts me? I slink back down into my bed, pulling the heavy comforter over my head in a pathetic attempt to protect myself from the onslaught of emotions that consume me. I tuck my phone against my chest, over what's left of my fractured heart.

I'm hurting. I'm angry. I'm so screwed up and broken, and yet, I'm still breaking. How is that even possible? How can a person continue to break when they're already broken? How can a person I haven't seen in four years still affect me like this?

I want to throw the traitorous device into the wall and smash it. Toss it out my window as hard as I can and hope it reaches the Pacific at the other end of the beach, where it will be swept away, never to return. But I don't. Because curiosity is a nefarious bitch. Because I have to know why the man who was my everything and now my nothing is contacting me after all this time, asking me to come home.

Unknown: **I'm sitting here in my old room, on my bed, and I can't focus. I can't think about what I need to be thinking about. So, I need you to come home.**

I shake my head as tears line my eyes, stubbornly refusing to fall but obscuring my vision all the same. Nothing he's saying makes sense to me. Nothing. It's completely nonsensical, and yet, it's not. I still know him well enough to understand both what he's saying and what he's not.

Me: **Why?**

Unknown: **Because I need you to.**

Me: **I can't. Too busy with work.**

That's sort of a lie. I mean, I *am* headed to New York for the Rainbow Ball in a few days. But he doesn't need to know that. And I do not want to see him. I absolutely, positively, do not.

2

Unknown: ***My dad had a stroke***

My eyes cinch shut, and I cover them with one hand. I can't breathe. A gasped sob escapes the back of my throat, burning me with its raw taste. God. Now what the hell am I going to do? I love his father. Jesus Christ. How can I say no to him now? How can I avoid this the way I so desperately need to? *Shit.*

Me: ***I'm sorry. I didn't know. Is he okay?***

Unknown: ***He'll live, but he's not great. He's in the ICU. Worse than he was after the heart attack.***

I shake my head back and forth. I can't go. I can't go home. I was there two months ago to visit my parents and my sister's family. I have work—so much freaking work that I can barely keep up. I don't want to see him. I won't survive it. I'll see him, and I'll feel everything I haven't allowed myself to feel. I'll be sucked back in.

Things are different now.

They are. My situation has changed completely, but I never had the guts to call him and tell him that. Mostly because I was hurt. Mostly because I felt abandoned and brushed off. Mostly because I was terrified that it wouldn't matter after all this time apart. If I see him now, knowing how much has changed…Shit. I just…Fuck. I can't.

I don't know what to do.

I'm drenched in sweat. The blanket I sought refuge in is now smothering me. I'm relieved his father is alive. I still speak to him once a month. Wait, let me amend that—he still *calls* me once a month. And we talk. Not about Jameson. Never about him. Only about me and my life. I'm a wreck that Jameson is contacting me. I can't play this game. I never could. It was all or nothing with him.

Unknown: ***I miss you.***

I stare at the words, read them over again, then respond too quickly, ***Liar.***

Unknown: ***Never. I miss you so goddamn much.***

I think I just died. Everything inside me has stopped. My heart is not beating. My breath has stalled inside my chest, unable to be expelled. My mind is completely blank. And when everything comes back to life, I'm consumed with an angry, caustic fury I never knew I was capable of.

Unknown: *Are you still there?*

Me: *What do you want me to say?*

Unknown: *I don't know. I'm torn on that. Please come home.*

Me: *Why?*

Unknown: *Because I need you. Because he needs you. Because I was always too busy obsessing over you to fall for someone else. Because I need to know if I'm making a mistake by hoping.*

I shake my head vigorously, letting out the loudest, shrillest shriek I can muster. It's not fucking helping, and I need something to help. Clamoring out of bed, I hurry over to the balcony doors, unlocking them and tossing them open wide.

Fresh air. I need fresh air. Even Southern California fresh air. A burst of salty, ocean mist hits me square in the face, clinging to the sweat I'm covered in. It's still dark out. Dawn is not yet playing with the midnight-blue sky.

I stare out into the black expanse of the ocean, listen to the crashing of the waves and sigh. I knew about him. I would be lying if I said I hadn't Facebook-stalked him a time or twenty over the years. Forced myself to hate him with the sort of passion reserved for political figures and pop stars. But this? Saying he misses me?

Me: *Seeing me won't change that. But if you're asking, you are.*

He responds immediately, and I can't help but grin a little at that. *You still care about me, Jameson Woods.* When I catch the traitorous thought, I shut it down instantly. Because if he cared, if his texted words meant anything, then I wouldn't be here, and he wouldn't be there, and this bullshit four a.m. text conversation wouldn't be happening.

Unknown: *I'm not asking. Seeing you might change everything. But more than that, I need you here with me. My father would want to see you. Come home.*

I hate him. I hate him. I hate him!

Me: *I can't come home. Stop using your father to manipulate me.*

Unknown: *It's the only play I have. You can come home. I know you can. Are you seeing someone? Before you respond, any answer other than no might kill me right now.*

I growl, not caring if anyone walking by hears. How can he do this to me? How can he be so goddamn selfish? Doesn't he know what he put me through? That I still haven't found my way back after four years? I shouldn't reply. I should just throw my phone away and never look back.

Me: *No. And you're a bastard.*

Unknown: *YES. I Am! Please. I am officially begging. Really, Lee. I'm not even bullshitting. I'm a mess. Please. Please. Please!!!!*

Me: ...

Unknown: *What does that mean?*

Me: *It means I'm thinking. Stop!*

My eyes lock on nothing, my mind swirling a mile a minute.

Lee. He called me Lee. That nickname might actually hurt the most. And now he's asking me to come home. Jameson Woods, the man I thought was my forever, is asking me to come home to see him. And for what? To scratch a long-forgotten itch? To assuage some long-abandoned guilt over what he did? Why would I fall for that?

I sigh again because I know why. It's the same reason I never bring men home. It's the same reason I haven't given up this house even though I don't fully live in it anymore and it's far from convenient. It's the same reason I continued this conversation instead of smashing my phone.

Jameson Woods.

The indelible ink on my body. The scar on my soul. The fissure in my heart.

Unknown: ...

I can't help the small laugh that squeaks out as I lean forward and prop my elbows on the edge of the railing. The cool wind whips through my hair, and I hate that I feel this way. That I'm entertaining him the way I am.

Me: **What does that mean?**

Unknown: **It means I'm getting impatient. Please. I need you to come home. I know I'm a bastard. I know I shouldn't be asking you this. But I am.**

Unknown: **Aren't you at least a little curious?**

YES!

Me: **NO!!!!!!! And bastard doesn't cover you.**

Unknown: **Please. It's spinning out of control, and I need to see you. I need to know.**

Me: **You already know.**

Unknown: **About you?**

Me: **Yes, or you wouldn't be texting me at four in the morning.**

Unknown: **It's seven here. Does that mean you'll come?**

Me: ...

Unknown: ...

Me: **Yes**.

My phone slips from my fingers, clanging to the hard surface of my balcony floor. My phone buzzes again, a little louder now since the sound is reverberating off the ground. I don't pick it up. I don't look down. I don't care if he's thanking me or anything else he comes up with. I don't care. I don't want to know.

Because I'm busy getting my head on straight.

Locking myself down.

I'm worried about his father and I want to see him, want to make sure he's okay with my own two eyes.

I'll go home and I'll see him. I'll see him, and I'll do the one thing I was never able to do before. I'll say goodbye. My eyes close and I allow myself to slip back. To remember every single moment we had together. To indulge in the sweet torture that, if I let it, will rip me apart piece by piece. Because I know what I'm in for, and I know that once I step foot off that airplane, nothing will ever be right again.

Chapter One
LYRIC

Six years ago

"YOU'RE NEW HERE," the girl on my right says just as my ass hits the hard plastic of my chair. Her accusation, mixed with the inquisitive expression on her face, makes me wish I had been a bit more discerning in my seating choice, but when you don't know anyone, you tend to find any seat in the middle. The non-stick-out seat as I refer to it. Evidently, it's not living up to its name.

"Is this school that small?" I question in return instead of answering.

I am new. First day of my first semester in this new school to be exact. A transfer student in my junior year, but I have a reason. This school is known for its music and business program. Both separate obviously, but considering I'm a music major and business minor, it's sort of perfect. I was at NYU, thinking that would be the best place for me, but it really wasn't. It was pretty fucking unhelpful actually. My father warned me about that. I hate it when he's right, but he usually is, so maybe it's time I start listening.

My pretty neighbor nods, her rose-tinted lips pinching up into something resembling a scowl, her dark blonde bob moving with her head like they're one unit. She has deep, soulful eyes, porcelain skin, and a hoop through her nose. She pushes up the bridge of her stylishly too-big, black-framed glasses and smiles. "Unfortunately, yes. I'm Cassia, but everyone calls me Cass."

"Lyric."

"Oh," she gasps, eyes wide. "Pretty name. Unusual. Do you do something with music?"

I get this question a lot. Every time I introduce myself to someone. Like the name given to me at birth dictates the meaning behind my life. The sad part? It does. And I kind of hate telling people that. It makes me wish my rock-star father hadn't been so literal in naming me. I'd much rather have been named something nondescript. Something like Jessica or Tessa or Julie or Megan. Something that wouldn't draw attention to my passion or his. Music.

My eyes inadvertently draw down and I catch sight of her T-shirt. Jimmy Eat World. I smile. I like them, too.

Instead of answering, I laugh it off, quickly changing the subject as I try to evade the question. I don't know her well enough to answer that one yet. "How did you know I was new?"

She shrugs like the answer should be obvious. "I've never seen you here before. Five thousand is small enough that you notice everyone, and you don't have that doe-eyed, new puppy look about you that suggests freshman. Plus, this is advanced corporate finance, which is an upperclassman course."

Observant little thing, isn't she? "Well, you're good. I am new. First day. Junior transfer."

She sits up straight, my answer supplying her with a burst of new energy. Her shoulders square as she shifts to face me, but before her eyes can meet mine again, her attention diverts to the front of the classroom. Her mouth pops open, and her cheeks pink up just enough for me to know she's staring at someone she finds attractive.

On instinct, I turn in the direction of her gaze and land directly on Jameson Woods the Third. How do I know his name and the fact that he's the third of his male ancestors with that exact name when this is my first day here?

I went to high school with him.

And now I sigh out loud. I can't even stop it.

For some reason, his presence in my fresh start irritates me. It's inexplicable, really. I never had a problem with Jameson Woods. Even when he ruined a friend of mine or six, I understood what he was. I even appreciated his brutal honesty when he told the girls he enjoyed his fun and wanted nothing more. In my mind, it was on them for getting attached to a guy they knew better than to get attached to. There is no taming the bad boy. There is no making the chronic player a monogamist.

He strolls aimlessly around the large, tiered lecture hall, his eyes filled with boredom and a blatant lack of desire to be here at nine a.m. on a Monday—day one of the semester. Before he catches me in the act, I take a few seconds to check him out. I'm not the only one. Every other female's eyes are glued to him. A few of the guys, too.

I allow myself to take him in.

Hair, thick and black like a raven. Short on the sides, long and tousled on top to the point of flopping onto his forehead in an I-just-rolled-out-of-bed-after-having-sex-all-night way. Strong, chiseled jaw with a hint of dark stubble, which he scratches absentmindedly. Eyes, the palest of blue like a freaking husky dog, framed in impossibly long, dark lashes. Tall, built, and tan with muscles for miles. The cotton of his t-shirt—the same shade of black as his hair—strains against his form.

Cocky swagger? Check. Confident smirk? Double check. Too good looking to be legal or even real? Unfortunately, yes.

Bastard has all of that in spades and knows it.

He's the equivalent of a king-sized candy bar. So deceptively tempting. Looks so enticingly ideal. Large, delicious, and promises endless pleasure—or so the rumors tried to sell it to you—while you indulge. But you know that once you give in, once you eat that whole goddamn candy bar, you'll regret it. Mostly because he unapologetically screwed every single girl in our high school while maintaining the persona of the nice guy and was hated by no one. Not even the girls he left in the dust with a smile and a broken heart.

I never got involved with his drama. I listened with patience and understanding when my friends cried on my shoulder and berated themselves for giving in to what they knew better than to taste.

I had a boyfriend for most of high school, which is probably why I can't stand the notion of one now. I have to admit, I've relished my freedom like a rogue fish in the ocean.

Jameson I-know-every-woman-is-watching-me Woods runs a hand through his perfect hair. I find myself rolling my eyes at him, a wry smile twisting on my lips. I move back to my neighbor, but she's still all googly eyes—something I would not have thought coming from a bad-ass chick like this—for the hot bod. I inadvertently roll my eyes again, wishing for the second time in ten minutes that I had sat somewhere else.

"I know you," a deep timbre wrapped in pure, heated sex says, rumbling through the room like thunder before the rain on a summer night. I don't have to look over my shoulder to know he's talking to me. I can feel his eyes on me, electrically raising the hairs on the back of my neck and causing my stomach to do an annoying swooping thing. I don't acknowledge him. In my estimation, he's gotten too much female attention in his life, and I like the idea of making him work for it.

Or maybe I'm being unfair to him. After all, it's been years since I've seen him.

"Melody, right?"

Or maybe I was spot on. *Dick.* Melody is my sister's name. She's four freaking years older than me and was the goddess of our school and town. He knows I'm not Melody. He was good friends with my boyfriend in high school, and by extension, friendly with me. He knows I'm Lyric. So yeah, dick seems to work.

The feet of the chair beside mine screech in protest against the linoleum floor before his large body descends into the seat and he slides himself in. I'm still facing Cass, whose dark chocolate eyes have officially bugged out of her head.

"You know him?" she whisper-shouts, like the guy is not actually sitting on the other side of me within hearing range. "Totally would not have pegged you for the hot jock type. No judgement, but really?" She scrunches her nose up in distaste now that she's past her physical admiration of him.

"Of course, Music knows me. We go way back."

I close my eyes and release a silent breath. Couldn't he just have kept going? Ignored me the way I'm ignoring him? I haven't moved, but I'm getting closer to turning and giving this arrogant prick exactly what he's after. My irritation.

"You do know him?"

I nod.

"Do you want me to get rid of him? I can be a scary bitch when needed."

Jameson chuckles, and a large, well-groomed hand extends beyond me toward Cass. "Jameson," he says smoothly. "Pleasure to meet any friend of Sonata's."

I can't stop my growl this time, and I hate that I just gave in to him because now he's laughing instead of chuckling, and his chair is moving just that much closer to mine. And hell, that laugh.

"I'm Cass. You do know her name is Lyric, right? I seriously cannot tell if you're just being a dick or if you really don't know her name."

"He's being a dick."

"You sure about that name, Cass? She looks more like an Opera to me."

"And by that, you mean artistic, classic, and timelessly beautiful?" I say in a saccharine sweet voice, unable to stop it. My back is still to him because I haven't dared to face him yet.

"Timelessly beautiful, maybe, but I'd say more like, overly dramatic, brightly colored, and larger than life."

I can't help the small bubble of a laugh at that. I'm wearing a bright yellow shirt, ripped pink jeans, and black Chucks. *Touché.*

His shoulder nudges into my back, rubbing up and down once. "Nice to see you again, *Lyric.*"

I turn, unable to resist the pull. I can't determine if it's curiosity or annoyance fueling me on. And hell, he's even better up close. I don't remember him looking like this when we were in high school. I remember him being tall, yes, but lankier and less defined. His hair wasn't this caliber of perfection, either.

College has turned Jameson Woods into a full-fledged man. He smiles at me, big and bright like he's actually happy to see me, showcasing his perfect teeth and the tiniest hint of a dimple in his cheek. "Are you done checking me out yet? If not, take your time, because it's giving me an excuse to do the same to you."

I roll my eyes at him and he gleams. I forgot what a flirt he could be.

"Football?"

"Soccer and baseball. Singer?"

"Producer."

"Living on campus or in private housing?"

"Campus in a single. You?"

"Off-campus house with two friends."

"Finance major?"

"Business and finance." Jameson leans in and whispers in my ear, his warm breath brushing across my skin. "Charlie mentioned you were transferring here."

I turn fully to him, scrunching my eyebrows. I'm still vaguely friendly with my ex, as I am with most people we went to high school with, but not *that* friendly. I definitely don't recall mentioning that I was coming here.

"He Facebook stalks you, I think." He throws me a wink and then grabs a beat-up notebook from his equally worn black shoulder bag and tosses it on the desktop, followed by a pen that has been chewed on and then some.

"I never go on Facebook, and I haven't talked to him in forever."

Jameson shrugs, popping the end of that pen into his mouth and rolling it around between his teeth a time or two before taking it out to speak again. "Don't know what to tell you about that. I've been avoiding that guy like herpes for over a year now. You're not the only one he stalks, and a straight dude stalking another straight dude is just fucked. So, what the hell brings you here? I thought you were in New York."

"I was. This school has a better program." I leave it at that without elaborating. And really, I like New York, but I didn't love living there. The constant hustle and bustle and overpopulation mixed with tiny, cockroach-infested living conditions grated on me.

"Wait. You left New York to come here?" Cass interjects, her tone incredulous.

I can only offer her a half-shrug and a placating grin. I don't have much of an explanation that I'm willing to divulge. My father is a music legend. Rock-and-roll royalty. His band, Burnt Tears, is on Rolling Stones' top twenty bands of all-time list. Every music conservatory I applied to only saw his name. The students and professors at NYU were only interested in him and not me. This school may be small and pretty much in the middle-of-nowhere Tennessee, but it has a dedicated music-development program that gave zero fucks about my last name or industry lineage.

"I knew you were a music person," she continues, satisfied in her previous assumption. "I am, too, actually, but I'm a pianist. I take it you haven't met Saylor, yet?" she asks cautiously.

I shake my head. Cass pushes up the bridge of her glasses and sags a little like she's relieved by this. "You will, and when you do, you'll know it. That's all I'm saying."

"Saylor Ramsey?" Jameson asks, and Cass nods. "Nice girl. I hang out with her sometimes."

"Of course, you do," Cass says, not even bothering to hide her sarcasm. "She's bitchy Taylor Swift goes to college."

I can't help but laugh at that.

"As entertaining as this is to watch, you both realize that class started like two minutes ago, right?" I interrupt, jutting my chin toward the front of the room. Cass and Jameson track my movement toward the professor, who closely resembles a neo-Nazi fascist complete with sharp features, brown tweed skirt suit that ends mid-calf, and a severe expression. Given the fact that this is an advanced corporate finance course, I give the woman my undivided attention.

I punch my password into my laptop and pull up a blank page in my finance folder, ready to take notes.

"Shit, I forgot how organized you are." Jameson leans over, trying to get a better look at my screen. His large frame brushes against mine, the heavenly scent of his body wash or cologne or whatever, permeating the air around me.

"Back off," I mutter, trying to elbow him back and getting nowhere in the process. He's too close. Too unexpected.

He offers me a sly grin, flipping open the first page of his notebook and scribbling something down on it before sliding it across the table and angling it for me to see. "Truth or dare?"

I read the words and then glance up at him with a raised eyebrow. He returns the gesture, his expression mocking, and I'm helpless to stop my smile. I reach over and point to truth.

He nods like he knew that's where I was going and then writes, "You're even prettier than you were in high school."

I do my best to ignore the flutters. And the butterflies. And hold in my smile this time. He taps on his first question, truth or dare, again with his chewed pen. I shake my head, knowing how fast this little game can go downhill. He does it again, nudging his elbow into my side. I follow the professor, who is going on about the syllabus and expectations for the semester, using my pen to point to dare.

"Study with me," he speaks aloud instead of writing it.

That's not what I was expecting after his pretty comment. I'm unable to decipher if *study* is a euphemism for something else, but then I catch the sober expression he's pinning me with, and I can't help but stare back at him, utterly baffled. He licks his lips nervously and then leans into me, pressing his chest against my arm and shoulder and whispers directly into my ear, his breath warm against my sensitive skin, "I need an A in this class, Lee, and I won't be able to do it on my own. You're smart and organized. Will you study with me?"

Lee?

He pulls back, watching me intently.

"I'm not fucking you," I warn.

He smirks, tilting his head to the side, his black hair falling across his forehead, his wolf-like eyes bouncing around my face feature by feature. "I'm not asking you to. Promise."

"Just studying?"

"Just studying."

"Okay," I relent with an exaggerated sigh. "But I have a feeling I'm going to regret this."

His eyes continue that inventory of me and then that smirk turns into an impish grin, his eyes twinkling with mischief. "And I have a feeling I'm going break my promise."

Chapter Two

JAMESON

"Dude, are you gonna answer your phone?" Cane asks, standing on the threshold of my bedroom door.

I'm lying on my bed with my arms tucked under my head, staring straight up at my ceiling. My stepmother has been calling me all afternoon about Thanksgiving, and I have no desire to join her and my father when they go to her family in Canada. Her family hates me. Views me as the bastard stepson—which I guess I sort of am. I already told her last week that I wasn't going, so I have no idea why she continues to blow up my phone.

"It's my stepmother, so no. I have zero desire to listen to her bullshit, half-hearted guilt trip about going to fucking Canada."

"Why the hell is she nagging you about that now? It's only September."

I shrug with one shoulder since my other arm is behind my head. Damn, I'm sore. "Because she wants to buy plane tickets and evidently me telling her I'm not going is not a good enough answer for her."

"I thought you told her you were coming home with me?"

I lower my chin and meet Cane's brown eyes.

"I did. Why do you think I'm not picking up? I'm tired. I'm sore as balls from practice, and the last thing I want to do right now is talk to the woman my father felt the need to marry."

"Right. So, should I tell the hottie downstairs that you're in a bitter, crappy mood and that she should come back another time?"

I furrow my eyebrows, propping myself up onto my elbows so I can see him better. "What hottie? I'm not expecting anyone."

Cane grins impishly, his eyebrows bouncing up and down suggestively. "In that case, I'll run back downstairs and entertain the little honey myself."

"Stop being a twat and tell me who's here."

"Go see for yourself, asshole. She said you were supposed to meet her in the library and no-showed. But this girl—"

"Shit," I mutter, flying out of bed and cutting Cane off as I push past him. I cannot believe I forgot about studying with Lyric. She's gonna kick my ass for this. "Lee?" I call out in a desperate rush of air, before I hit the stairs, running down them as fast as my aching leg muscles will take me. "I'm sorry," I say as I hit the floor and zip around the corner.

Lyric is standing in my living room, wearing light blue jeans, a bright pink blouse, and a pissed-off scowl. Her long, blonde braid hangs over her shoulder, and her fiery hazel eyes narrowed with a look that says don't bullshit a bullshitter. She's way too pretty when she's angry. If I didn't need her help so much, I might push this a bit further just to see where it could go.

"You're a dick," she says, pointing a stern finger at me.

I nod. I am a dick. But today I was an unintentional dick, so that has to count for something, right?

"I waited in the freaking library for over an hour. And since you're not dead or have some crazy disease that renders you incapable of moving or answering a call, I'm done with you."

"I'm so—"

"Don't say you're sorry," she snaps, interrupting me. "I seriously do not want to hear it. It was not my idea to study with you. It was yours, and then you don't show up?" She shakes her head, folding her arms across her chest and pushing up her tits enough to make my eyes drop down to look, before coercing them back up to her face under threat of losing her completely. "I don't even know why I agreed to this with you. There is nothing in it for me. You didn't even pick up your phone when I called."

Shit. It was Lyric calling and not my stepmother.

I walk across the room and grasp her shoulders, her neck craning to meet my eyes. She tries to step back, to force me to release her, but I can't do that. She'll bolt on me. I know she will. I've known this girl since I was six and we started kindergarten together. We were never what you'd call close or even friends per se, but that doesn't mean I don't know her. That doesn't mean I didn't watch her from the sidelines for years.

And she chose to date douchebag Charlie.

"I fucked up," I say, staring deep into her eyes and trying hard to concentrate on my apology instead of the different patterns of green, gray, and brown. "I had a shit practice, and the team had to run stadiums for an extra half hour. My stepmother has been calling me non-stop about going to Canada for Thanksgiving with her family. She's already called four times today. When my phone continued to ring, I assumed it was her and ignored it. Please don't go," I beg. "I didn't mean to ditch you, and I am so sorry that I did. I promise it won't happen again."

I release her shoulders and hold my hands up in supplication, knowing this gesture— along with my big, contrite, puppy dog eyes —might seal the deal for me. She still looks angry. Or maybe like she is questioning why she's here when she probably doesn't need studying help. Crap. That's not good. Because as I stand here, looking down on her, I realize I really want her to stay, and it's for more than just helping me study.

I've always had a crush on Lyric Rose. Every guy did. She's beautiful and smart, funny and cool. At least, to high school kids she seemed very cool. Confident and always herself. Sexy as sin in that unapproachable, unattainable way.

But she's not unapproachable. She's sweet. So goddamn sweet. I like talking to her. I like looking at her. And if I can do both of those things and have her help me study, well, then I can't think of a better way to spend an evening.

But I have nothing to offer this girl. No real incentive to make her stay.

"I'll do anything if you help me out. Anything. Name it and it's yours."

She shakes her head again, her teeth sinking into her full bottom lip. She's softening. I know she is. I smile at her. I give her my most charming look. The one that disarms women completely and makes them mine when they don't even want to be. The one that has them forgiving me when they should hate me. But Lyric isn't just any woman, and she knows me well enough to know all my tricks.

"I'm hungry," she says and now I do smile, but this one is genuine because how cute and random is this girl?

"I can buy you dinner. Whatever you want. We'll eat and study. That can be our thing. You help me study, and I feed you because the cafeteria food isn't all that great. You've probably already figured that out. But I live off-campus and I have a car. So yeah, I'll feed you, Lee. Whenever, whatever you want." This is the ramblings of a desperate man, but I don't have it in me to care, not if it gets her to stay.

She's smirking now, hopefully finding my crazy babbling endearing. I think I just won her over. "I want veggie tacos from that excellent Mexican place in town."

I nod, moving my hands firmly back onto her shoulders. I can't let go, because if I do, I might hug her. It's the most bizarre sensation. One I have definitely never experienced before. But I want to hug Lyric Rose. She's like a soothing balm on my ravaged soul. I knew it the second I saw her in class two weeks ago. Hell, the first minute I saw her in kindergarten with blonde, braided pigtails and a brightly colored dress. There's just something about her. Maybe it's the familiarity of home without the stress and agitation that typically comes when I think about that place. Maybe it's her unassuming beauty and quick tongue. Maybe it's the fact that she's a giant softy, even when she's trying to be tough. I don't know. But whatever it is about her, I like having her around me.

"I can get you veggie tacos. Will it bother you if I eat ones with meat?" I vaguely recall her being a vegetarian.

She smiles, those teeth still embedded in that supple, full, bottom lip that I have a tremendous urge to nip on just to see if it tastes as good as it looks. "No. I don't care if you eat meat, as long as I don't have to."

"We'll never have a happily ever after with you being a vegetarian."

She laughs and pushes me away. I release her, because I'm about ninety-eight percent sure she's not going to run out the door, and because if I don't let her go and step back, I might do something really foolish. Like kiss her. "I think I'll survive. Order my food and I'll set up what we need to study before the exam on Monday."

"You got it, babe."

"No sour cream, and guacamole on the side. And please ask them to cook the onions. Oh, and I don't like that pico sauce thing they put on them, so please have them omit it."

"Done. My phone is upstairs, but we can study in the dining room unless you want to do it in my bedroom."

"Definitely not." She scrunches her nose like the idea of going upstairs with me is gross. I hold my hand up to my chest like she just shot me. "You're not wounded. Your ego is far too big for little old me to hurt it." *If only she knew.* "Hey, Jameson?" she calls out, the moment my foot hits the first step.

I lean over the half-wall that separates the stairs from the living room. "Yeah?"

"Thanks for not commenting on my weird food order." She's serious, and she must be reading the confusion on my face because she continues with, "Sometimes I can be a bit...particular with things."

"I know," I tell her because I do. Like I said, I know her. She's a perfectionist. She always has to be in control of a situation. She has OCD tendencies that I'd be willing to bet run deeper than she'd like people to know. At least, that's how she was in high school. In the two weeks I've had class with her, she hasn't shown me anything different. "Doesn't bother me, Lee. I like that about you." I wink at her and run up the stairs, not even giving her a chance to comment or look embarrassed, or whatever it is girls do in that situation.

I grab my phone off my desk, as well as my notebook and pen. Popping my pen into my mouth, I roll it around, grinding my teeth into the worn plastic as I scroll through my missed calls. There is two more from Dianne, my stepmother, and three from Lyric. I feel terrible about that and am surprised she caved on studying with me so quickly.

I dial up the Mexican restaurant because I know their number by freaking heart and order our food. Veggie tacos for her and chicken for me, then I head back down to her. She's already set up at my dining room table, the way I expected her to be, laptop open and ready, notebook set up with pen across the paper at a forty-five-degree angle. But what I didn't expect was Travers to be standing over her, smiling like the damn Cheshire cat as his eyes feast on her like she's the dessert after the meal he's been waiting for.

"Called in the food," I say louder than I need to. Travers doesn't budge away from her, even though I'm positive he just understood my back-the-fuck-off tone. "Should be here in less than an hour." Lyric twists around his large body to find me, but she doesn't comment. "Do you want a beer or anything to drink?"

"Water. We're studying."

I should have known. "Are you going to scold me if I have a beer?"

She shrugs as I approach her other side. "It's your house. But if you wait, I'll have a beer with dinner."

"Deal."

"Is this your super-secret girlfriend none of us know about?" Travers asks, his eyes still on Lyric.

"Study partner," the two of us say in unison. "Lyric, this is my roommate, Travers. Trav, this is my childhood friend and study partner, Lyric. She's going to help me get an A in our corporate finance class."

"You've got your work cut out for you, sweetheart."

"Dick," I mutter and he laughs, reaching out and slapping my shoulder like he's swatting away a bug.

"Childhood friend, huh?" Travers asks with more interest than I would like and Lyric shrugs. I really don't have anything to add to that one. "Okay then. We'll leave it with a vague, uncomfortable silence. I gotta jet to meet up with Sam and Tony, but it was a pleasure to meet you, Lyric. I hope I get to see you again real soon."

He goes to take her hand and I reflexively smack him away. "Back off my study partner. She's immune to your charms."

"No woman is immune to my charms." He runs a hand through his blond hair and winks one of his green eyes at her. "It's the southern gentleman in me."

"And as long as you don't try to put your southern gentleman in me, we'll get along just fine."

Travers laughs, loud and hard. "How did you know that was my next line?"

"Read you like a book," she teases, smiling back.

"I like you. You're a lot fun, Lyric. Enjoy studying with this sulky bastard."

I flip him off and he blows me a kiss before leaving. Cane is already gone so now I'm alone with Lyric. It feels…I don't know. Not awkward. Not necessarily that. But I'm definitely more hyperaware of her. Of her sounds. Of her scent. Of the way she moves and where her eyes go. Why? I think I'm affected by her. I want her. I sit down next to her and find myself moving my chair closer to her than I probably should.

I don't want to want her. I genuinely do not. We grew up together. We're from the same town and know the same people. We now go to the same college and I absolutely do need her help to get an A. Lusting after her is not an option.

"Why do you need an A in this class?" she asks, opening her textbook to coincide with the class PowerPoint that's pulled up on her laptop.

"Are you reading my mind now?"

She looks up at me, her hazel eyes swimming in confusion.

"I was just thinking about how I need an A in this class." *And about what you'd look like naked and sprawled out on my bed as I made you come with my mouth.* Fuck, now I'm getting hard.

I. Cannot. Lust. After. Her.

She leans back in her seat; the spine of the chair is tall and stiff without a lot of give to it, so she doesn't have far to go. She's waiting me out, I realize, and typically, I don't talk about my family. I don't talk about my situation with them, but maybe her family life is far crazier than mine? Her father is a rock star after all. That has to come with its own set of challenges. It certainly got her a lot of attention growing up. So, if anyone can understand me, understand the demands placed on me, it's her.

"My father requires an A in all of my business and finance classes if I want to work for his company."

She stares me down for a long moment, a lifetime of questions scrolling across her face, then asks, "And that's what you want? To work for him?"

"Not *him* necessarily, but his company, yes. I want his company to one day be mine, and the only way that's happening is if I earn it."

She smiles softly, liking that answer. "Then I think we should get started. There's a lot of material to go over."

"Can I ask you a question before we get into this?" I pop my pen in my mouth, chew on it a couple of times to break the buildup of tension inside of me.

"Sure. Go for it."

"Why are you in college?"

She lets out a small, bemused laugh. "Where else should I be?"

"Making music." She frowns, and I wonder if her dismay is directed at me or the fact that she's not making music professionally yet. "You could be in Hollywood making albums."

"Do you like trading on your father's name?"

I shake my head. "I don't mind having to work my way to the top. It means I earned it. That nepotism didn't play a hand in my success."

She points at me with an ah-ha expression like I just got her. "I don't like trading on my father's name, either. That's all anyone cared about in New York. 'When is the Great Gabriel Rose coming to visit the school?'" She puts air quotes around the words, a sarcastic inflection in her tone. "Would he perform there? Would he come and help teach the students? On and fucking on. It was infuriating. And yeah, I do intern for Robert Snow at Spin Records over the summers. Obviously, he knows my father as they have a long history of working together. But Robert made me show him what I could do before he even considered taking me on. And if I don't get a degree and my desired career in music doesn't pan out, then what would I do?"

"I don't think you have anything to worry about."

She smiles, leaning forward until she's practically in my personal space. I lean forward, too, most definitely invading hers. However, instead of blushing or catching her breath at our proximity—as other girls might when I pull this particular move—her grin turns mischievous. Sinfully sexy. "And I think you can get an A all on your own. I can't tell if you're selling yourself short academically, intellectually, or if you're the sort of guy who likes to cover his ass."

Before I can stop myself, I draw in closer, our faces, noses, and mouths only inches apart. Her eyes widen, but just barely. She's trying so hard not to pull away. To throw the game she started back at me. But I'll never lose this. Not with any woman I find as fuckable as I find her. Our eyes lock for a moment, the corner of my lips perking up as I skirt along the flesh of her cheek until I reach her ear. I blow out a warm breath, her body trembling with the smallest of perceptible shudders. I inhale, savoring the uniqueness of her fragrance. It's not perfume. It's not even body wash or shampoo. It's all Lyric. And it's amazing.

"You'll just have to wait and see."

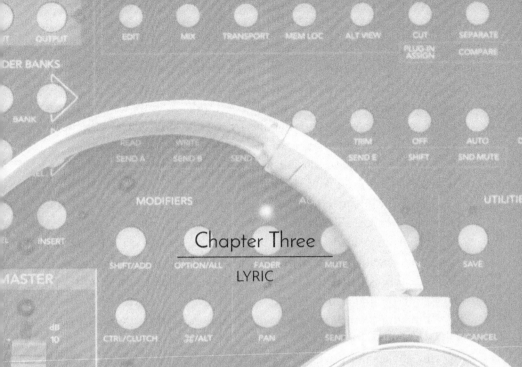

Chapter Three

LYRIC

Comprehensive Music Theory is probably one of the most annoying classes a music major can take. Especially since there are like three levels to it here. And yet, it's imperative for any artist. Mainly because they all have a different style. A different strength and skillset; learning the foundation of something that can be so instinctive is a good thing.

I'm not an artist. Not traditionally, anyway. I don't sing. I mean, I *can* sing and I'm not bad at it, but it's not where I excel. I can play several different instruments, but none of them at a professional level. I make music. I write music. I compile, blend, and alter it until I've created music the way it's meant to sound.

So, this course is sort of ridiculous for me.

I don't need to learn about the elements of the score—clefs, intervals, naming octaves, downbeats, upbeats, the list goes on and on. I don't need that. I know it. It's in my soul, it's been my life's education, and I believe excessive classical training isn't always the best if you do have that innate ability. It can confuse you. Make you second guess things about your talent that you probably shouldn't second guess.

But even so, I take notes and follow along, doing my best to work on the keyboard or whatever instrument our professor has us working with that class. Some students sing. I try to avoid that.

Mostly because I have a pretty good indication that everyone in this class knows who my father is. I get looks and watch as people quietly whisper in that obvious, I'm-talking-about-you-and-not-doing-the-best-job-at-hiding-it way. I keep to myself in here. Cass is in this class with me, and she makes it much easier to tolerate. This class, and our advanced corporate finance class, are the only two we have together, but I'll take it.

"What are you doing after this?" Cass asks as we pack up our stuff. She's eyeing my finance book like it's the incarnation of evil. I don't disagree with her on that sentiment. I hate finance and am glad Jameson makes me study it.

"I'm supposed to meet up with Jameson in the library to study. Do you want to join?"

She shakes her head like I just asked her if she wants to drive to Nashville and perform nude at a honky-tonk with drunk, sweaty men surrounding her. "No freaking way. What's with the two of you always studying together anyway? It's been like six weeks now. It's weird. And maybe a bit disconcerting, since I didn't know guys like Jameson utilized places like the library. Or studied for that matter. I always assumed they got by on their good looks, especially with the female members of the faculty."

I throw her a look as I lift my heavy bag onto my shoulder and adjust it until it's as comfortable as can be. "He needs an A."

"Right. That still doesn't explain why you two study together like four days a week."

I have no answer for that. Especially since we don't always study when we're together. Sometimes we get caught up with other things. But I'm not about to admit that to her right now.

"He likes you."

I snort, rolling my eyes. "No, he doesn't. We're friends. We grew up in the same town and we hang out. That's it. His house is nice and off-campus, and I like his roommates. They're funny in an annoying, misogynistic, overly flirtatious, big brother sort of way."

"That doesn't even make sense. And it sounds a bit incestuous. And I don't know about——"

"Lyric?" A male voice interrupts her from behind me, and I see Cass's eyes widen and her lips break out into a smile as I turn around. Matt, one of the kids from our class, is standing at the end of the aisle next to Saylor, the girl Cass warned me about. And after meeting her a time or two in this class, and another one I unfortunately have with her, I understand the warning.

"Hey," I say with a warm smile for both of them. I feel Cass come to stand next to me on my right, and I wonder if it's so she can see the show better or if it's an act of solidarity.

"How's it going?" Matt asks, but before I can open my mouth to respond, Saylor cuts in.

"Are you signing up for the holiday showcase?" Does she have to ask that with an accusatory tone?

"Nope. Not my scene. What about you?"

She smirks, tossing her bleached blonde hair over her shoulder. Saylor is pretty. A bit too thin, but in a model way that makes her stand out. Especially since she's very tall and has pretty blue eyes.

"Of course. Matt here thinks you should, too, but doesn't know what you'd do in it, considering you don't sing or play a particular instrument with any proficiency."

God, she's such a bitch.

I peer over at Matt, and I feel Cass bumping her elbow into my back intentionally. Matt looks stricken and slightly annoyed. "That's not what I said," he clips out, throwing Saylor a death glare. Matt has dark hair and eyes, and a great smile complete with adorable boyish dimples that you kind of want to stick your finger into. He screams boy-band mock-up in every way imaginable. "I think you'd be great," he says with a softer note. "but I know you don't perform. I just thought it would be cool if you wrote something for a specific person or helped a few of us arrange a piece."

Saylor glares at him, clearly not liking that answer at all. Her arms cross over her chest and her hip juts out. If looks could kill, Matt would be very dead by this point. "I thought we were going to do a duet," she snaps at him. "I hardly think we need *her* to help us. It's not like she's that good anyway."

"Probably not," I say, not having any interest in working with her. Or speaking to her. Or being in the same general vicinity as her. "But thanks for thinking of me," I add for Matt's sake. I'm not about to get into a bitch fest with this girl. She's not worth the effort. I move to step around them, wanting to get away from her and this awkward tension that seems to be bubbling up to something ugly.

"If you change your mind, though…" Matt trails off and I pat his shoulder as I pass him.

"Thanks, but I think you two have it figured out. I'll be there to cheer you on."

He looks like he wants to say more, but Cass is pulling me by my arm toward the exit of the class. "Jesus, I thought she was going to cut you with one of her talons," she whispers in my ear. "Did you see the look she was giving you?"

"I don't think I could have missed it," I laugh. We step outside into the mild fall day, my lungs automatically inhaling the sweetness of the October air before I practically slam into a tall, hard body. "Hey," I say to Jameson, surprise leaking from my voice. "What are you doing here?"

Before he can answer, Saylor walks up to him, slinking her fingers into the crook of his arm in a way that screams 'this is mine and you can't have it.'

"I didn't know you were coming to see me today," she coos, staring up at him adoringly. Matt is standing there next to her, his eyes bouncing back and forth between Jameson and me. I don't know what I'm supposed to do here. Is he here to see her? The thought twists my stomach in a way I don't appreciate.

"Actually, Lyric and I have plans to study together," Jameson states, standing up taller while staring at me in a way that makes my heart beat just a little faster. "I finished up in my class early and thought I'd meet you here. It's nice out, and I don't want to sit in the stuffy library to study."

"I didn't know you were friends with Lyric, Jamie," Saylor says, still holding on to his arm like he's her prized possession. "She hardly seems like the type of girl you spend time with. You usually like us less...rough around the edges. No offense," she sneers, looking at me with the fakest smile in the history of fake smiles.

"Right. Why would I take offense to that? It's not like it was rude or anything."

Cass snorts and tries—poorly, I might add—to cover it up as a cough. I pat her back which only makes her choke harder.

"You see, Saylor, that's where you're wrong. Lyric and I have been close for years." Jameson winks at me, and I can't help but laugh if for no other reason than the scowl pinching up Saylor's face.

"Really?" Matt questions, his gaze still shifting between Jameson and myself. "How's that?"

"We grew up together," Jameson and I say in unison. How annoying is that? I scrunch up my nose and roll my eyes, but Jameson is smiling widely at me. "Yup. Lee here is my favorite dirty little secret."

"Don't you wish."

Saylor's nose wrinkles like she's smelling garbage, and Matt appears a little confused.

Cass slaps Jameson's arm and my back, trying to cut the tension. "Well, this is fun and everything in a totally non-awkward ass way, but I need to get going. There's a cup of coffee out there calling my name. I'll catch you later, Lyric."

I cock an eyebrow at her, and she throws me a small bow and a shit-eating grin.

"I'll call you."

"Oh, you better." Her eyes flicker to each of us, then walks off, throwing a small finger-wave over her shoulder.

"Since you're boringly busy with studying now, maybe we can get together later and actually have some fun?" Saylor asks Jameson, who's checking something on his phone. He tucks it into his pocket at her words. "It's been a while since we've...spent alone time together," she purrs suggestively, her eyes on me as she does.

Lame. That's so freaking lame. *Grow up*, I want to shout at her. Why does this feel like high school? I mean, she's practically feeling

Jameson up just to prove…what? That she fucks him? Please. Like I didn't already know that.

Her hands are running up and down his arms, squeezing his huge man-muscles, and petting his chest like he's made out of cashmere. Her big eyes lock on his face, and really, Jameson just looks uncomfortable at this point. "I'm not sure I have the time right now, Saylor. I have a lot going on with soccer practice and studying."

"Did you really grow up together?" Matt asks me, mercifully diverting my attention away from the two love birds, while they continue their back and forth.

"Yep. Same town. I've known him since kindergarten."

"That's cool, I guess." He shifts his weight, looking over at Jameson, who is still engrossed with his hag, and then back to me, indecision on his face. "I meant what I said about working with you. I know we could write something amazing together. Maybe we could work on my sound and see what we come up with?"

"Sure," I shrug. "You have a really good voice with tremendous range. I think there's a lot you could do."

"Awesome." He beams. "Can I grab your number? We could meet up and talk about it over coffee or something."

"You ready, Lee?" Jameson interjects, his tone sharp, his eyes hard with something unspoken behind them.

My head whips in his direction. "Uh, sure. Just give me a sec."

"*Lee?*"

"It's a nickname," I supply, adjusting my heavy bag and wrapping my arms around my chest.

"It's a term of endearment. Something just between us, if you know what I mean." Jameson winks at Matt before his playful expression deviates and he stares him down. Something unspoken passes between them. Matt shakes his head, a small frown marring his handsome face before it's gone just as quickly.

Matt pivots to face me fully, his dark eyes sweeping over me like he's trying to figure me out. Saylor is gone, leaving just the three of us standing here. And now it really is getting awkward as an unspoken hostility begins to build like smoke from a fire.

"Go ahead," Matt says coolly before his stoic mask transforms into a broad smile, aimed directly for me. He steps into me, closer than I expect, considering I hardly know the guy. "I'll get your number next class."

"Okay. I'll see you then." I step back and Jameson maneuvers in beside me. Matt shakes his head, scowling and then walks off, and suddenly, I find myself peering up at a very satisfied Jameson.

"I'm thinking lunch and then some outdoor studying. I'm starving, but I have all afternoon. What about you?"

What just happened? Why did that have the look and feel of a pissing match between Matt and Jameson? I can't imagine that being the case since Jameson just practically set up a date with the poison princess right in front of me. And more to the point, why do I care about either of those two things? Jameson is free to do whatever he wants with whomever he wants. But even as I force myself to think—and possibly believe that's exactly what happened—I'm struck with the bitter taste of jealousy.

And I do not like it.

"I want a salad," I say, forcing those thoughts far from my brain and consciousness. "The one that has goat cheese and all those chopped vegetables in it."

"Of course, you do. I've never seen a woman eat more vegetables than you. You're like an adorable little bunny rabbit." He takes my heavy bag from my shoulder and puts it onto his since all he has is his standard notebook and chewed-up pen. "Come on. Before another asshole tries to join us."

I let out an incredulous scoff. "You're the one who just set up a fuck date with Evil Barbie."

"That's where you're wrong, Lee. It's why she stormed off in a bitchy huff. If you hadn't been playing footsie with the guy who is only interested in using you for your musical talents, you would have seen that."

I peek up at him, squinting against the intrusive sun as I take in his profile. I wish I were taller. I'm not short, but Jameson has to be well over six feet. He's a good six or seven inches taller than I am which makes my not-so-casual observation of him difficult as we walk.

"I don't care if that's what he's after. He pretty much told me he wanted my help on his sound."

"You can't really be that clueless."

I bump my hip into him, but of course the brick of a man hardly misses a step. "You just told me that's all he's after," I bark, growing more exasperated with him by the second. "And why did you tell Saylor no? I saw your tongue down her throat, like, a month ago."

"Keeping tabs on me, baby?" I roll my eyes at his cocky smirk and he taps the tip of my nose with his finger like I just answered my own question. "Because Saylor is starting to develop expectations, possibly an attachment, and that's the last thing I want."

We make our way to the edge of town where there's a sandwich shop that we frequent. It's one of the only places in town that has anything vegetarian. Southerners are not known for avoiding meat. I get a lot of puzzled expressions when I ask them to alter my food to make it vegetarian. It's like I'm speaking in Russian. They just can't wrap their heads around it.

"From her?"

"From women in general. At least for now. I'm young and I like having fun." He glances down at me, one eyebrow raised as he guides me around a couple standing in the middle of the sidewalk peering into a store window. "Don't pretend you don't feel the same. I heard you telling Cane something similar."

He opens the restaurant's door for me, holding it so that I have to duck under his arm to enter. "I'm not judging. Just curious."

We move to get in line, and he throws his arm around my shoulder, just like that. Like it's the most natural thing in the world for him to touch me, to hold me in such a way. Butterflies. Dammit, I have excited butterflies like a small child about to go on her first roller-coaster. *Did the guy not just tell you he doesn't form attachments? That he likes his fun? Are you not in the exact same mindset, foolish girl?*

"You're the only girl who doesn't irritate the shit out of me in under twenty minutes. Saylor is pretty, but there's not much to her other than her bitchiness. I'm not against monogamy or girlfriends. I just don't have much desire for that yet."

"I get it. I'm sort of the same. I like my freedom. I like having fun. I had Charlie for most of high school, and there was a guy I was seeing at NYU for a bit. But like you said, we're young. I don't want to feel guilty about spending so much time on my music or hanging out with my friends or going to California for my internship this summer."

Jameson pulls me in closer to his side and just...holds me there. He doesn't say anything else as we move and shift up to the front of the line. And when we get there, he orders for me. Not in a macho, asshole way. He just does it, and he remembers that I want the dressing on the side and don't like raw onions, so he has them hold them. And he makes sure they don't put any chicken on it.

I wasn't lying when I said I don't want a boyfriend. I really don't. But still, there is that part of me that loves that he turned Saylor down. And none of that has to do with her attitude and blatant disdain for me. Then there's that whole scene with Matt. The more I think on it, the more I know Jameson was trying to get him to fuck off. But why? Why be a dick like that if you're not interested?

Is it a territorial thing? An alpha 'I don't want her, but I don't want anyone else to have her either' thing? I don't know. But I do know it's not the sort of thing I can bring up. Mostly because it will change our dynamic, and I'm not sure I want to do that. And really, what would I ask? Some questions are better left unanswered. Some truths better left unsaid.

He leads me over to a table by the window, and I stare out at the lunchtime rush. "I don't want to study today," he admits, his voice distant as he also stares out the window.

"We don't have to. It's not like we have an exam or anything this week." Or next week, for that matter.

He nods, but his gaze doesn't deviate. "What do you want to do instead?"

I smile and with that smile, I realize this could turn bad for me. Because I'm smiling that he still wants to hang out even though we're not studying. I'm smiling because I don't annoy him the way other girls do in under twenty minutes. I don't even seem to annoy him after hours together, because he keeps coming back for more and always gets that frowny face when we say goodbye. This smile is dangerous, and I force it from my face before it does something stupid like turn into feelings.

Then he pivots to me. "Whatever you want. Like I said, I have all afternoon, and I'd like to spend it with you."

And just like that, my smile is back.

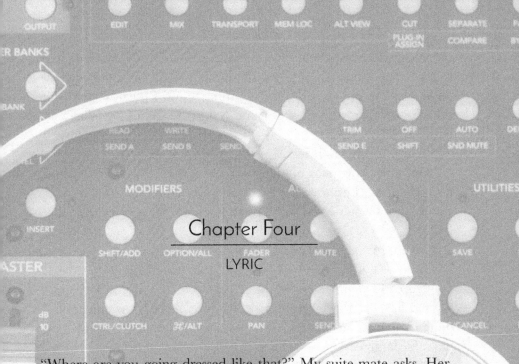

Chapter Four

LYRIC

"Where are you going dressed like that?" My suite-mate asks. Her obvious disdain for me and my outfit should be off-putting, but it's not. I feel bad for her. She's the type of girl who eats her feelings in the form of her hair and fingernails. She wears all black—sort of depressing if you ask me—has dyed black hair, thick black makeup, and too many piercings for me to count.

Honestly, I dig the goth look. I think it's pretty rad, and if I had the ability to pull it off, I might do it a bit more. But this girl is a downer. I mean, there's a reason she's a junior and voluntarily living in campus housing. She's sort of a nasty, bitter bitch. But I think that's all a big coverup. I think she might just be a sad girl.

"I'm going out to a bar and then a party with my friend Cass. You want to come with us?"

Daria stares at me like I just asked her if she wants to be bitten by a venomous snake. "You do understand that guys drug girls at those parties."

"Not all of them," I jest. Only she's not laughing, and I wonder if that happened to her. I finish applying my mascara while she watches. We're in my room. She came in uninvited and watched while I changed my outfit twice, did my hair, and now while I finish my makeup. I don't get her fascination, but it's there. I'd love to help this girl come out of her shell of darkness. "I'll be super vigilant about holding onto my drinks," I promise, and I mean it. Bad shit does go down at college parties, and I didn't mean to downplay that with her.

"Are you going to bring a guy back here for sex?"

Hmmm…how does one answer that question? Especially since it's none of her business who I fuck and where I fuck them. "Maybe. But if I do, I assume you won't be in my room, so it really shouldn't bother you."

"I've seen you with Jameson Woods."

Here we go.

"Yup." I catch her eye in the reflection of my mirror as I apply my red lipstick. I love red lipstick. It's just…hell, it's so fun. And I don't care what anyone says, whenever you wear it, you feel pretty, desirable, and sexy.

"He sleeps around."

I shrug. I don't care that he sleeps around. I mean, *I do*, but I try *really* hard not to. We don't have that kind of relationship. We've become friends who flirt. And friends who flirt rarely cross that magic, irreversible line. Mostly because they like flirting. They also know sex will destroy whatever good thing they have going. Jameson wants me to study with him, even if he really doesn't need me the way he thinks he does. And as Daria pointed out, he sleeps around. And because he sleeps around, he's not looking to sleep with me.

You only sleep with your friends if you want to make them more.

In the months that Jameson and I have been friends, I know he does not want to make me more.

"You're wearing a dress."

"Yup." What I really want to say is, *aren't you a perceptive little thing?* But I don't. I keep my mouth shut, because like I said, I think she's just sad under her layer of bluntness. I am wearing a dress and she did state the obvious. My dress is short. Mid-thigh and a deep purple with these fantastic cutout lines in turquoise. My shoes for tonight are also purple. I'd call them hooker heels because they pretty much are, but I feel like that might be selling the exorbitant price of the shoe short.

My mother likes to dress me as she would herself if she were twenty-one. Every week—seriously, every freaking week—I get a new box. Last week it was the shoes that match the dress I'm wearing tonight. The week before, it was a psychotically expensive purse that I'll more than likely never use and will either donate to a charity to auction or give to my sister.

"When you bend over, I can see your ass."

"Good to know. I'll try not to bend over too much then."

Daria blows out a frustrated puff of air. She's sitting on my bed and I sort of wish she wasn't. It feels too personal for a woman who continuously criticizes me. "I think you're making a mistake in going."

Closing up the tube of lipstick, I tuck it away into my purse and smack my lips together. "Why's that?" I ask, spinning on my still-bare feet to face her. Her eyes are down, staring at my orange comforter. "Did something happen to you at a party?" I ask gently.

"No," she says quickly and then goes quiet. I walk over to her, keeping my distance, but letting her know that she can talk to me. "You're the only person here who doesn't call me a freak, and I'd like to spend more time with you."

Well shit. "I don't think you're a freak at all. Why do people call you that?"

She shakes her head, her eyes still down. "Because of the way I dress and because I'm bisexual."

"Well, they can eat a dick when it comes to how you dress and who you like." She doesn't say anything or even really react, and I wonder if it's because she said she wants to spend more time with me. Maybe she's waiting on my direct answer to that? "I'm cool with hanging out with you, Daria. But you know I'm not gay, right?" She nods. As long as she knows. "Do you wanna go out for brunch with me tomorrow when I'm super hungover and needing greasy food?"

"Will you bring Cassia?"

Now I'm starting to get it. "You like her?" A very reluctant nod.

37

"Can I ask her if she's into that?" A more reluctant nod. "If you change your mind about coming tonight, call or text me. I don't give a fuck what you wear or how you wear it."

She smiles and it's the first time in the history of the world that's happened between us.

"Not tonight. Maybe another night."

"Okay. I'll ask Cass if she's into girls. I think she might be, but don't quote me on that yet."

"Thanks."

I take that as a victory and leave to meet up with Cass, who also doesn't like parties but is learning to appreciate the horror show they are. I go for the spectacle. I don't go to rub my tits up against some willing guy. I don't go to get trashed on nasty, cheap beer. I definitely don't go to dance to horribly mixed trick-hop bullshit. But I am in college. When I left NYU, I promised myself I'd relax my uptight tendencies and have more fun.

Tonight, Cass and I are going out to a bar first, and then we're hitting up a party at one of the large houses on the outskirts of campus. I meet her outside my dorm building and we walk—me in my freaking five-inch hooker heels—down to the main strip where the bar we want to go to is. I like Cass. In the months I've been in this school, we've gotten closer.

She's a pianist. A talented one, but I'm trying to get her to branch out to bass guitar. She has phenomenal rhythm and a knack for hearing what other musicians are putting out and following along. She'd be killer on the bass, and I happen to know an up-and-coming band that's looking for someone, but I don't know how interested she is in that.

But that's what I do. It's what I freaking love. What I get high off of. Music. Making music to be exact. Bringing multiple instruments—sometimes even electronics—together into something that gets people moving their heads and singing along in their cars. Gets them feeling shit they might not want to feel. Or crying. God, if I can get someone to cry, I'm the happiest person ever.

Before you think I'm a cruel bitch, it only makes me happy because you only cry when you're truly feeling.

I can mix together anything and make it sound so goddamn good you didn't even know your soul needed it until I'm literally feeding it to you and you're begging for more.

I'm in a great mood. I spoke to Melody tonight, and she's moving in with her boyfriend. She's in love. My father is signed up for a very limited world tour with his band, and now that we're all out of the nest, my mom is talking about going with him for once.

I may have grown up with rock-and-roll glory, but my father, and especially my mother, made sure my sister and I had the most normal upbringing that any wealthy girls could. They put us first,even to the point that my father put his music career on hold. Imagine that. Seriously try. You're on top of the world. One of the biggest bands since the Beatles, the Rolling Stones, or Journey, and you meet this woman who tells you that she's really not into the scene. Would you give it up?

Well, my father did. Without blinking an eye. He gave up the touring. He gave up the crazy production schedules and long absences from home. Groupies? Never looked at another woman again after meeting my mother. And once Melody was born, that was it. He became a daddy. My tattooed, long-haired, rock star father held our hands as he took us to school and threw us princess birthday parties. Melody isn't into music. She's into dance and her boyfriend. But I think my father likes that I'm into music as much as I am. Even if he's proud of us no matter what we do.

The bar is loud and overcrowded with college kids, and there's some ridiculous karaoke thing going on in the back.

"Beer?" Cass shouts to me as we make our way into the fray.

"No," I scream back. "Shots."

She shakes her head as I nod mine. She blows out a frustrated breath. "One shot and then beer."

"Deal. And for the record, you look super hot without glasses, but I think I also like your daytime persona with them. I honestly cannot decide which is better. You're like Superwoman versus Clara Kent."

She laughs, rolling her eyes at me. "*Clara* Kent?"

I shrug. "I couldn't go with Clark. It wouldn't work for you."

"It's easier to go out without them. What kind of shot are you making me drink?"

I think on that for a minute, and just as I'm opening my mouth to speak, someone behind me says, "Tequila."

I shake my head without even turning around to face Jameson. "No. Whiskey."

Cass shakes her head this time. "Kamikaze."

Jameson groans behind me. His hand grasps my hip, his thumb gliding along the bare skin peeking out of one of the cutouts. "Too girly."

I spin around to face him, and immediately wish I had stayed put. His black hair is brushed back and off his face. His wolfish blue eyes are piercing, and his beautiful angled jaw is clean shaven. He's easily the most gorgeous man I've ever seen on a regular day. But like this? It's just unfair. He's a freaking Adonis. He's wearing a blue-and-black plaid shirt over dark, low-hung jeans. I can't stop myself from staring at the way the shirt fits his chest and arms.

"What are you doing here?"

He laughs, extending his grip on my hip. I thought for sure that once I spun around, his hand would drop. No such luck. His touching me like this—in an intimate way in a not-so-intimate setting—is doing things to me. Funny things. Lightheaded, heat-producing things.

"Same thing as you. Getting shitty before the party. But damn, Lee." He gives me a slow, languid once over. His eyes raking across every square inch of me. He's doing it intentionally to annoy me, but that doesn't mean I feel those eyes any less. I might, in fact, feel them more since he's making a show of it. "You're…" he shakes his head like he's at a loss for words.

"Too much woman for you?" Cass offers, and I laugh despite myself. The coil of desire his heated looks are producing unravel in the pit of my stomach. And other choice places as well. Can one look make a woman's panties wet? The answer is a resounding yes.

"Probably, but that was not what I was thinking." His eyes find my red lips. "At. All." He squeezes my waist, that thumb brushing against the bare skin of my hip once more. He steps forward, those eyes of his dancing all around my face before he pulls me in—not even caring that we're in a crowded room, and Cass is standing right here—against his chest as his mouth descends to my ear. I close my eyes, knowing no one can see me fall into this moment. Knowing he can't tell I'm breathing in the scent of his cologne, or savoring the sensation of his warmth against my overheated body.

"You're so beautiful my chest hurts," he rasps into my ear and my eyes cinch tight, my breath catching in my chest. "So beautiful I can barely breathe. The idea of another guy simply talking to you makes me deranged and violent."

I step back. If I don't, I'll lose myself in him. "Shots," I whisper, my voice thick and low from the impact of his words, but I know he hears me. Or at least he reads the word on my lips.

"Shots," he agrees, his hand leaving my hip and snaking up to mine, intertwining our fingers as he holds my hand. *As he holds my hand!* He leads me—us—over to the wall-length, ancient townie bar, lined three layers deep with waiting patrons.

It's been eight weeks since school began. Eight. That's not a lot. But week by week, I give more of myself over to him. Whether it's in the library where we study and talk for hours. Or in his bedroom where we study and watch Netflix shows for hours. Or when we walk all around town and hang out under a tree by the lake for hours.

Everything we do together seems to end up in that increment of time.

Hours.

He rarely touches me when we're casually out in public, and never on campus. But when we meet up like this, in a bar or at a party, he most definitely touches me then.

Intimately. Tenderly. In a way that unequivocally tells any other interested guy to fuck off.

And you know what? I don't stop him. I like it. I like it so much my skin thrills with electricity. My heart palpitates. My brain shuts off all sensibility and rationality and gives into the physicality of the moment.

I know I'm turning into one of those high-school girls I used to feel sorry for. I know I'm becoming another college-girl cliché. I've seen him with other women. Saylor Ramsey—the biggest bitch in the world multiplied by five. Jordan Presley. Kayla Gold. The list goes on and on. He hooks up with them a time or two and then they're done. I've watched him kiss them. I've watched him full-on make-out with them. I've watched them walk off together, headed to do things I don't want to ever think about.

But I make myself do it. It's a reminder. A necessary slap in the face.

A way to keep my head on straight where he's concerned.

So, this hand-holding thing? Yeah. It doesn't mean anything.

Cass and I talk about Daria while Jameson orders our shots and beers. Cass is also bisexual. I knew this about her, but I didn't want to tell Daria in case Cass wasn't interested.

"You know Matt has been asking about you?" Cass says with a wicked grin, louder than she should. Matt is a fellow music major. He's a singer. A somewhat talented one. A gorgeous one. The one who has been asking me to work with him. The one who had a pissing match with Jameson a few weeks back.

"What has he been asking? The usual?"

Cass shakes her head. In the two months we've been friends, we've developed a shorthand of sorts. She knows that *the usual* refers to my family. A lot of people have asked. I've told practically none. Doesn't mean they don't know who I am. It's like saying that you don't know Paul McCartney's daughter is a major fashion designer. Like saying that you don't know Steven Tyler's daughter is Liv Tyler. My sister and I try to keep a low profile, but in a school this small with a bunch of music majors, the secret is bound to get out.

"No. He's been asking about your situation with…" she trails off, jutting her chin in Jameson's direction. His back is still to us, but I get the impression he can hear everything we're saying. Mostly because his back is now stiff as a board.

"What did you tell him?"

"That you're as single as Jesus was and nowhere near as pious."

I choke out a laugh just as a shot of something amber is thrust into my face by an angry hand. Cass's expression is something along the lines of I-knew-it mixed with a satisfied devil.

"Do you disagree, Jamie boy?" she asks tartly, accepting her pale green shot with something akin to fear and nausea as she takes it in.

"I wouldn't know," he clips out, holding his small glass filled with clear liquid up that I know is tequila. "Cheers. Let's drink up, ladies. I need to get back. My boys are waiting on me."

Is now a bad time to tell him that Travers invited me here tonight? Not as his date, of course. Travers and I have become friends. I'm thinking yes, and I'm also thinking that joining him and his friends tonight, whether here or at the party, is a bad idea. Something is shifting between us and it's not a good idea to feed into it.

He slams the shot down the back of his throat without waiting on us to join. I want to say something, but for the life of me, I don't know what.

Because I don't know what this is.

There is no description for it. No road map to follow. No way to understand the rules or comprehend how to not trip on the mine-field and have this all explode in our faces. I want him. I'm attracted to him. I might even like him more than I should.

But I'm not about to give in and commit emotional suicide.

And he hasn't tried anything other than that handhold just now, which was the first of its kind. Not only that, he's made his position on relationships known. He doesn't have the patience or desire for them. "I'm having fun" is what he always says about the revolving door of women. So, whatever he's expecting from me, I do not know.

"I'll see you later." He storms off. Angry. Gnashing a wide path through college kids on his way across the bar.

"Oh shit." Cass laughs, covering her mouth. We're both watching his retreating form. "You're so screwed."

I nod. I think I just might be. This feels like it's headed some-where neither of us should go.

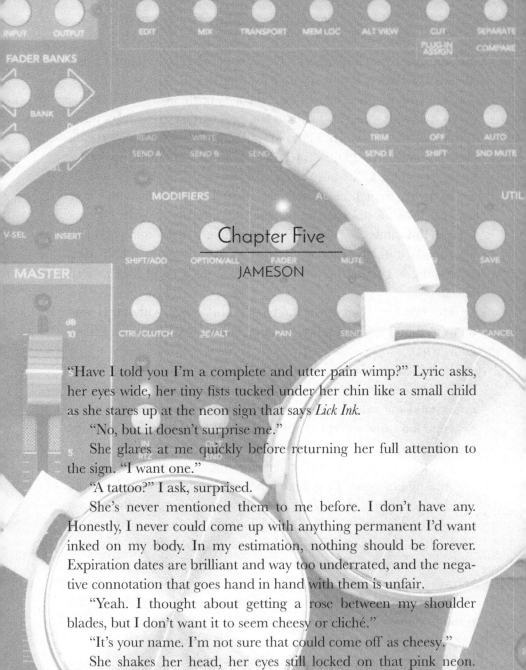

Chapter Five

JAMESON

"Have I told you I'm a complete and utter pain wimp?" Lyric asks, her eyes wide, her tiny fists tucked under her chin like a small child as she stares up at the neon sign that says *Lick Ink*.

"No, but it doesn't surprise me."

She glares at me quickly before returning her full attention to the sign. "I want one."

"A tattoo?" I ask, surprised.

She's never mentioned them to me before. I don't have any. Honestly, I never could come up with anything permanent I'd want inked on my body. In my estimation, nothing should be forever. Expiration dates are brilliant and way too underrated, and the negative connotation that goes hand in hand with them is unfair.

"Yeah. I thought about getting a rose between my shoulder blades, but I don't want it to seem cheesy or cliché."

"It's your name. I'm not sure that could come off as cheesy."

She shakes her head, her eyes still locked on that pink neon. "My dad wrote a song about Melody and me when I was fifteen."

I turn to face her, cataloging Burnt Tears' songs one by one.

"Day Dreamer's Life," she supplies when I can't come up with anything.

I smile at that. That song is all about love and life and finding the true meaning behind both. I had no idea he wrote it for his daughters. It makes me like her father more than I already do. "I see my soul through your eyes. The way you strip me of my lies. I've come undone. I'm forever on the run."

"That's the one," she interrupts. "I know the notes by heart. I can play them on every instrument within my power, and I think I want the chorus tattooed on my body along with a rose."

"Now?"

She nods, and I think I just swallowed my tongue. I don't know if I can watch that. If I can be a part of something so intimate with this girl. I'm trying. I'm trying really freaking hard.

And I'm failing.

I know I am. I spend so much time with her. Studying. Classes. Just hanging out, the two of us or with other people. She's a fixture. A current running through me. A harmonized note, to put it in her terms.

I want to give in to this thing between us so goddamn bad. I want to kiss her. Possess her. Make her mine.

And yet. I don't want any of those things with her.

Because Lyric could never just be a fuck. Never just a girl who I sleep with a few times and then move on from. She's Lyric, and Lyric is someone very rare and special to me.

But where would that leave us? A relationship?

Neither of us is interested in that.

I like my life of unattached freedom. That's how it's supposed to be when you're twenty-one and in college. And before you think I'm an asshole for that, Lyric feels exactly the same.

My few guy friends that have girlfriends always complain about them. About the things they get suckered into doing in the name of regular pussy.

But I get regular pussy, and I don't have the aggravation of someone dragging me to a rom-com or feeling obligated to spend my free time with them instead of hanging out with my boys.

I've never really had a girlfriend, and honestly, it doesn't sound all that appealing. At least not the way they describe it. It's not like I have the best relationship role-models the way Lyric does. When I was ten, my mom died after a grueling, five-year battle with breast cancer. My father married Dianne—the bitch who pretends to tolerate me while badmouthing my very existence—three years later.

"I'm afraid of pain," Lyric says, this time a bit more urgently. She reaches out for my hand and I give her mine freely. I want to absorb her fear. Annihilate it. Because she's so strong. This woman is so goddamn strong. And smart. God, is she smart. She makes me outline chapters and sections and comes up with questions I didn't even know I needed answers to. All about corporate finance.

I mean, can you think of a more boring subject?

It's the least favorite of my current classes, and yet, it's the one I look forward to the most. It's the one I haven't missed, not even once. Not even when I had a cold and felt like crap.

"You don't have to do it." I'm stalling. I'm trying to find a way out of this. Because I know her. She's going to want that ink on an intimate part of her body. Which means she's going to have to remove articles of clothing to reveal her chosen canvas. Hell, my cock is hard just thinking about that.

"Will you come with me?" she asks, finally turning her body to face mine, her pretty eyes filled with hope. Damn her for this. Doesn't she know what she's asking?

"Of course, I will. What are friends for?"

She smiles, and I hate myself just a bit more for that last bit. But I'm not her boyfriend, and I am her friend. Even if it tastes all wrong on my tongue. Especially given this particular situation.

"Come on." She squeezes my hand and leads me inside. The door chimes overhead as we enter. The walls are lined with pictures and ideas of tattoos. The ubiquitous buzzing sound associated with a tattoo parlor fills the vanilla-scented air. The furniture is a glossy art deco mixed with hipster chic. The woman at the counter is a colorful variety of fun between her tattoos and piercings. It's everything I ever expected it to be and more.

"May I help you?"

"I want a tattoo done, but it's something very specific."

"Can you draw it?" the acid flashback asks, propping her elbows onto the counter and taking in Lyric with a skeptical eye.

"Yeah. I think I can. But I need someone who understands music to be able to do this."

The woman smiles and nods her head. "What sort of music we talkin' about?"

Lyric whips out her phone, pulls up the song and hits play. Another guy, who, if possible, has more ink on his body than his female counterpart, joins us. "You want me to put the lyrics on your body?" the guy asks, a bit too gleeful over the prospect if you ask me.

"No," Lyric says, shaking her head, her expression so very serious. "I want the notes. They were written first. He felt those notes before he wrote one word. I also want a rose incorporated in it somehow."

The dude's eyes narrow, but he doesn't question her on that. "Draw it out, fill out the form and we'll get started."

Thirty minutes later, we're in a backroom listening to Moses— that's the guy's name—explain the procedure and the aftercare, and everything we need to know about getting a tattoo.

Then she takes off her shirt.

Then she unhooks her bra.

Then she covers her full, beautiful, perfect tits with her forearm.

Then she blushes when she catches my eye.

I can't look away. I've been begging myself to do just that for the last two minutes, but I cannot force the action. I have to look. I have to take her in. I have to memorize every curve, every dip, every pink, peaked bud and every freckle. A lust I have no right to burns inside me.

She swallows softly. I swallow loudly.

She blows out a heavy breath. I suck one in.

"Lay on your stomach," he instructs, and I haven't averted my eyes from her once. She follows his direction, and once her chest is pressed into the vintage red plastic, she reaches out a hand for me, her face tensing up at the impending sting of the needle.

I take her hand in mine, lowering my body onto a rolling stool and scooting up until I'm practically nose to nose with her. Our breaths become one. Our eyes see only each other's. Our lips are tasting without kissing.

"You okay?" I whisper the moment the buzzing begins and the needle impales her porcelain skin. The moment her body stiffens up and he tells her to relax.

"Yes," she half-pants, half-whimpers. "It hurts."

"What can I do?" I ask, feeling so helpless. So consumed. So desperate.

Her eyes somehow search deeper into mine, and I know exactly what she's thinking. God help me, I know exactly what she wants because it's exactly what I want.

I press my forehead to hers and close my eyes. Our noses rub, back and forth, back and forth. Our lips brush on the last swipe of our noses and her breath hitches.

"Relax," the guy demands again, and I can't tell if he's speaking to her or me. I can't relax. Relaxing is giving in. How can I kiss her like this? With another man less than a foot away. While that man has his hands on her body.

I open my eyes and hers are right there, swirls of green and gray and brown. Beautiful. Unique. Lyric is a fingerprint on my soul. "I want to break my promise," I mouth, the words inaudible, but they're finally out there and I won't take them back. But we're so close that she misses it, and I can't figure out if I'm relieved by this or not.

Lyric begins to hum the melody of the song the guy is permanently etching into her back. The notes, the sound, reverberate through me. Light me up. Her voice is so achingly sweet. I don't know what's happening between us. She's become my best friend. And I need her. I need that friendship and I need her in my life.

You just want to bag her, I convince myself. *Keep your dick in control*, I plead. *Don't do something you'll regret*, I demand. *She'll only ever be your friend*, I force.

After the longest two hours of my life, she's done. Black music notes gently floating with a bright red rose intertwined between her shoulder blades, the thorny vines twisting and twirling outward. It's angry and mean-looking right now, but when her skin calms down, it will be exactly what she dreamt it would be.

I turn around this time as she gingerly puts back on her shirt sans bra. I don't think about that. About the fact that her breasts, her nipples, are more than likely visible beneath the thin layer of her tangerine blouse. She pays, and we leave the shop, and I take her out for an ice cream because she was brave, and I need something to keep my mouth busy with other than her lips. Or her nipples.

"Do you think that was a mistake?" she asks, spooning a bite of hot-fudge-covered vanilla into her mouth.

I bark out a laugh. "You ask that *now?*"

She shrugs and then winces at the pull of her smarting skin.

"No. I don't think it was a mistake. Are you going to tell your dad?"

She nods, running her spoon through her melting dessert. "I'll show him when I go home for Thanksgiving."

"Will he be pissed?"

Lyric lets out an indignant snort. "It would be hypocritical as hell if he was, considering it's his song and he's already covered in tattoos."

"What about your mom?"

"Not much she can say. I'm twenty-one. I'm an adult and I made the choice with my eyes open. I don't regret it. I don't think I ever will. It's not something I have to look at every day and grow tired of."

"I doubt I'll ever get one. Your song feels different because it's timeless and was written for you by your father. But nothing in my life feels like forever, and the things that could aren't worth making permanent."

"Wow," she says, the corner of her mouth twitching up, her eyes glowing. "That's pretty damn depressing, Jameson. Maybe you should have 'nothing lasts forever' inked on your chest."

I laugh, reaching across the table and swiping her spoon before I take the dollop of ice cream and shovel it into my mouth.

"Hey. That's mine." She tries to grab at my spoon, but I'm faster than she is. I cram them both in my mouth, making a show of licking them, moaning as I do. "Gross." She scrunches her nose up in disgust.

Standing up, she reaches over and yanks one of the white plastic spoons from my mouth before dropping it back into her ice cream, scooping some up and then popping it into her mouth.

"Not so gross then, baby. You're sucking on my spit."

"And I'm sure I'll need a series of shots and antibiotics as a result."

"Such a brat. I thought you were an OCD germaphobe."

She shakes her head, proving her point by licking the spoon I just had in my mouth. I like that she's essentially, willingly, eating me. It's like kissing her without the drama and causalities. "I'm not a germaphobe. I just like things the way I like them. That does not make me OCD."

"Fine. A control freak."

"That I'll give you. But you know, the world would be a better place if it were run by control-freak women."

"I can't argue with that. I always like it when women try to control me. Especially when they fail."

She rolls her eyes at me, reluctantly smiling around the spoon we just shared.

"Next week is Thanksgiving. Three weeks after that, we have finals."

I nod, unsure where she's headed with this.

"We don't have any classes together next semester."

Ah.

"Nope. You'll be rid of me and my dependence on your brilliance."

"That's a shame. I was just starting to really like Travers. Even Cane is growing on me."

Brat. "When do you leave for Thanksgiving?" I ask, changing the subject away from my roommates.

"Tuesday after class. Why, do you need a lift home?"

"Are you driving?"

"No." Her cheeks color and I love it when she blushes. She

50

doesn't do it often, but when she does, it's freaking awesome. "My dad's coming to pick me up."

"In a private jet?"

She nods, her attention suddenly very focused on her ice cream.

"Damn. That makes me wish I was going home instead of to Cane's for the holiday. We already bought our plane tickets."

"I thought you worked things out with your stepmom?"

"About Christmas. Not about Thanksgiving."

"Oh. I didn't know. I would have invited you home with me."

"Nah. I'm good with going home with Cane. He lives in New York City, but I doubt we'll leave the city. We're only there for three days. I'll catch up with everyone from home during Christmas break."

"Thank you for coming with me." She looks up at me, her eyes bleeding with sincerity. "I know sitting there like that for so long wasn't your idea of fun, but it means a lot to me that you were there. I'm not sure I could have done it on my own."

I reach across the table and take her hand. "Anytime you want to get half naked and have a man ink your body, I'll be there."

She laughs, but it's not her real laugh. It's an uncomfortable, possibly embarrassed laugh.

"In all seriousness, you're my girl, Lee. I can't think of anything I wouldn't do for you."

She squeezes my hand and I squeeze hers back. We fall silent, reveling in this magic flashing between us. Completely unsure where it could possibly lead us.

Chapter Six
LYRIC

Christmas is in three days. Three. The semester ended this afternoon after our advanced corporate finance final. I happen to know that both Jameson and I aced it. I'd be willing to bet Cass did as well since the three of us studied our asses off for it. But now the semester is done and we don't have to be back at school again until January third.

Typically, I'd be thrilled. But not this year.

My dad decided to go on a limited tour that has him in Australia at the moment. They invited me to go with them, but they're going from Australia to New Zealand to Southeast Asia and back to California, all in the span of ten days. It's going to be one hotel after another.

More days and hours of travel than I care to think about.

It's not like we'll be celebrating the holiday as a family because Melody is with her boyfriend's family, and my dad has a show both Christmas Eve and Christmas Day.

So, I opted out.

But I didn't want to go home, either. That just felt too depressing to me. Right now, I'm sort of regretting that decision.

The dorm closes tonight. As in, no students are allowed to stay on campus over the holiday break.

Most of the students are already gone, including the few friends I have. Which is why I'm in the process of standing outside the nicest hotel in town. That's not saying a lot. It's really just a glorified motel. I'm not a snob. I'm not, I swear. But I wouldn't mind a spa where I can get a massage. Or being pampered with room service and indulging on chocolate and alcohol from the minibar.

This hotel has none of that.

So yeah, I'm a bit depressed.

A horn blares from behind me, startling me out of my lost-girl moment. I move toward the mechanical doors, pulling my suitcase behind me.

"What the hell are you doing?" a familiar voice yells out. I roll my head over my shoulder to catch Jameson, leaning across the passenger seat of his car, staring at me like I'm crazy through the window.

"What the hell are *you* doing? Heading to the airport?"

He shakes his head. "My flight was canceled. They're getting snow up in Connecticut, so I decided I'm not going." I furrow my eyebrows, spin around and walk over to his car. I let go of my suitcase and prop my forearms across the bridge of the lowered window.

"Why not?"

He blows out a breath, running his hand through his hair and looking as exhausted as I feel. "My stepmother convinced my pussy-whipped father to go on a cruise last minute. They leave in two days and don't come home until after the new year."

"Shit," I say, shaking my head. "I'm sorry. That sucks."

"Yeah. It sucks, but what did I expect? She hates me and is trying to get back at me for not going to see her shitty family over Thanksgiving. My father didn't even put up a fight."

"What are you going to do?"

He chuckles and shrugs like he has no idea. "Hang out at my place? Order a lot of takeout? Drink a lot of alcohol? I don't know."

His eyes track back to mine as he tilts his head. "Why aren't you going home? Isn't that what you told me you were doing?"

"I lied." His eyes narrow, and now it's my turn to shrug a shoulder. "I didn't want the pity-party or the obligatory invitations. I don't want to crash someone's Christmas, and I don't want to go home to an empty house, so I'm parking my ass at a hotel for the break."

Jameson growls out something unintelligible before he throws his Jeep into park and gets out of the car. He's on me in a flash, grabbing my suitcase and carrying it to the back of his car.

"What the hell?"

"You're not spending almost two weeks in this hotel. No fucking way. You're going to come and stay at my place. Both Cane and Travers are gone. You can sleep in one of their rooms. We'll spend the vacation together."

I hesitate. Not because that doesn't sound good, but because it does. "You think that's a good idea?" I have to ask. One of us needs to be thinking rationally about this. After I got my tattoo, he pulled away. Not a lot, not even a perceptible amount to anyone else. But I noticed it. I felt it. I think it's because I not only bared my breasts to him but part of my soul.

And he didn't want it.

It hurt, but it was the wakeup call I desperately needed. I put him squarely back in the friend zone and that's how it's been in the weeks since. But if we're sharing a space like that? I just don't know.

"I think it's a great idea." He pauses and catches my eye. "I'm not letting you stay alone in a hotel. Come stay with me, Lee. We'll go to the grocery store and grab a shit-ton of food and booze. We can even get Christmas decorations if you want."

I smile, sinking my teeth into my bottom lip to hide it. It's so damn tempting.

"Come on. I know you want to." That grin. Christ almighty, that grin of his.

"Okay. But I'm buying the food."

He sighs and shakes his head. "We'll split it."

"I'm buying an expensive bourbon that you'll share with me."

"Deal."

I get in his car as he puts my suitcase in his trunk. I call the hotel to cancel my reservation. Then, we head to the grocery store. We load up on enough food to feed an army for weeks. We decide to try and cook a Christmas dinner. We even get a tiny plastic tree, lights, and multicolored ornaments.

"I have a present for you," he says as we make our way to the register. "I thought you were going to be home, so I was planning to give it to you there."

I smile to myself, staring away from him and out into the grocery store, so he doesn't catch it. "I have something for you, too."

I feel a poke in my side, and I turn back to him. He opens his mouth to say something when the woman in front of us catches our attention with the words 'ice storm'. "Yes," she asserts, nodding vigorously at the checkout lady. "I heard it's supposed to start tomorrow night and last through Christmas. It's why I'm getting all my shopping done now. The weatherman on channel eight said *six inches* of snow before it turns to ice. Can you believe it?"

I glance over at Jameson and he's grinning. "Good thing we have food and alcohol. But I think we might need to get some batteries, flashlights, and candles. We will lose power. We do every time it gets like that. Especially with ice. This town will shut down the second the flakes start to fall."

"This is the south," I protest, dumbly not comprehending how snow and ice can find their way here.

"Yeah. But it's not *that* south, Lee. It can get as nasty as an unpaid whore in Nashville." The woman in front of us turns, scowling at Jameson. "Sorry," he says with a contrite, charming grin. The woman forgives him instantly. I don't think anyone can be mad at the bastard when he smiles like that.

"Fine," I groan, not pleased at all. "I'll run and get what we need." I grab everything I can find, readying for the apocalypse of snow and ice. At home, six inches of snow and some ice isn't that big of a deal. I live in New England, after all. But I guess southerners aren't as well versed in winter weather as we northerners are.

"Here," I say, tossing my findings onto the belt and adding it to our booty.

We pay for the groceries, load everything up into his car, and then we silently ride to his house. It's eerily quiet when we get inside. His roommates left this morning. Now it's cold, dark, and lifeless. So unlike how it typically is. Both Cane and Travers keep this place buzzing with loud, crude conversations wrapped in women and debauchery.

I head directly into the kitchen, which isn't all that big. It's little more than a galley with a large counter separating it from the dining area. "I have no idea where your stuff goes, so I'm just going to put it where I think it should go."

Jameson looks at me, the corner of his lips quirking up. "I have no doubt you'll have my kitchen whipped into shape in no time."

He's right. This place is a disaster. Nothing makes sense. I mean, he has pots mixed in the same cabinet as food. I go through everything. Mostly because I need the distraction. I'm in Jameson's apartment, and apparently, I'm staying here for more than ten days. Alone. With him. Part of that is going to be through a storm, which means I'll have trouble leaving and getting some no doubt much-needed space.

"I put your suitcase up in Traver's room. It's cleaner than Cane's. I also changed the sheets because I can't even think about what was on the ones he had on his bed. I washed my hands three times in scalding water after touching them."

I laugh and then scrunch my nose as I face him. "That's sort of gross. Are his sheets clean?"

"They're my sheets, actually. I promise you, they're clean. But if you'd rather sleep in my bed, I'll sleep in his."

"Right," I snort out. "Like your bed is any less covered in bodily fluids than his is."

Jameson glances away, and for the first time in all the years I've known him, I think he's embarrassed. "I haven't had a woman in my bed in almost two months."

My jaw has officially hit the floor. My eyes might be bugging out of my head. I know I'm frozen in the middle of his tiny ass kitchen.

"Don't look so shocked. I've never liked bringing girls home to my bed."

I blink and try to clear my head. I want to ask when the last time he was with a woman was, but honestly, I don't want to know. It's none of my business anyway.

"It's fine. If you changed the sheets, I'll sleep in Traver's room."

"What are we making for dinner?"

"Margaritas."

He laughs, nudging into me as he takes the bottle of tequila from my hand. "I'll make those. What about for food? Don't tell me we're ordering out?"

"I was thinking Israeli couscous with vegetables and pesto. We can add some sort of meat product for you."

"What the hell is Israeli couscous?"

I laugh at his expression. "You'll like it. Just trust me."

"I'm going to need a lot of alcohol to get through this week."

"Then mix it up. I'm waiting."

Jameson gets to work on our margaritas that don't work all that well with the dinner I have planned out, but who cares?

He hands me one, but before I can take a sip, he holds his glass out to me. "I'm glad you're here. I was not looking forward to this break."

"I'm glad I'm here, too. I was not all that into the hotel situation."

We clink glasses and each take a sip. I set my glass down and go back to chopping up vegetables. "Where are your parents?"

"On tour. They start in Australia and then work their way back to America before finishing up in Italy sometime around the time when school lets out. He couldn't say no to this tour. The venues are too big and the payday too great." I look over at him, taking another sip of my delicious drink. "But really, I think he missed it. The touring, the crowds, the music."

"Why didn't you want that? I've heard you sing. You're good."

"Not that good," I say with a smile, and he shakes his head at my self-deprecation. He moves in next to me, taking over chopping some of the veggies while I get to work on the couscous. "In all seriousness, it was never my thing. I don't like being the center of attention. I don't like the limelight. I like being in the background. I like making the music, not performing it."

"And you're going to Los Angeles this summer?"

I glance over at him; there's something in his voice that makes me. Something wistful. "Yeah. You'll be in New York, right?"

He nods and our eyes lock. "I don't know how I'm going to get through next semester without you studying with me."

I smile, trying for some levity. I don't feel any. I feel heavy, weighed down. "I'll still help you outline and study. You know, I will. Even if I'm not taking the class."

He takes a step in my direction, and I turn to face him, my neck arching back to meet his eyes. They're swimming with an ocean of emotion. Something drastic has changed in Jameson. It both excites and terrifies me. I am going away this summer. And once I graduate —though that's not for over a year—I'm going to move to California. And he'll be in New York. And we'll be separated.

Even though that's months away, we both know that whatever this is between us isn't casual enough to withstand that sort of time limit. That sort of self-imposed distance.

"I'm going to set up the bullshit hack of a tree we got."

I nod.

"I'll make my chicken, though. You don't have to touch it."

"Thanks."

He bends down. I tilt up. Our eyes meet in what I can only describe as combustible heat. I suck in a rush of air. He lets out his and I swallow it down. I can't help it. He spins around quickly and stalks off, leaving me standing in his kitchen with the sound of vegetables sautéing.

Twelve days. How will I ever survive it?

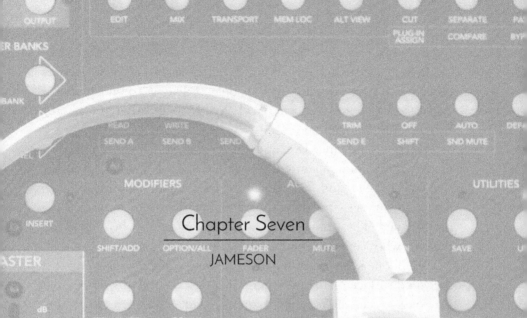

Chapter Seven

JAMESON

It started snowing at four in the morning. How do I know that you might ask? Because I was awake. It's been two days since I brought Lyric home with me. Two days of not a whole lot mixed with too much sexual tension. She cooks. And she hums while she does. Her food is really freaking good. Even that crazy couscous shit she made me was delicious.

She's also cleaned my entire apartment, including Cane's room. I have no idea how he'll react when he comes home to a spotless room, but I couldn't stop her. I even let her in my room. Our place has never smelled this good. She's been doing laundry and listening to music and working on her computer—making music, I think. She's everywhere and yet, so goddamn easy and agreeable. She hasn't demanded anything of me. Never asks for my time or my help with anything.

Which only makes me want to give it to her more.

She just does things.

It's the control freak in her, I know. It's busywork, so she doesn't have to think about spending Christmas away from the family she's so close with, I know.

But I like having her here.

I like it so much, I invited her to tag along on my run yesterday morning. I hate running with people. I like it so much that I suggested lunch and a movie. We'd already spent twenty-four hours together, pretty much non-stop.

Today is Christmas Eve, and as I stare out my bedroom window at the falling snow against the dark gray sky, I have a lot on my mind. My father and the woman he perpetually chooses over me. The Christmases and other holidays I've been left out since my mother died. The woman sleeping in my roommate's bed just down the hall, who seems to be unraveling me seam by seam.

My phone rings, vibrating and sounding generally pissed against the wood surface of my nightstand. I pick it up and answer without checking to see who's calling. I know it's not my father. He's some-where at sea, I think. But still. It would be nice if it were. "Hello?"

"Hey, man. How's it going?"

"What the hell are you doing awake at eight in the morning, Cane?"

He laughs, loud and excited in my ear. Maybe even a little psychotic. "Dude, I haven't fucking slept." *That makes two of us.* "Are you forgetting what today is?"

I wrack my muddled overworked brain for a moment and then, "Oh shit. Happy birthday, big guy."

"Thanks, man. But I wasn't calling for that. Do you remember what we talked about a couple months back? About starting our own financial company and taking on larger corporate interests?"

"Yeah," I laugh the words. "And if I recall, the three of us pretty much acknowledged that we'd be doomed from the start."

"Things have changed as of today, my friend."

I wait. I stand here, staring out at the falling snow because the way he says that? It makes me believe him. Something has changed. It's subtle, but there is an assured confidence, a giddy knowledge that wasn't there before. "Are you going to make me beg for it?"

"I don't talk about this shit with you guys. I know you come from some money, but Trav does not. He's on a full-boat athletic scholarship and still needs to work. So, I don't talk about my family situation."

"Do you really think we don't know you're loaded? You wear fucking designer beanies."

He blows a breath into the phone, the sound crackling against my ear, Then he says, "I inherited sixty million dollars today as part of my trust fund from my grandparents. I get another sixty when I turn twenty-five."

I manage to make it to the edge of my bed before I collapse, my knees giving out on me, my forehead hitting the palm of my hand.

"You still with me?"

"Barely. Jesus," I breathe.

"Yeah. Jesus just about sums it up. But you know what this means?"

I choke out a laugh. "Yeah. You need an excellent financial planner."

"I have one man. It's you. You may be young, but you know your shit. I know you play around in the stock market, and I know you've been earning some serious dollars with it."

I don't respond to that. When my mother died, she left me some money. Not a lot, but when I turned eighteen and started interning regularly for my father's hedge fund, I learned a thing or two.

"I'm serious about this company shit. I think we can do it. We have the capital to start. Trav wants to go to law school. Cool. He already said he'd be into corporate and tax law. Between you and me, I think we can really get this going."

"You're serious?"

"One hundred percent, bro. One hundred percent. And if we fail, well, I get another sixty in a few years. I'm not worried about me. My parents are sitting pretty on Forbes already and I'm their only child. I know you have something potentially going with your dad's company. But I also know you don't want to work for him."

I feel like I can't breathe. Like the cream walls are closing in on me. It's something I'd love to do. Something I've always sort of dreamed about. But the risk? Shit. The risk of failing is so goddamn high. And we're young. So freaking young. Who the hell is going to invest with us?

"I don't have your kind of money. Nowhere close. And Trav isn't in the same universe."

"I'll be fifty, and you each can be twenty-five. We need a lawyer, even a future one, and you're much better at this stuff than I am. I'm the guy who can sell manure to a cow farmer. I can close any deal, but I can't do any of this without you two. I don't want to do it without the two of you."

"Okay," I say, even though I don't know if I'm really agreeing to this. If it's something that's even possible.

"Awesome," he says and I can hear the elation in his voice. The belief. "I'm going to call Trav. Have a good Christmas if I don't catch up with you again before that."

"You too, Cane, and happy birthday."

"Right. Later."

He disconnects the call, and my phone slips out of my hand, landing on my bed with a gentle thud. A slow, reluctant smile begins to curl up the corners of my mouth. Our own company. Christ, I can hardly imagine it. But the moment I think that I know it's a lie. I love my father. I love him endlessly, but Cane is right, I don't want to work for him. I don't want to spend the next thirty years slaving away for him until he decides to retire, then hope he hands over the reins to me. There are other guys there already. Guys who are older and better positioned for that than I am. Guys my father knows and trusts.

Probably a hell of a lot more than the son he abandoned on Christmas.

Cane lives in New York City. He's already there and I've been to his family's place. It's huge. Massive for not just New York, but for pretty much anywhere. It's a good place to start. I stand up and walk back over to the window, staring out at nothing. Thinking. Strategizing. Coming up with names and logos and business models and—

"Hey," Lyric's timid voice calls out from the edge of my bedroom. I know that's exactly where she is even though I haven't turned around. She's too considerate to enter my room before I give her permission. "It's really coming down out there. A white Christmas."

I nod and smile at that. A white Christmas with her. I spin around and face her. Her gorgeous blonde hair is wet like she just got out of the shower, clinging slightly to the fabric of her lime-green blouse. She's wearing bright red leggings and red-and-white candy cane striped socks.

I laugh. I can't help it. "You look like an elf."

She glances down, a smile playing on her lips and brightening her hazel eyes. They look greener today. Maybe it's the blouse.

"That's the point. It's Christmas Eve. Wait till you see me tomorrow." I walk across the room and wrap my arms around her, pulling her soundly into my chest. I have no idea where the impulse came from. How my body actually made the ten-foot journey over to her. How she ended up here.

But God, I need this. I need this comfort. I can't remember the last time anyone who mattered hugged me. Probably not since my mother.

My father was never the most affectionate.

It's not really his fault and I don't blame him. Well, not fully anyway. His wife died, and he was left with a depressed adolescent son he didn't know how to relate to. He was hurting too, and coping has never been his strong suit.

So, there was never an abundance of hugs in my house.

Lyric freezes for a moment, clearly as caught off guard by the physical gesture as I am. But then she does the most amazing thing. She snakes her arms under mine and wraps them around my back, her hands sliding up to reach my shoulder blades, pulling me closer into her small, warm body. I sigh. I can't help it. I don't think anything has ever felt so good in my life. So fucking *right*.

She smells like strawberries and mint from her shampoo. Like a cool cocktail on a warm summer night. She doesn't question me. She just sinks into me, letting me melt into her. My forehead drops to her shoulder, my face burying into the crook of her neck. The tips of her fingers reach up, playing with the too long ends of my hair. I kiss her sweet skin. It's impossible not to. Just a small taste and her breath hitches, but more in bewilderment than anything else, I'm sure.

"Jamie," she breathes, and it's the first time she's ever called me anything other than Jameson. I can't tell which I like better from her.

I can't let her go. I don't know if my name on her lips is her way of saying 'let go' or 'I'm okay' or 'what the fuck are you doing.' I don't have answers for any of that. Because I thought I was okay. I really did. I thought I was more than just getting by. I felt like I was kicking ass.

But then the only family I have left me at Christmas. And then she came to stay here. And then Cane called with his crazy plan for our lives. And now I don't know. I just don't know.

"Are you okay?"

I nod against her.

"Do you want to talk about it?"

I shake my head.

"Okay." She squeezes, holding me so goddamn tight.

I think I'm absolutely crazy about this girl. Like insanely over the top in trouble. Because I'm going to New York. That's where my life is headed as opposed to hers laying three thousand miles west. But I don't know how to keep this up. How to pretend like I don't want her.

You'll hurt her.

I will. I know it. I feel it. That's where our story is headed.

I want to break my promise.

"Are you hungry?" I ask, my face still plastered to the sweet skin of her neck.

She giggles and I smile at the sound. "That's what I was coming to ask you. I wanted to go out because I feel like we're about to be stuck in your house for the next few days, but I'm not sure if we're too late for that."

I suck in one last deep breath and then I pull away, ignoring the way I suddenly feel like a pussy for losing my shit on her like that.

"It's not supposed to get bad out until this afternoon. They changed the forecast. Eight inches of snow and another couple of ice."

"Yikes. That's a real storm. Then let's go. You have a big Jeep. We can make it."

"We can make it," I agree, meaning that for so much more than breakfast.

Chapter Eight
LYRIC

"Do you open presents on Christmas Eve or Christmas day?" I ask as we finish picking at the last of our dinner. I cooked meat for the first time in my life, but Jameson ate it and said it was good. He could have been lying. I really wouldn't know, and I never will since I'm not about to try it. But my mother always made ham on Christmas eve, so I felt like I needed to.

I miss them. I miss my family. It's the first Christmas we're not all together as a family. I'm not mad at them for not being around this year. I get it. They deserve this time. My father put his life on hold for us for years, so I don't begrudge him this time. It just sucks.

I lift my glass of bourbon, the same brand my father always drinks, and take a small sip. We had wine with dinner, but now that it's done, we're both enjoying a glass of the good stuff before we clear our places and clean up. Jameson has been quiet today. At breakfast he was practically mute. I don't know what that hug was all about, and I haven't brought it up since. He needed it. That's all I know. I did, too, if I'm being honest about it.

Jameson's eyes come up from his plate to meet mine. "Lee, I haven't opened presents since I was a kid."

"Oh," I say, feeling a little foolish. I forgot that his family situation is a lot different than mine. "Does that mean you don't have a preference either way?"

He shakes his head and then shrugs, his eyes dropping back down to his plate as he shifts the leftover ham and mashed potatoes around with his fork.

"Do you want me to shut up?" I ask, not even being a bitch. I get it. He's had me here, and even though I've tried to stay out of his way, it's a lot of time together. He might just want a break. He glances back up, his eyebrows knitting together. "Seriously. I get it. Do you just need some space tonight?"

He blows out a breath and drops his fork onto his plate with a loud clank. He runs a hand through his inky hair and leans back in his chair. "I'm sorry. I'm being a total ass. You made this amazing dinner for me, and I'm glad you're here. I am. I don't want you to shut up and I don't need space. I just have a lot of my mind."

"Do you want to smoke a joint and watch a movie?"

He bellows out a stuttered, incredulous laugh. "What?"

"What?" I say back. "I don't smoke all that often, but we're not going anywhere. It's snowing its balls off outside and it could be fun."

"You have a joint?"

I tilt my head and wink at him. "I just so happen to. Daria gave me some as a Christmas present before she left. I got her new Doc Martens and she gave me two joints."

Jameson grins so big, that tiny hint of a dimple that only comes out when he smiles like this is there. It's the happiest I've seen him look in days, and it has me returning his smile with the same enthusiasm. "Go get it, baby. I'll clean up the kitchen. then we'll smoke a joint together. But I don't want to watch a movie. I want to play a game instead. We can watch a movie tomorrow."

I hop off the chair and head for the stairs. "That's if we don't lose power," I call out just as the fucking lights flicker. Like seriously. The exact same second the words left my mouth. "You've got to be kidding me. Do I have a super-secret power I didn't know about?"

Jameson laughs but gets up quickly. "Move your ass," he says. "I'll get the candles and flashlights ready. If it's already flickering, it won't last much longer."

"Fuck," I hiss. I hate losing power. Actually, I've never really experienced it before. We have a generator at our home in Connecticut. But it scares me. Probably because of that. "What about the heat?"

"Right. Well. We have a fireplace that runs on gas, and we have a lot of blankets."

I run up the stairs. By the time I hit the top step, they flicker again. I grab one of the joints Daria gave me and a blanket because I have a feeling we're going to need it, and then I head back downstairs. Jameson is in the kitchen doing the dishes, so I deposit the blanket on the couch and toss the joint onto the coffee table. Then I light some candles. I bought a ton, so I doubt we'll run out.

Besides, it's already dark out and if the power does go out, I don't want to be fumbling around trying to find them. "Do you want me to top you off?"

Jameson rolls his head over his shoulder and finds me. "How fucked up are we getting tonight?"

I shrug. "I'm not drunk, and I'll probably just have a little more. I doubt I'll have more than a hit or two of the joint."

"If you're having more, I'm having more."

Can't argue with that. I pour us each another two fingers and just as I'm pushing the cork back into the bottle, the lights flicker again, go out for a beat and then come back on. "Get ready for it, Lee. It's coming."

"It's fine. I'm fine."

I'm not fine. I'm nowhere close to fine.

"You're nervous."

Damn perceptive bastard. "Yep. I'm nervous. But really, we have food and flashlights and candles and the fireplace and blankets. We'll be fine."

"You convincing me or yourself there?"

"Dick," I mutter under my breath, and he laughs, turning off the water and wiping his hands with a dishtowel. Jameson is a clean boy. Thank God. Cane, on the other hand? Not so much. I told him I cleaned his room this afternoon when I called him to wish him a happy birthday. He told me he was pledging his undying love and devotion to me and offered to give me multiple orgasms as payment, so I don't think he was all that pissed that I did so without asking.

I like Jameson's friends. They're good guys. Even if they do flirt like tomorrow is the apocalypse, and this is their last chance to get a woman in their bed.

Taking two candles and a flashlight over to the coffee table, I sit down, tucking myself under the comforter I brought down. Jameson turns on the gas fireplace and then comes and sits down right beside me.

"Merry Christmas, beautiful Lee. I cannot think of a better person to spend it with."

I smile, lifting my glass the way he is, and we clink before taking a sip of the smooth buttery bourbon. "I'm glad I'm not at the hotel. This is so much better."

"May I?" he asks, picking up the joint. I wave my hand in the air, indicating that he can go ahead. He puts the tip of it into the flame of a candle, puffing a few times to get it lit. The lights flicker again and this time, they don't come back on. "You okay?" he asks, taking a drag and then handing it to me.

"I'm good. But I'm thinking we'll sleep down here in front of the fire."

"Probably a good idea. I'll grab more blankets later. Truth or dare?"

"What?" I laugh, coughing and choking some on the smoke in my lungs.

"You heard me," he grins, taking the joint from me and sucking in another hit before passing it back for me to do the same.

I breathe in another hit and then wave him off, letting him know I'm done. I like a buzz, but I don't love getting really high. He stubs it out on a plate he brought to the coffee table and then turns on me, facing me fully, his glass still in his hand. "Come on. What the hell else do we have to do?"

He's got a point. "Truth."

"Wimp."

"Hey." I slap at him. "You can't rate my choice."

"If you had to choose between going naked around campus or having your thoughts appear in a bubble above your head for everyone to read, which would you choose?"

I laugh, leaning back into the couch. "Naked. My thoughts are rarely fit for people to read. Truth or dare?"

"Truth."

"Wimp."

He chuckles, taking a sip of his drink.

"What's the craziest sexual thing you've ever done?"

"Threesome," he says without hesitation and my eyes widen. "I was hammered, unfortunately, but I was at a party sophomore year where these two senior girls came on to me. They led me to an empty bedroom and started making out with each other. It went on from there."

"Sounds hot."

He nods, a wicked gleam in his eyes. A gleam that has me squirming under the blanket. It's dark in here, but not uncomfortably so. The warm glow from the candles and fireplace dance across us, providing just enough light to see by.

"What about you?"

I shake my head. "That's not how this game is played."

"Adapt with me."

I turn away from his penetrating stare, over to the flames of the fireplace. It's gas, so there isn't that lovely crackle and pop that you get with a real wood fire. This one just has a gentle hiss to it and the flames are sort of lackluster, but it's better than nothing and provides an easy distraction.

"You're blushing, Lyric. Even in this dark room, I can see that."

I laugh despite myself. "It's nothing great. I really don't have anything all that fun to share."

"Tell me."

I sink my teeth into my lip. Why is this so difficult? Right, like I don't know. "I used a sex toy with a guy I was seeing back in New York."

He's silent and it takes every ounce of bravery in me to look over at him. "What did you do with the sex toy?" he asks, once my eyes find his. His expression is pure heat. His pale blue eyes are darker. Sexier. He's getting off on what I'm telling him and now he wants a visual to go with it.

"He watched as I made myself come with it."

Jameson closes his eyes slowly, licks his lips, and then opens to find me once more. "Truth or dare," he whispers, his voice thick with the mounting tension. It's like a hypnotic dance with a snake. Dangerous. Forbidden. Exciting. I can't look away. I'm utterly entranced. My chest is fluttering. My stomach is coiling. My skin humming.

"I thought it was my turn to ask you that?"

He shakes his head slowly, leaning forward and setting his glass down on the coffee table. He reaches out, taking mine and doing the same.

"Dare."

He grins and shifts closer to mine. The blanket is still covering my body, my feet propped up on the couch between us. His hand finds my knee and even through the blanket, I can feel the warmth seeping into me.

"Let me break my promise."

A bemused chuckle floats out. That's not where I thought he was going. "What promise?"

"The one I made to you that first day in class."

I stare at him, completely at a loss.

"The one where I told you I wouldn't ask to fuck you."

Oh. *That* promise.

He raises up, his knees pressing into the couch. "I know you feel it. I know you know how good it will be between us."

I nod. I do know. But I also know this will end badly if we give in to it. "I don't know if I can just have sex with you," I admit.

"I don't want to *just* have sex with you."

"That's not what I meant."

He comes closer, spreading my knees under the blanket and crawling up in between them. My heart is galloping out of my chest and he reaches out, touching the pulse at the base of my neck, his eyes on that point of contact. His fingers are warm and his touch feels like lightning.

"What are you looking for then?" I hate that question. It makes me feel like I'm asking for something he's not willing to offer on his own. "A relationship?"

I hesitate on that one. Because I know, if we start this, there will be no going back. He's right about us. We have something, and it's not the sort of something that diminishes with time. It's the sort of something that grows.

"I'm going to California in five months."

"I'm going to New York in five months."

His fingers trail up from that spot on my neck, gliding across my collarbone, up the back of my neck and into my hair. He grips it, holding it firmly in his possession, forcing me to face him head-on. My breaths are coming out in short, erratic pants. My mind is swimming and drowning and giddy and terrified all at once. I'm on overload.

"I dream about you," he says, slingshotting his words into me and forcing me to swallow them down. "About kissing you. Touching you. Fucking you. I haven't been able to look at another girl in weeks. Probably longer. I want you so badly; I'm crazy with it. But our lives are headed in different directions. So, how's this? We try it. We give it our best shot, but we take it one day at a time. We don't place expectations, and we don't talk about the future, and we see where we end up."

Yeah, with a broken heart.

But if I go into this with my eyes open and the knowledge that it can't go anywhere serious, can I hold myself back from truly falling for him? I don't know. I don't. If I said yes, I'd be lying. But screw it. I want him too damn badly not to try and find out. And if I do get hurt, well, I can't say I didn't know it was coming beforehand.

"Are we exclusive?"

"The thought of another man touching you makes me homicidal, so I'm going with yes."

"One day at a time?"

"It's the only way."

I stare at him. Breathe him in feature by feature as I try to clear the fog of lust and think rationally about this.

"What do you say, Lyric? Do you want this with me?"

Chapter Nine
LYRIC

"Yes," I say, agreeing to what we both want, and the most beautiful smile lights up Jameson's face, his clear blue eyes sparkling with lust against the flicker of orange flames. "We're going to ruin each other for everyone else," I warn him.

"I'm counting on it," he practically growls the words before his lips slam into mine, his body pushing me back into the couch as he covers me. It's the sort of kiss that's commanding. That zings down your spine and curls your toes and makes you moan just as you think, wow, he can really kiss.

And then it hits me.

This is no ordinary kiss before more. He turned my words into a dare. A challenge. Asshole is, in fact, trying to ruin me for everyone else. But two can play at that game. I can shred him of other women. I can rock his world upside down. And when this is over, he'll compare every girl from this moment on to me.

Every. Single. One.

The sad reality of that? I can already tell I'm going to compare every future man to him and we're still only kissing. I could stop this. But I'm already too addicted to his kisses. In fact, if he stops kissing me, I might die. He groans into my mouth, that hand in my hair begins pulling just a bit more as he adjusts me to get the position way he wants.

I hum, raking my fingers up his back.

"This has to go," he says, leaning back.

He yanks the blanket off me, tossing it to the floor before he's back on me. His length stretches over me as he holds most of his weight up with his elbows that are sinking into the couch, on either side of my head.

"Mine," he whispers against my mouth, his hand cupping my jaw.

He draws back, his eyes catch mine, our noses touch and the intensity, the raw, vulnerable passion has me woozy.

"Mine," he repeats, this time it's a demand. An order to comply with. I am his. I think I've been his since that first moment in class when I saw him walking up the steps before he even noticed me. When I disregarded him as an arrogant jerk who ate through women like a premenstrual teenager eats through calories. I'm not wrong in that description of him. He does do that. And now I'm his next victim.

I know what day by day is code for: Not serious.

But it's better that way. I have no room for serious and neither does he. Instead of giving voice to the millions of tiny bombs exploding within my head about just how stupid this is, I say, "Mine."

"Yours."

"Yours."

The fire in the hearth has nothing on his eyes. He reaches behind his back and tugs his shirt over his head. He grins when he catches me taking in the musculature of his arms and chest. I don't have access to the full picture at this angle, but damn, this man. Adonis really doesn't come close.

Leaning back, he sits me up and then takes my blouse off, unbuttoning each button with care. He takes his time, starting from the bottom and working his way up. But once he reaches the fabric covering my breasts, he cups me, squeezing me hard. "Do you like this shirt?"

"Pardon?" I don't think I can make sense of anything other than his hands on me.

"Do. You. Like. This. Shirt?"

"Oh. Well, ye—"

He tears at the remaining closure, snapping buttons left and right. "I'll buy you a new one," he says with a wicked grin.

He tosses the shredded material to the floor and then takes me in, staring at my bra-covered tits like he's fourteen and has never seen breasts before. Like I'm art and poetry. Like I'm the lyrics to a song he never knew he needed to hear.

"Breathe."

I shake my head. "I can't," I say, only now realizing that I'm a pant away from hyperventilating.

"Do you not want to do this?"

"I want to do this more than I've ever wanted to do anything." No truer words have ever been spoken.

His mouth finds mine in a fevered kiss, his hands back on my breasts that now only have lace separating us. His thumbs glide across my nipples that are desperately straining against the fabric. Diving his head down, his mouth takes over, nipping, biting, and sucking at me through the lace, his hands slide across my ribs until they reach the clasp in the back, removing it with ease.

My bra flies somewhere and then he devours me, taking my breasts into his mouth and hands. Like he needs to acquaint himself with every single inch of flesh. Testing every kiss, pinch, lick, and bite for my body's reaction. Fingers press into the soft leggings covering my pussy, fingering me, rubbing me through them. "You're so wet. Even through two fucking layers, I feel how wet you are. You're soaked. Dripping for me."

"Yes," I pant out as his mouth continues its torture on my needy nipples.

"Take off your leggings and touch yourself, Lyric."

Christ almighty. I don't think I've ever been this turned on. I didn't even know it was possible to feel like this. This...combustible. Explosive. My leggings find themselves somewhere. I don't care enough to look. One hand slides beneath the lace of my thong. I'm so desperate for release, my fingers start off at a wild rhythm. My other hand cups his hard cock over the thick layer of denim still covering it.

"Please," I moan, beg, plead. "I need you."

"God, you're perfect."

I open my eyes and find him watching me, unsnapping the button of his jeans, his eyes locked on the movement of my fingers inside my body.

"Harder," he commands, and I obey. I'm so close. "You smell so good, Lee. I can practically taste you."

"Taste me," I moan, not even sure who I am anymore. I never beg like this. I never make demands like this. But hell, I love how insane he has me. How close to the edge he's driven me with his words and desire.

He flicks my nipple and I come. I come loud and hard and wildly. I come so hard I see stars dancing behind my eyes. In a flash, before I can even comprehend the movement or what's happening, he has me on my back, my panties now gone and his mouth on my pussy.

"So sweet," he whispers into me, the sound driving me up the wall in ecstasy. He eats me like a starving man presented with a buffet of his favorite foods. "This," he says, his finger gliding against my backdoor, "is also going to be mine."

Oh God. My eyes roll back in my head.

"Every hole, every inch, is mine, Lyric Rose. And in five months, when we're forced apart, you'll touch yourself while thinking about all of the naughty, dirty things I did to you."

He sucks on my clit and I'm done. I scream this time, tugging on his hair and twisting my body. The sensation is too much and yet... shit, there are no words for what this is. Wrecked is the closest I can come up with. His mouth finds mine, his lips taking without asking. His hard cock grinds into my overly sensitive parts.

"Are you ready?"

"Yes," I breathe, barely able to formulate conscious thought patterns.

"Good," he says as he thrusts into me, hard and deep, taking no prisoners as he moves, our skin slapping with only a condom between us to keep us sane and smart. My fingers find his hair. His back. My nails mark him. Brand him. He is mine and I need the world to know it. I want him to feel it tonight when he lies on his back and tomorrow when he showers. I want his blood. His flesh.

And fuck my life, his heart.

I want that, too, and as a result, I do the stupidest thing on the planet. I open my eyes. I watch him screw me. I watch him possess me. I watch his face move, twist, exalt in bliss. I watch as he opens his eyes and finds mine. He moves my legs up to his shoulders and drills into me even deeper. I watch it all and he watches me.

Enraptured. Star-fire and dancing midnight.

And when we come, it's together. I've never experienced that. A man who watches, learns, and waits.

"That was only our first time," he pants against me when we're both covered in sweat and sated smiles.

No words have ever terrified me more.

"I don't think I'll ever be able to give you up."

No words have ever made me feel more alive.

"I didn't know it could be like that."

No words have ever made me want to cry so hard.

I'm going to love you, Jameson Woods. And then I'll get my heart broken.

I sigh and close my eyes, sinking into him. His arms wrap around me, holding me so very close. So close I never want to move again. So close I'm not sure I've ever been this content in my life.

Hold off, I say to myself. *Detach*, I beg.

"Too late," he says, his hands running down my hair. I said those words aloud. But I don't think I care, mostly because I know he's right. It is too late. Because I'm his and he's mine, and there is no going back now. The die is cast.

Chapter Ten
LYRIC

"Remind me what we're doing at a baseball game again?" Cass asks, her dark eyes surveying the crowd with equal measures of amusement and revulsion. "Those guys don't have any shirts on, Lyric. And their stomachs are painted yellow and red with the letters of our school on them."

"I know," I laugh, checking out the scrawny freshman who are yelling and heckling the other team.

"Do they know our school name is misspelled?"

"Not sure," I muse, taking a sip of my soda, shifting my weight to my other ass cheek. These stadium bench seats are mad uncomfortable. It's probably why most people are standing. "But they're entertaining nonetheless. Who knew people got this crazy over a baseball game?"

"What time do your parents come in?"

"They land at the airfield in an hour."

"Does anyone else know? Other than Jameson, I mean?"

I shake my head. I haven't told anyone. Not even Daria. And I swore Jameson to secrecy, so he hasn't mentioned it to Travers or Cane. My parents are literally stopping here for a few hours on their way to Las Vegas. It still makes me smile. My rock star father is nominated for Song of the Year at the Academy of Country Music Awards. He wrote a song for Jeremy Straight and it's been played nonstop on the radio—at least here in Tennessee.

I can't wait to see them, to take them all around campus. They've been here before, but that was back in September when they brought me here, so I didn't really know it the way I do now. And if I thought it was pretty here in the fall, it's downright gorgeous in the spring. The trees all have new leaves, and the air is sweet and fragrant with budding flowers. The sun is high and bright in the sky, with only a few clouds that don't dare to obstruct it or it's warmth. So much warmer here than it is up north this time of year.

"Is your dad the sort that beats up boyfriends? Because if he is, I'd really like front-row seats to that. It would be much more entertaining than this shit show. I get that your man love is the catcher, but why do *we* have to watch? It's not like he can talk to us or anything. He probably wouldn't even know if we left."

"My dad is definitely not the sort to beat up boyfriends. It's bad PR." I wink at her. "He'll just interrogate him some, but I doubt it will be all that much. He's known Jameson as long as I have. And you're here to suffer through with me because you're a good friend, and you owe me for that nonsense with Saylor last week."

She huffs out a breath, pushing the bridge her sunglasses up her nose. "Fine. But why do you have to be here?"

"He asked me to." I shrug, taking another sip of my soda. "And watching your boyfriend play baseball is what good girlfriends do."

The pitcher strikes the batter out and the inning ends. Jameson stands up, removing his face-guard and wiping away a trail of sweat from his forehead with the sleeve of his uniform. He looks…well, he looks fucking hot. It's not even the uniform, though admittedly, that's not bad. It's the sexy sweat and the flushed cheeks and the disheveled hair. He looks like he just had sex, so maybe that's what this giddy feeling at the sight of him is.

He searches the crowd, spotting me, and one of his big smiles before throwing me a wave. I wave back, smiling equally big. You'd think it'd been days since we'd seen each other based on the amount of butterflies I have right now, but it's only been a few hours.

"God, you two are so nauseating."

We sorta are. I can't even deny it.

"Did I tell you he's insisting on buying all of us dinner tonight?"

Cass looks over at me, her eyebrows at her hairline. "He's in love with you."

I shake my head, trying to ignore the way those words make me feel, my gaze focused on the field.

"Yes. He is. This is so much more serious than you play at."

"It's not serious," I protest, maybe a bit stronger than I should, given the audience, but it's the freaking truth. Well, at least it's the truth we keep feeding ourselves. Or at least I do with myself. I swallow that pill daily. It's become my morning vitamin. Especially when we leave each other's bed. Especially when I find myself thinking about him constantly and looking forward to the hours we spend together like they're my elixir to a happy life.

It's been months since Christmas, and as anticipated, I've fallen so hard for him. So. Hard. So impossibly hard that there is no stopping this for me. Even though we're barreling at an alarmingly fast rate toward the end of the semester and an entire summer apart. I try not to let my mind wander to such caustic territory, but it's impossible. I'm a planner. I like to have every situation figured out to the best of my ability. But there is no figuring this out.

Because we're on a day-by-day plan.

Stupid fucking day-by-day plan. I knew that would come back to bite me in the ass, and it most certainly has. I have to play it cool and casual when I am anything but. The stupid, insecure girl in me is afraid to bring it up. And I hate that almost as much as I hate obsessing over it because I am not a stupid, insecure girl. I'm not. But Jameson has inadvertently altered my neurochemistry and day by day—I really hate those words—I come up with more excuses to keep my mouth shut.

I have no idea if Jameson even gives our situation any thought. Because we don't talk about it. We don't say 'I love you' or 'I'm crazy about you' or anything remotely similar. We live in the moment with each other. And while I'm content to do that ninety-six percent of the time, that pesky four percent is eating me alive, occasionally overshadowing that much larger ninety-six percent.

"Lyric, any man who wants to buy his girlfriend's parents dinner is in love," she says with conviction. "I know we're not talking about this, but what happens when you go to California, and he goes to New York?"

I hate the way she just asked that. It's not even the question; it's the concern in her tone that's gutting me.

"I don't know," I answer truthfully. "I'm assuming we breakup."

"Seriously? And you're cool with that?"

"No. I'm not cool with that, but I don't see another way. Do you?" I stare her down, knowing she doesn't have any answers. Same as me.

"Yeah, I do actually," she grins, nudging her body into me and jutting her chin towards the field.

Reflexively, I turn to look and find Jameson next up to bat. But before he heads for the batter's box, he stops dead in his tracks—the whole stadium waiting on him—he finds me again and winks. But it's more than a flirtatious gesture. It's the gleam in his eyes that stops my heart. It's the way he continues to watch me for another couple of seconds before he heads over and gets ready for his turn at the plate that has my whole body humming with an infusion of dopamine.

"You stay together and ride out the distance. I've been at this school for three years, Lyric. And Jameson Woods has been here with me the entire time. Like I said to you on the first day, it's a small school. You pretty much know everyone, and even if you don't, you know Jameson. Or at least *of* him. He was a party guy. A guy who slept his way through two-thirds of the female students. Until you came along. You can deny him being in love with you all you want. Maybe that's how you mentally get through the ambiguity of your relationship, but he worships you."

I swallow hard, my throat feeling like it's closing up on me, the swell of emotion lodged in it, threatening to become something else.

Something like hope.

"I needed to hear that," I whisper, feeling a little foolish for admitting that.

"I know." Cass grabs my forearm and gives me a squeeze. "But that's not why I said it. I said it because it's the truth. You need to talk to him, Lyric. The two of you need to figure this out."

I nod. She's right. I know she's right. "Big girl panties."

"Yep. But more than that, you need to remember that you're a smart, beautiful, worthy woman. He's the one who's lucky to have you. He's the one who would be a fool to let you go."

"Stop," I laugh-cry. God, I'm freaking crying at a baseball game. Could anything be more pathetic? Cass rests her head on my shoulder, and we both watch as Jameson faces the pitcher with single-minded focus and determination. "Thank you," I manage once I get myself back under control. "I really love you and shit."

"I know. I really love you and shit, too." She sighs out. "This is for the win, right? Like if Jameson gets a hit right now, they win, and we can leave?"

"Huh?" I look over at the scoreboard and sure enough, it's the bottom of the ninth, only one out, but a runner is on third, and the score is tied. "Oh. Crap. Yeah, we should probably cheer him on and stuff."

"I'm not yelling anything, Lyric. That goes against every cool-girl code I have."

I scrunch my nose up. "I know. I feel sort of lame yelling, *go Jameson*. Do you think he'll notice if we don't?"

"No, he'll—" A loud clang sounds as his aluminum bat smacks the ball, and it goes careening through the air like a bullet on a mission. Jameson starts to run full steam ahead towards first base. "Oh my God," Cass screams. "Get down. Get down!" I think she's talking to the ball that's still in the air, and I'm trying so hard to suppress my laughter, but it's bubbling out of me anyway. "Yes! That's a hit. We won."

Now I'm hysterical, because she's on her feet, jumping up and down, the same as everyone else, wearing black shorts and a t-shirt that says, *I don't ask, I tell*. I also stand up because my boyfriend just won the game for his team and our school, and it's the sort of moment you cheer. Even if it makes you feel silly to do so. Jameson comes around the base, and the whole team is out there, jumping up and down with gleeful smiles. Crowding around him before they launch on him, mauling him like they just won the freaking World Series. They didn't. They just suck, so I guess a win is a big deal. But they're treating Jameson like he's their god right now, which I can't help but love.

Pride swells in my chest. My guy did it. He won the game.

"Don't worry," I say, nudging my elbow into Cass's side. "I'll keep my mouth shut. This moment shall forever remain between us."

"It better." We both laugh. Then Jameson is at the bottom of the red partition between the field and the stands, smiling like a guy who just won the game. He waves for me to come over to him.

"That's my cue."

"Go. I'll catch up with you tomorrow."

I lean in and give Cass a kiss on the cheek. "Thanks for coming with me."

She winks at me. "Anytime. Now go."

I do go. I practically skip down the large cement steps that separates my seat from the field. "Hey," I say as I get within hearing distance. "Congrats. That was freaking awesome. I'm so proud of you."

When I reach him, he wraps his arms around me, holding me as close and as tight as the barrier will allow. "I cannot believe I got that hit," he says into my ear, his tone pure elation mixed with astonishment. "I've never done that before, Lee." He pulls back and cups my cheeks, the cloud nine smile on his face not going anywhere anytime soon. "It's you. You're my good-luck charm."

"Kiss her," one of his teammates yells from behind. Jameson and I laugh, but then the whole team gets in on the action, chanting, "Kiss her, kiss her!"

My face turns beet red, but Jameson just laughs harder. "Gotta give the crowd what they want," he says before he crashes his lips into mine, lifting me off my feet and pulling me over the barrier until I'm on the field in his arms with his mouth pressed to mine in front of hundreds—maybe thousands—of fans.

We're awarded whistles, cheers, and catcalls, causing us both to laugh into each other. But I'm not embarrassed enough to stop kissing him. I love that he's this happy. I love that he has this moment to shine. It's contagious. Infectious. So goddamn perfect that I never want it to end for him.

His tongue sweeps into my mouth for a quick taste, my feet dangling off the ground as he pulls back and drops his forehead to mine, breathless and still grinning from ear to ear. "*Now*, this was officially the best game of my life."

"Just game?" I ask incredulously. "Not moment?"

He shakes his head no. "All my best moments belong to you."

Stop it, heart. Stop it now.

He gives me another searing kiss and then sets me down, his forehead staying on mine. *Say it. Don't say it. Say it.*

"I need a shower, baby. But will you wait for me? I want to go with you meet up with your parents."

I love you. So much it scares me.

"How could I say no to the man who won the game?"

His eyes shine, and his lips press to mine once again. "I'm so glad you were here. It wouldn't have been complete without you."

"Wouldn't have missed it."

He's sincere and I'm playful, and this moment is so bittersweet. So perfectly painful. So divinely dangerous. "Okay. I won't be long." He kisses me again, rubs his nose against mine and then releases me. By this time, most of the crowd has filtered out, and the team has gone into the clubhouse or the locker room or whatever the hell they call that place. I watch Jameson go. Just before he reaches the steps that will lead him down into the dugout, he turns back to me and just...looks at me.

But this look is so completely different than any other. This look is everything. This look says he loves me. Even if he hasn't said the words yet. Even if he doesn't even realize that's what this is. It's love. I know it and I hold on to it. I store it away because, in the very near future, there may come a time when I need to pull it out and cradle it next to my heart. Shove it into the forefront of my consciousness to tell myself: See, it was real.

There may come a time when I hurt too much to remember this look and his words and the way he loves me. He ducks down and heads inside, and for a few extra moments, I just stand here, holding on to that. *You love me, Jameson Woods. Let's hope we can both remember it when our distance becomes so much more than we bargained for.*

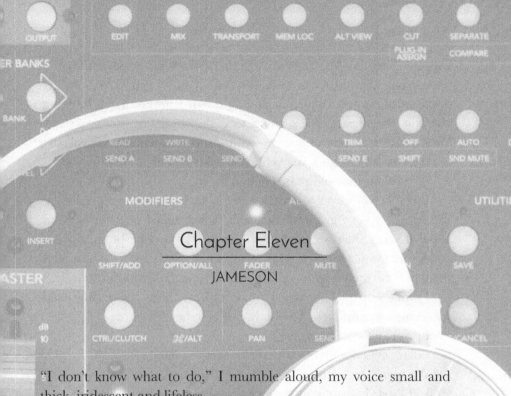

Chapter Eleven

JAMESON

"I don't know what to do," I mumble aloud, my voice small and thick, iridescent and lifeless.

"Marry her," Cane suggests dryly, his eyes on his computer as he types away. We've got this going. Our company. He tucked his sixty million and my million into it, and Trav has promised his first-born child as well as a kidney, and we're going. Moving. We have shit already spinning and we're still so young it frightens me.

I haven't told my father.

I don't plan on it yet.

Cane suggested continuing my internship that starts in a few weeks, learn as much as I can, and then next year, we're going to go in full-steam.

"Shut up," I say, mindlessly staring at a Braves game on television. Our baseball season wrapped up yesterday with a stunning loss. It really wasn't that stunning. We pretty much suck, but it's still fun. I like playing baseball much more than soccer, but I'm much better at soccer than I am at baseball. Go figure. I'm stalling. Even in my own goddamn mind, I'm stalling. I give zero fucks about sports in this minute.

We're supposed to leave for a party in a bit. Lyric will be there with her friends. We've been…together since Christmas, and we've done what we said we would. We take it day by day. We haven't discussed the future. But that doesn't mean I haven't been thinking about it relentlessly. She's going to California. I'm going to New York. Neither of us will have any time, and cross-country travel isn't all that convenient for a weekend visit here or there.

And really, it wouldn't be enough for me.

I feel Traver's eyes on the side of my face, but I can't face him. I should never have given in. But hell. How could I not? I'm so wild about Lyric. She's so ingrained in my blood. My brain. In my goddamn essence that I don't even smell like myself anymore. I smell like me mixed with her. No matter how many times I shower.

I can't stop fucking her. I can't stop touching her. I can't stop spending every moment I possibly can with her.

I just can't stop!

I can't get enough because there is no enough.

We spent our entire Christmas break in bed, only coming up for air and food. I was an animal. Insatiable. I fucked my dick raw and all I could think about was the next time I could be with her. And since then, either she's here or I'm at her place. Every night. I have lunch with her most days. I walk her to class and she meets me after mine.

I've never had this with anyone before. Never.

I was convinced it would feel like an obligation. That spending all this time with her would be a drag. But it's not. Because when she leaves my bed in the morning, it feels empty and cold. And when I leave hers, I'm dragging ass all the way to the gym or class or wherever I'm headed. I spend all this time with her because I *want* to. Because I don't know how not to.

Does she have to be so perfectly flawed? So absolutely right for me? Couldn't she just have been a regular girl?

"Break up with her," Cane says, flipping the tables.

"Never gonna happen."

"How do you think this summer will go? You're talking four months apart," Travers points out, oh so unhelpfully.

My fingertips dig into the denim of my jeans. I have no answer for that. Mostly because I can't think about being away from her that long. I'm screwed.

"He's in love, dude," Cane declares. "It's too late for any of that crap."

Again, I stay silent. I can't be in love with her. It's not even possible. We have a day-by-day plan. We haven't said anything anywhere close to that to each other. Yeah, we have a lot of sex, and we spend a lot of time together, but we don't talk or act like we're serious. Besides, love is for the blind and daft. I am neither. That doesn't mean I won't try to find a way to get to California a few times at least.

Cane passes Trav a joint, the cloying scent hitting my nose. Trav offers it to me after he takes a hit but I shake my head no. "You knew this was all coming. I don't get why you're all messed up about it."

I shrug, leaning forward to grab my beer from the coffee table. I take a slow, easy sip before I return it to its previous resting place.

"Because she's Goldicocks and our boy Jamie here is her just right." I turn to glare at Cane and he laughs. "Right. Tell me again that you're not in love with her. Admit it, dude. She's got you by the short and curlies."

"Shut up, twatlick," Trav snaps at him before turning back to me, the joint hanging loosely from his lips as a slow curling stream of smoke floats up. "When does she leave?"

"Right after finals."

"They do have studios in New York," Cane offers like he's brokering a deal. Like I haven't thought of that already. "Her gig might be more flexible than yours."

I finish off my beer, kicking my feet up onto the coffee table. "Robert Snow hates New York. He stays in LA, so that's where she's going. She going to be an assistant producer on the new 5 album."

Their eyes widen, and they exchange impressed glances. It's big time. She's big time. Or at least she will be. I don't feel big time. I feel like a college kid playing at being a startup. Only instead of doing something cool and techy, we're playing with other people's money. Would you trust the three of us with your cash? No. You wouldn't. So yeah, I can't imagine this ending the way we want it to. She'll be miles ahead of me, and I'll be so far behind she won't be able to see me, not even if she squints.

"She has access to a private jet, right?"

I shake my head. "Nope. Her father has it with him in Europe where *Blind Tears* are touring."

"Then you'll see her in September."

Yup. September. Awesome.

I get to my feet and Trav snuffs out the joint as Cane closes up the laptop. Time to go.

The party is for the baseball players. Our team captain, a senior by the name of Jonas Oswilder, lives in a big off-campus house with a few of the other senior baseball players. It's why he's standing on his kitchen table, which looks like it's about to snap under his weight, with a red plastic cup in his hand, yelling out some bullshit about our team while everyone cheers and shouts.

That's what drunk athletes do.

But I can't relax. I can't get into the spirit and the mood of the party. I don't care about being here. I need to talk to Lyric and see where her head is at. We've been avoiding it, but with only a couple more weeks before we go our separate ways, it's time.

The clock strikes midnight and as I turn—for what feels like the millionth time—to the front door, she walks in. Finally. She's smiling, taking in the organized chaos and drunken bedlam with a sense of humor.

Daria, her roommate, is clinging tightly to Cass's arm. I'm not quite sure what the two of them are, but I know it's something. Lyric is wearing a dress that makes my cock instantly thicken in my jeans. Short. Hot pink. Low cut. Her blonde hair is down, sweeping along the crest of her shoulders now that she cut it off last month. Her lips match her dress and her eyes are bright and clear.

She might just be my fantasy come to life. My wet dream personified. My midnight magic.

She looks around the open room teeming with people, and I watch her, waiting for the moment when she finds me. But somehow, she doesn't. She just walks further into the party, going in the opposite direction from me. I don't call out to her. I have a better idea for my girl.

And yeah, I just called her my girl. Because at this point, I might as well swing from the noose like I mean it. I'm done with the game I created. With the one that neither of us are particularly good at playing. I sneak back, away from the roaring scene in the kitchen, over to the bedrooms. I know which one is empty because no one dares to enter Oswilder's room. But he's so damn drunk and busy, I doubt he'll ever find out.

I open the door and sure enough, it's dark and quiet. Ignoring the scent of sweat smothered in cologne, I wait, the door partially ajar so I can see. It doesn't take long. I hear her talking to Daria about something while Cass laughs. I'd know that crazy laugh probably anywhere. She passes by, her blonde hair swinging. I reach out, wrapping my arm around her waist and tugging her into me, pulling her into the dark room. I wink at her friends, their expressions shifting from startled to scared to amused.

Lyric yelps, but I quickly stifle her cries of protest with a searing kiss. It doesn't even take her a full second to catch up before her hands are all over me, running through my hair, pulling up my t-shirt so she can slink her hands along my abs. I flex under her touch, pressing into her before I drop to my knees.

"You wearing this dress to taunt me?"

She nods, her head back against the wall, chin raised, mouth open on a silent moan. God, she's so sexy. I raise up the short hem of her skirt, inch by inch, enjoying the hell out of the smooth skin of her thighs as I go. "Jesus, matching panties, Lee. You are trying to taunt me."

I bury my face in the thin hot pink satin covering her pussy. She lets out a long moan, unable to stop it escaping her lips. Lyric gets loud if I don't shush her, but right now, I don't care if the whole damn party knows how good I'm about to make her feel. Inhaling deeply, I nip at her over the fabric. She's soaked. It only takes her seconds to be ready for me.

"This is mine," I breathe into her and she whimpers, her thighs already starting to tremble, and I haven't even gotten started with her. "No one else's."

"Mmmm."

"Tell me, Lee. Tell me you're mine. Tell me you want this to continue." Her chin drops to her chest and she meets my eyes, my face still right where we both want it, but I think I've successfully managed to distract her. "I don't want this to end when the semester does."

Her eyes sparkle against the light that seeps in through the seam of the door. "But—"

"I don't care. I know it's going to be shit. I know I won't see you and barely talk to you. I know all of this, but I don't want you to be with anyone else."

"You're willing to make that same promise? Four months apart with no other women?"

I nod, running my nose up and down her panties.

"This is epically stupid. We're going to end up fighting. We're going to end up getting jealous and wanting things neither of us can deliver."

I stand up because this is the sort of conversation that has to happen face to face. I cup her cheeks and hold her gaze. I open my mouth, but I can't make the words come out. I can't say them. I'm paralyzed. Because in this moment, looking into her eyes, I realize just how far my lies have extended. I do love this woman. Like no one has ever loved anyone before. But I can't tell her. I can't tell her how badly I need her. I don't even know why. The harder I try to force words out, the more impossible it becomes.

"See," she says, completely misreading my silence. "I don't want to place expectations on you and then hate you if you don't deliver on them."

I shake my head, but still, I stay silent. *Speak, dammit.* Why the fuck can't I tell her? But I know why. Because if I give her that piece of me, when this ends, I'll end with it. How can we succeed? We're only talking about four months, but it feels like an eternity and that's just this summer. What about next summer after we graduate when she permanently moves to Los Angeles and I permanently move to New York City?

What then?

"No expectations," I say and hate myself for it.

Her eyes glisten and I know I just said the wrong thing. I know it. I just indicated that I want my freedom to fuck other women when other women don't even show up on my radar.

"So, this is ending?"

I shake my head and press my lips to hers. "Never," I breathe against her, kissing her so she doesn't doubt my need for her again. "We can make it work, Lee. We just won't place expectations on our time. We'll talk when we can. We'll see each other if the timing works out. And come September, we'll pick right back up."

"Until the next time we reach this point."

"A lot can happen in a year, baby."

"Kiss me, Jameson. Because I'm so tired of thinking about things I promised you I wouldn't. I'm a planner. I'm the girl who always has to be in control of a situation, and I have no control over this. It's killing me. I hate that I think about it so much. That I don't want these four months apart to happen even though my dream job is waiting for me. But all the jobs I'm interested in are in California and I—"

I quiet her with a kiss. I kiss her so she knows I understand. That I'm not asking her to choose between her dream and me. Just like she's not asking me to pick her over my dream. We're so young. Just at the beginning of our lives. If we deviate from our dreams now, we don't know if we'll find our way back. The world is too crazy. But I meant it. A lot can happen in a year. So, tonight, I'll comfort her with my body. With my reticent heart.

I kiss her mouth and infuse her soul with mine. We become one, and for the first time—at a baseball party in my captain's room—I make love to her. I tell her with my body what my mouth can't. I make promises I wonder if I'll be able to keep. I guess that's why I hate time so much. The bitch is unyielding. Can't rewind her. Can't speed her up or slow her down when you really want to. She's an impenetrable force out to get you.

Lyric clutches at me, holding on tight after we finish, both of us breathing hard. We may have figured out a plan for the summer, but everything between us still feels unsettled. Shaky. Like even though we're both giving everything over to the other person, we're still holding everything back.

"Four months, Lee. It's nothing. Just a blip."

Her eyes find mine and she smiles softly, her hand running across my cheek and through my hair. I love it when she does that, and I automatically close my eyes before reopening them.

"We'll be back in no time."

I nod. But inside, I wonder what we'll look like when we are.

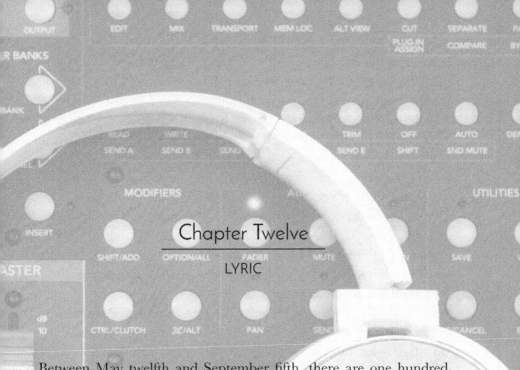

Chapter Twelve
LYRIC

Between May twelfth and September fifth, there are one hundred and fourteen days. Out of those one hundred and fourteen days, I saw Jameson a total of four. Four days out of a hundred and fourteen. We didn't talk much, either. I mean, we did talk, but not nearly as much as I would have liked. Not every day or even every other day. Sometimes we'd go three, or even four, days without speaking.

This summer was rough. As predicted, we fought a lot. I tried not to get angry. I tried not to place demands on him or his time like we'd discussed before we went our separate ways. But God, it was so freaking tough. Because when you're crazy about someone, all you want is to have them in your sphere. Physically with you. And when that can't happen, you settle for things like Facetime and phone calls. Even texts, though those fall last on my list.

Jameson didn't like the guys in one of the bands I worked with. He didn't like the long hours and me living in my father's Malibu house by myself. He really doesn't like my relationship with Robert Snow.

In reverse, I hated his long hours. It drove me nuts when he went to clubs with Cane and Travers. I'd cringe every time I heard women in the background of his office because I knew they saw exactly what I see when they looked at him.

We made plans to see each other more time than just those four days, of course. He canceled on me twice. I canceled on him once. Those four days we spent together was over the Fourth of July.

I understood he was busy. He was working long hours at his father's company and trying to get their startup going with any spare time he had left. So yeah. He didn't have a lot of time. The time difference didn't help, because he'd want to call at six in the morning New York time when he'd first wake up—three in the morning California time. By the time I woke up at seven, he was already well into his workday. Nighttime wasn't much better for us.

I tried not to think about what he was doing and who he was doing it with. I trusted him. I knew he cared deeply for me even if he never told me directly, and I held on to that during some particularly dark moments. But in all honesty, I was too busy to think much about our relationship status.

I was doing twelve, sometimes fourteen-hour days, working on two different albums. Both were so very different. One was for an up and coming alternative band called Wild Minds, whose songs were written like a beautiful poetry yet they liked to pair to a slightly heavier rock sound. Sort of like a cross between Imagine Dragons and Kings of Leon. The other was a female soloist who has more of a hip-hop sound. We were able to incorporate a few tracks with some really kick-ass trick-hop beats so they will light up clubs when this album goes live. Her soft voice mixed in with the heavy techno beats really made you feel the soul behind it.

In truth, I didn't want to leave Los Angeles for Tennessee. I love it there. I love what I was doing there. I love producing music and working with artists, and I have no desire to go back to school other than to be with Jameson. In fact, Robert suggested that I stay. That I don't need an education. That I already have all the tools I need to succeed in this world, in this industry, and that I'm wasting my time studying. Part of me, a very dark part, agrees with him.

I really don't need the degree. It's not like I'm getting much out of my music courses anyway.

But Jameson is here, and if I didn't come back, well, then I'm essentially giving up on us. Not that we won't have to make that call next summer. But I can't stomach that now. Not when so many things can change between now and then.

Now I'm back on campus, headed to my dorm. I'm still on campus. Mostly because it's really convenient. I'm sharing a suite with Daria again; Cass said she'd rather die than live in a dorm with a shared bathroom. I sort of get her point on that, but we only share it with four other girls. It's not that terrible.

The late summer air is sweet and warm, the sun just starting to set, lighting up the sky with gorgeous shades of pink, purple, orange, and gold. Jameson sent me a text this morning, informing me that his flight didn't land until ten, and it's an hour drive to campus. Disappointed? You bet. It's just another thing to add on to the pile of bullshit that makes me wonder if I'm the only one invested in us. I mean, what the fuck? He couldn't get an earlier flight to be with me for a few hours before our classes started tomorrow?

I sigh, staring up at the pretty puffy multicolored clouds, trying not to obsess about the guy.

"Hey Lyric," a voice calls out to my right, and I spin, startled as I come face to face with Matt. "Nice running into you. How was your summer?" He stands over me, a little closer than I'd expect him to, tall with a broad smile that brings those boyish dimples out in full force.

"It was good. Busy. How about you?"

If possible, that smile grows. "Awesome, actually. I was in New York, working on an off-Broadway show."

"Cool," I say. "Sounds great."

"Yeah," he nods enthusiastically. "It was a huge success. As one of the stars, I feel like I got a lot of notoriety for it. I even had some agents and other interested parties approach me. They saw the show and heard me at open mic nights."

"Nice. Sounds like things are starting to come together for you."

He steps closer, and I have to resist the urge to step back. After Jameson and I got together, Matt sort of backed off. Sort of. He continued to push me about working with him on his sound. I know what this is. I'm not stupid or naïve. I know what he's after.

"I'd like you to work with me on that. I know with our talents combined, we can make something amazing."

Right. Um…how do you tell someone you have very little interest in working with them or having them trade on your name? "Not sure if I'm the best person to help you with that, Matt. I know there are a lot of other more talented producers out there that I bet your interested parties would rather have you work with."

He grins like he's reading me, but I don't think he really is. In fact, that smarmy grin makes it feel like he's about to try and drop a bomb on my head. "Is this about Jameson? About him not liking the thought of you working with me? Because I heard the two of you weren't seeing each other anymore."

I hate it when I know things before they happen. It never turns out in my favor. And does Matt really think that pointing out my troubled relationship is the way to enlist my help? "I'm not sure who told you that—"

"Saylor did," he quickly interrupts, my stomach dropping at her name. "Didn't you know she was in New York with Jameson?" Does he have to look so satisfied? I didn't know Saylor was in New York this summer. It's not a name Jameson and I use all that often. "She told me that he told her the two of you were over. I'm not sure what happened between them, but—"

"Nothing fucking happened between them," Jameson's loud, angry voice rings through the twilight of the evening. I feel his hand slide around my waist. I feel the warmth of his body infuse my ravaged, insecure soul as he settles himself against me, practically nose to nose with Matt—who has yet to step back. "Clearly, Saylor was talking out of her bony ass because Lyric and I are still very much together, and that's not about to change, Matt. So how about you take your untalented, opportunistic self and fuck off." He shifts, gazing down at me with something close to adoration in his pale blue eyes. "Lee and I have a lot of catching up to do."

Matt steps back, but he laughs harshly as he does it. "I wouldn't trust him I were you, Lyric. Saylor told me all about the times she had his cock in her mouth over the summer and the late-night sex at the club."

Asshole. Why? Just why does he have to do that? Why do people feel the need to be so inherently mean to others? I seriously do not get it.

Jameson removes his hand from my waist, balling up his fists until his knuckles turn white, stepping in Matt's direction. "You have two seconds. I'm bigger and taller, and though fighting isn't typically my style, I won't hesitate to knock your lanky ass to the ground and spit on you while you bleed."

Oh shit.

"One."

Matt stares him down, trying to hold onto his precious pride, but deep down, he has to know he's outmatched. Jameson easily has three inches and fifteen pounds of muscle on him. He starts walking backward, all the while maintaining eye contact with Jameson. Once he's a good ten feet away and just before he turns to walk off, he refocuses on me and smiles. "I'll see you around, Lyric. Remember what I said."

With that, he's gone. Walking briskly away while trying to preserve an air of nonchalance. Jameson turns on me, and in a heartbeat, I'm in his arms. Not just being held but lifted up until my feet dangle inches from the ground.

"He's a liar," he says in no uncertain terms. His words are clear and direct, sincerity and desperation bleeding from his eyes as he begs me to hear him. Believe him. "I swear to God, Lee. I swear on everything there is that he's lying. Saylor had Cane's dick in her mouth all summer." I blink at him, shaking my head slightly. He lifts me higher, forcing my legs to wrap around his waist and my arms to encircle his neck until we're eye to eye and inches apart. "Saylor was in New York this summer. I didn't mention it to you because I didn't want you to worry about her. I know how you feel about each other. She tried with me, okay? She did. I probably should have told you, but you were in California, and we were barely talking as it was. I didn't want to fight over nothing. I brushed her off immediately and she didn't try again. I didn't want her, Lee. I only want you. She latched onto Cane because, as you know, he has money. Thankfully, his mother installed a gold-digger alarm in him at birth, so he didn't do much with her other than let her suck him off as often as she was willing. He didn't even fuck her."

"Okay," I say, believing him, but still not all that happy that this conversation had to happen in the aftermath. Or at all. Or that he filled me in on the details about her with Cane. That feels like a bit of a TMI, but I won't mention that. But really, Jameson knows I'm friendly enough with Cane and Travers that these would be verifiable facts. And I don't think he'd ever ask his friends to lie to me for him.

"Is that 'okay' as in you believe me?" he asks warily, his eyes bouncing back and forth between mine.

I nod. "Yes. I believe you. I know you wouldn't cheat."

"Thank Christ." He blows out a huge breath of relief. "Because I've missed you so goddamn much." His lips find mine, reclaiming what is only his. "Come home with me. I know we need to talk. I know things have been...not right. But I've missed you, and I want to pick up where we left off last spring."

I pull back and meet his eyes. *I love you*, I think.

This is not the first time I've thought those words. Or even mouthed them silently while he was inside my body. But I haven't dared to speak them aloud. And it's not even because he hasn't said them first. It's because I know that once I give into them, allow them to take over and become part of our fabric, our relationship will change.

There will be no more holding back.

I want that with him. I want him forever, I think. I can't imagine not wanting, loving him. But this summer might have scarred me. It might have been my worst fears realized. Part of me is screaming to get out now. To leave this school and this life and go back to California. To save myself from the inevitable heartache. But I can't make myself do it.

It felt like a part of me was missing all summer, and instinctively, I knew that part was Jameson.

How do you walk away from the man who makes you feel like you weren't really living before he barreled his way into your life? Like all you were doing was going through the motions, oblivious to how good it could really be. I feel complete in myself. I won't even say he completes me or makes me whole because I like to believe I am that without him. But he escalates me to an entirely different plane of existence.

Now that I've had a taste, I don't want any other flavor.

I want to go home with him. I want to say yes to everything he's offering me. But instead, I ask, "Should we stop this now?"

He sets me down on my feet, taking my hand in his and placing it over his chest. "Do you feel this?" he asks, pressing my fragile hand onto the strong muscles of his chest, his heart thrumming beneath me. "Do you feel the way my heart is beating right now?"

I nod, staring at my hand covering his heart, my throat thick with emotion to the point that I have to clear it away.

"This rhythm is the fear of losing you."

Jesus. I can't...breathe.

"This rhythm is something I've only ever felt with you. I'm crazy about you, Lyric."

Tears build up behind my eyes, but I can't let them fall. Not until he says it. I won't cry over him until that point, and I know, I fucking know, he's not going to stay it.

Because he sees that line too. Even though he's showing me, expressing it, he's not saying those three words that are not nearly as simple as some might have you believe.

His hand comes over my chest, pressing into my heart. His other hand grasping the bottom of my chin and forcing my face up to his. Forcing my eyes to meet his.

"I don't think I can stop now. I know what you're saying. I get it. I felt that too—the impossibility of us. But I know there's a reason you're my first real girlfriend. I know there's a reason I don't want to let you go." He pauses. Takes a deep breath. "Day by day?" he asks, watching me intently, measuring my response.

"What if I can't do day by day?"

He smirks like he knew that's what I was going to say. "Then, we have a lot of months to figure out a plan."

Chaos dances in my chest, seeping through my blood, igniting a slow, burning heat. It's in this moment I realize that Jameson Woods will be the end of me. I just can't figure out if that end will be in the form of salvation or ruination.

Chapter Thirteen
JAMESON

My phone sounds off like a foghorn, startling me out of my heavy slumber. I groan, rolling over to slap at it, only to realize it's not my alarm. Lyric moans next to me, murmuring something I can't hear but can guess at, into her pillow. I answer the phone with a swipe of my finger, opening one eye to check the caller. It's just numbers and though I know it's familiar, I can't place it in my hazy state.

"Hello?" I answer, my voice sounding and tasting like sand and ass—not the good kind at that.

"Jamie?"

I sit up straight, rubbing furiously at my eyes before I pull my phone away from my ear to check the time. 3:42. What the hell? "Dianne?"

"I don't know what to do," my stepmother cries, her voice panic mixed with an earthquake.

"What's wrong? What happened?" I feel Lyric sitting up next to me, her hand on my shoulder, but I can't turn to acknowledge her or answer her silent question.

"He's not waking up. I heard a crash in the bathroom. When I got up to see what the noise was from, I found your father on the floor with blood coming out of the side of his head."

Jesus! Fuck!

"Did you call 911?"

She puffs out a torrent of air into the phone. "No...I..." And then she falls silent like her brain has officially shut off and all higher logic and common sense are gone. "Why won't he wake up?"

"Hang up with me and call 911!" I bellow, terrified and helpless, losing the last shred of my sanity. Lyric grips my arm so tight, my head automatically whips in her direction. She's on the phone, I realize.

"Yes, we need an ambulance. There is a man unconscious after hitting his head. His wife is unable to rouse him."

I stare at her, listening as she relays my dad's address to the operator on the phone. She locks eyes with me as she repeats what the operator tells her. That they're going to get in contact with a local Greenwich dispatch and will have help sent over immediately.

"Jamie!" my stepmother screams, and I realize she's been trying to get my attention.

"Lyric called 911, Dianne. They're on their way. Just stay on the phone with me until they get there. I need you to tell me where they're taking him."

"Okay," she sobs, crying harder and harder into the phone. "I can't handle this. He's the strong one. Not me. I'm not cut out for this." She continues on and on, but I don't have words to comfort her. I don't have any words for anything right now.

The lights are on, and Lyric is up, moving about my room. My eyes mechanically follow her. She's packing a bag. She's throwing socks, boxers, t-shirts, and jeans in it. My hairbrush and deodorant go in next. Then she's zipping it up.

"I'm going back to my dorm to grab a bag. I'll call the airline on my way, but if there are no flights out of here in the next few hours into New York, I'll call my father and get the jet here for us."

Us. She's coming with me. Lyric just called 911 for my father who is unconscious. Lyric just packed me a bag. Lyric is getting her stuff and calling the damn airline for me.

"Get up, Jameson. Go shower or just get dressed. Get yourself together and I'll be back in twenty minutes." She turns around and leaves. I watch her go, my heart so full and my mind so lost.

I do get up. I follow her instructions, but I can't shower because Dianne, who is on the edge of her sanity, is still on the phone. I throw on a t-shirt, jeans, and a hoodie. I listen as the paramedics and police arrive. I listen as Dianne tries to explain what happened with my father.

My father is unconscious on the floor, bleeding from his head.

"He's going to Greenwich hospital, Jamie," she says after I've listened to them work on my father for far too long.

"I'm coming. Tell him I'm coming."

The phone disconnects. I don't even know if she heard me.. I collect everything I think I will need, my laptop, a few textbooks, notebooks, fucking pens. I shove them all into my messenger bag, grab the suitcase Lyric packed for me and then I'm flying out my bedroom door, stomping all the way down the stairs. I consider waking up Cane and Travers but decide against it. I'll text them later. I can't answer the questions they're going to ask.

I swing open the front door, a cool late-fall breeze hitting me square in the face.

Lyric isn't back with my Jeep yet, and I'm forced to wait when waiting is the last thing I want to do. The last time I saw my father was the day I came back to school, nearly two months ago. He took me to lunch before my flight and told me he was proud of me for all the hard work I put in over the summer. It was the first time he had ever given me praise like that. More than just a 'good job' or 'keep it up' or a pat on the back sort of thing.

This was real. This was genuine, and it made me feel like a two-timing piece of shit. I told him about the company Cane, Travers, and I have been working on. Once he got over the initial shock, he reminded me that his company would one day be mine. And then I'd really have my hands full. That lunch, in that small diner in midtown Manhattan, was one of my happiest moments. Because what I discovered in the cab to the airport is that my father finally saw me as more than just his son. He saw me as a man.

A man he was proud of.

Tears burn the backs of my eyes, my throat so thick I can hardly breathe or swallow past it.

He has to be okay.

I catch sight of headlights headed in my direction. They're stopped at the traffic light a few blocks down, and I know it's Lyric in my car. I stare at my car as I watch it idling, patiently waiting for the light to change because Lyric isn't the type of girl who would blow through a red light, even in the middle of the night.

We haven't talked about this past summer. Not once. Not even that day when we first got back when I told her about Saylor and how much I missed her. She hasn't asked any questions. She hasn't said anything about what's going to happen with us next. I know it's already starting to weigh on her, though. Because it's weighing on me.

This Christmas will mark our one-year anniversary, but it feels like a million lifetimes have happened in between that time. The months fly by too quickly when I'm with her, and too slowly when I'm not. Time, man. I hate time. But I love Lyric, and I'm at the point where I can't imagine myself without her by my side. My future is set for New York, and I know that eventually, she might be able to get herself there as well.

And if this summer proved anything, it proved that we can make this work. Four months apart have not impacted us. We're as strong as we were when we left last spring.

Maybe more so.

Definitely more so because I've given up on the idea that she's not my world. That the excuses of being too young and just wanting to have fun are just that. Excuses. Bullshit excuses at that. I've had my fun. I've slept with plenty of women. Not one of them made me feel a tenth of what Lyric does when I'm just standing in the same room as her.

The light still hasn't changed, but she must get fed up or too impatient, because she drives through the red intersection and down the couple of blocks before she's pulling up right in front of where

I'm sitting on the front steps. I stand, wordlessly toss my suitcase into the trunk, and when I approach the driver's side door, she shakes her head and yells at me through the glass to go around.

I don't have it in me to argue with her. When I get in, she turns to me for a second before twisting around completely, looking out the back window and pulling out onto the road.

"I'm driving," she starts like she's gearing up for me to fight her. "You have enough on your mind. I got us a six-a.m. flight to JFK, and my father's driver is going to pick us up at the airport and take us to the hospital."

"I love you," I say it simply, and her head whips in my direction, her eyes wide and startled like she never in a million years expected these words to come from me. That sort of makes me feel like an asshole because she deserved these words from me so many months ago. "I know this is the worst moment for this. I know I'm not doing it in some big romantic way that shows you just how much—but I can't hold it in anymore. I love you, Lyric Rose. You're the best thing to ever happen to me. And as long as I live, with a world and lifetime of experiences ahead of me, that will never change."

She's smiling softly, looking out the windshield as she focuses on the road. She's not a crier. She's not one of those girls who gets overly emotional and breaks down. Instead, she pulls the car over to the side of the empty road, throws it in park before she turns to me.

"I love you, too. I've loved you for a very long time. So long, in fact, I'm starting to get to the point where I don't remember ever not loving you. Jameson Woods, you might be stuck with me."

I take her face in my hands and kiss her. My tongue sweeps into her mouth and I taste her. I worship her. Devour her. If we weren't in such a rush, and if the world wasn't coming down around me, I would show her that her threat of being stuck with her is a promise I intend to keep.

"Thank you for taking care of everything this morning. Thank you for taking care of me when I need you the most."

She smiles against me, kissing my lips again. She doesn't say anything back. She didn't do all of that for me to thank her. She did all of that because that's the sort of person she is. I kiss her eyes. Her nose. Her cheeks, her forehead, and finally, her lips. We part reluctantly, as she throws the car back into gear, racing off into the darkness.

"Did you book a return flight?"

"No," she says with a small shake of her head. "I didn't know how I could with so much uncertainty around your father. John, my father's driver, is also his bodyguard and pilot. When I called him, he told me he'd fly us back whenever we're ready. The plane isn't scheduled for anything for a couple of weeks."

"I've never been on a private plane."

Lyric grins, her face illuminated in a blue glow that makes her look like some sort of beautiful sci-fi fairy. "It's pretty rad. At least, my father's plane is. I actually like it better than the one Robert has. It's big with a seating area, a dining room, office, and a bedroom in the back."

"Not bad being a rock star," I muse. While Lyric doesn't like to talk too much about her father's success, she does with me. She's told me about his career. About the album he's working on and how he's letting her produce a few of the songs. I think that might be her dream come true. She grew up in a world that most don't know and only have the luxury of dreaming about. But it's her life, and you'd never know it if you met her.

She does not scream rock star's daughter.

Though that tattoo she got last year on her back is pretty badass.

"I wrote a song," she says after a few minutes of silence, her words coming out as a whispered confession.

"A song?" I parrot. I knew she played around with other people's stuff, but I had no idea she wrote.

"Yeah," she hums, cutting to me quickly and then back to the dark highway.

"What kind of song?" I push when she doesn't say anything else.

"It's sort of Sonic Youth meets The Lumineers, if you can possibly wrap your head around that sort of sound. I don't really have words for it. Just the notes."

I smile, reaching out and taking her hand. God, this girl. My chest clenches so tight, I have the strongest urge to reach up and rub the spot. Just when I think I've seen all she can do. I mentally shake my head. There is no limit with Lyric. Nothing she's not capable of. "Will you hum it for me?"

She laughs, the sound buoyant, and the heavy weight I've had in the pit of my stomach since I got that call feels just a bit lighter. "No. Definitely not. But when we get on the plane, I'll play it for you. It's on my computer."

"I'm so glad you're coming with me. Something isn't right. It's more than him falling and hitting his head."

Lyric's eyebrows hit her hairline. "How do you know?"

"Because I heard the paramedics while they were working with him. He's the only family I have left. No grandparents. My father was an only child, like me. My mom never had a father that she knew, and both her mom and sister also died of breast cancer."

"Seriously?" she gasps, covering her mouth with one hand, her eyes filling with pain. "I had no idea. They must have had that genetic link."

I nod. "Yeah. She died before there was regular testing for it, but I know that must have been it. In any event, my dad is it. Dianne is not my family."

Lyric squeezes my hand. "Family is not always what you're born into. You have me. You have Cane and Travers. You're not alone in this world, Jameson. I know you feel like that sometimes. I see that darkness in you, but you're not. Not even close. I'm not going to spew bullshit platitudes or words of comfort about a situation I have no knowledge of. Your father is going to be okay, but if for some awful reason he's not, well, then we'll get through it. Together."

"I've known you practically my whole life, Lee. Since we were six." I shake my head. "I always saw you. Always watched you and secretly pined after you. Every fucking guy in school did. But I didn't know you. Not really." I lean over the center console and bury my face in her neck. "I'm so glad you transferred schools."

Her fingers glide up, slicing through my hair and holding me against her. "Me too. 'I have waited a lifetime, spent my time so foolishly. But now that I found you, together we'll make history'," she quotes. "Foreigner was never my favorite band, but those lines always stuck with me. I think maybe that's us."

"I certainly hope so, baby. I certainly hope so."

Chapter Fourteen

LYRIC

When we land, my father's driver is there waiting for us. I've known him since I was a small girl, so when he wraps me up in a big bear hug—because the man is the size of a bear—I release the breath I've been holding since Jameson got that phone call.

Jameson is exhausted. I tried to get him to sleep on the plane, but he couldn't. I think he was a little upset with me. I purchased first-class tickets because that's all they had left next to each other. I was not going to have him sit in some random middle seat without me there with him.

Even so, the comfort was nice to have and allowed him to practically lay across my lap as I ran my fingers through his hair, trying to lull him to sleep. He listened to my song, and after he heard it, kissed me crazy while praising a genius I do not feel I possess, then he fell silent for the remainder of the trip.

He greets John with a friendly handshake, and then we're quickly ushered to my father's large Mercedes sedan. In addition to having an airplane, my father also has an arsenal of cars. He's also one of the most generous men on the planet. I received a slew of texts from him once we landed and I turned off airplane mode, asking how we were, offering us the house to sleep in and food and whatever else we could ever need.

My father has met Jameson plenty of times growing up, but when he and my mother came to Tennessee, they fell in love with him. Even if he and my father did fight about who was going to pay the dinner bill for over five minutes. Jameson won. My overly possessive father, who is slow to like anyone his girls date, has accepted my boyfriend as part of our unit. And that means anything Jameson needs, my family is there to help with.

As we sit in New York rush-hour traffic that doesn't stop, even after everyone is already at work, Jameson calls the hospital for an update. I note he doesn't call Dianne, and I wonder if that's because of their tenuous relationship or something else. I hold his hand as he listens to whatever the doctor or nurse is telling him. When he closes his eyes like whatever they're saying physically hurts him, I move closer to him.

"He had a heart attack," he bewilderedly breathes out once he ends the call. "He's up in the ICU. They gave him some medication that dissolved the clot in his heart, and tomorrow they're planning on doing angioplasty."

"They dissolved the clot." I smile and he nods. "Sounds promising."

He doesn't say anything else. Not even as we pull up at the hospital and John shakes his hand, offering his sympathies. We're directed upstairs. As we walk down the hall of the ICU—a terrifying place to visit even if we didn't have a loved one here—and enter his room, I do my best to hold in my emotions. Jameson squeezes my hand so tightly I can feel the blood draining from my fingers.

My fingers match Jameson, who is suddenly white as a sheet with wide eyes and an expression that relays both of shock and terror. His father is asleep, his eyes closed, but for such a strong man, he looks small and meek.

His black hair—the same shade as Jameson's—is disheveled. There is a large, stitched-up gash on his right temple. There's tubes and wires protrude from his arms and chest, and he's hooked up to machines that drip medicines and fluids into his body. A monitor flashes green numbers at me, various wavy lines dancing across the small screen. I have no idea what any of it means, but I'm hoping it's good.

"Dad," Jameson whispers, his voice hoarse like he hasn't used it in years. His father doesn't open his eyes, and Jameson starts to tremble. I swallow hard, pleading with myself to hold it together.

"You must be Mr. Wood's son, Jameson?" a voice behind us asks, and we both spin around to face a young, pretty woman dressed in light blue scrubs. "I'm Doctor Landy."

"Nice to meet you." Jameson shakes her hand. "This is my girl-friend Lyric Rose."

She greets me before turning her full attention back to Jameson. "Would you mind stepping outside with me for a moment so we can talk?"

"Uh...," Jameson hesitates, clearly not wanting to leave his father's side.

"I'll stay," I offer.

He gives me the smallest of perceptive grins before following the doctor out into the hallway. I don't know what to do with myself. Where to go or how to move. I'm terrified that any misstep will be like tripping over the proverbial plug, even if I know that idea is ridiculous. It's just the overwhelming nature of the room and the situation.

There is an empty seat beside his bed, which I slowly sink into, realizing as an afterthought that Jameson's stepmother isn't here. Tentatively, I reach out and place my hand on top of Mr. Wood's. And then I smile because even though I know his name is Jameson, like my Jameson's, I've only ever heard him referred to as Mr. Woods.

At my touch, his eyes slowly flutter open, and I realize just how much Jameson looks like him. Same pale blue eyes. Same black hair. Some chiseled, handsome features.

"You're not my son," he whispers softly, his voice gravely and weak.

"No," I say, leaning forward. "Jameson is out in the hall speaking with the doctor. I'm—"

"Lyric. Yes, I know all about you." I blush a little at that and I'm not typically an easy blusher. "You're my son's girlfriend."

"Yes," I say, even though he didn't pose that as a question. I get the impression Mr. Woods knows and sees everything.

"I'm thrilled I'm finally getting to meet you, Lyric. I'm sure I've seen you before, around town or in school with Jamie. But we've never been formally introduced. You make my son very happy."

I smile. I can't stop it. Even in the middle of this grave situation, something about his father's statement fills me with giddy bubbles. "Me too, Mr. Woods. You have an incredible son."

"You can call me Jameson. But if that's too confusing since I know that's what you call him, you can call me Jamie and my son Jameson."

I smile. Laugh a little. "How are you feeling, Jamie?"

"Like I had a heart attack and hit my head." I frown at that, so he reaches over, covering the hand that's holding onto him with his other ice-cold hand. "I'm glad you two came, though you really should turn around and go back. You both have school."

"I don't think that's going to happen until you're on the mend."

"I'm grateful my son has you, Lyric. I don't know you well. Not yet, anyway, but you remind me of Jameson's mother, Lily. The way you love him and the way he loves you. It makes this old man very happy."

And I'm crying. Big, fat ugly tears. I can't stop them. They're rolling down my cheeks like a tsunami crashing to the shore. I feel so foolish and am beyond embarrassed, but God...how can I not cry at that?

"What did you say to make my girlfriend cry, old man?" Jameson comes in, his tone playful and eyes bright. I love that he just called him old man. Especially after his father called himself the very same thing.

"Come over here," his father says.

I wipe furiously at my eyes that are still leaking like a faucet. Jameson kisses the side of my face, stopping me when I try to rise

114

out of the seat so he can sit in my place. He lowers himself onto the arm of the chair instead, closer to his father. He doesn't touch him the way I am. He just sits there, stiff and uneasy despite the light-hearted moment they just shared.

"I'm fine, Jamie. I'm going to be fine. Stop looking at me like I'm about to die any second."

Jameson shakes his head, rolling his eyes and growling something under his breath.

"We need to talk," his father states, and now I do stand up. They need time alone.

"I'm going to go home and shower," I declare, shifting from Jamie to Jameson. Shit, that's going to get really confusing. Especially since his father—and everyone else—call Jameson Jamie. "I'll be back in a bit with some food."

Jameson—my Jameson—turns to me and nods. "Okay. Thanks, baby." He leans in and kisses my lips, right in front of his father. I've never kissed a boy in front of an adult like that, and I feel myself coloring again. Jameson laughs at my reaction. Then I say my good-byes to his father and get the hell out of there.

I don't bother calling John. He just dropped us off, and I already woke him in the middle of the night to have him pick us up at JFK. Instead, I take an Uber home, anxious to see my parents.

I step out of the car at the gate of my parent's house. The driver pulls away and I punch in the code, the large black iron gates swinging open for me. I don't even make it up the driveway to the front of the house before the front door bursts open and Melody comes flying out. She's laughing hysterically, practically skipping and galloping at the same time until her arms are wrapped around me, and she's jumping up and down, giggling and screaming in my ear.

"You fucking bitch," she squeals. "Why didn't you call me?"

I pull back, my smile as glorious as hers. "And when was I supposed to do that?"

She sighs, some of her enthusiasm slipping. "I don't know. I guess you had a lot on your plate. How is he?"

"Jameson the Third or Jameson Junior?"

She glares at me, her muddy green eyes narrowing. "Both, slut wagon."

God, I've missed my sister.

"Hanging in there and hanging in there. I left so they could talk and spend some alone time together. I'll go back after I visit with you, Mom and Dad."

"Am I the worst sort of person if I show you this?" she asks, extending her elegant, manicured hand out to me so I can see the massive, emerald-cut diamond that looks like it could sink a battleship, prominently displayed on her fourth finger.

"Oh my God!" I scream, wrapping my arms around her again as we do that jumping up and down, giggling thing that only really close sisters or friends can do. "You cunt. When did you get engaged?"

"This morning, actually. Can you believe it?" She pulls back, wiping at her happy tears. I have some of my own going too. "It was the craziest thing. I woke up to this elaborate breakfast José made me. I mean, everything, right down to the damn scones, was homemade. Just as I took a bite, he got down on one knee."

"You choked, didn't you?"

She bursts out laughing, throwing her head back and everything. "Yes! I did. I totally freaking did. But luckily, I got control quickly, because that is not a story to tell the grandkids. I said yes, obviously." She wiggles her fingers and the massive diamond glints at me again.

"I am so happy for you. When's the wedding? And what hideous dress are you going to force me into as maid-of-honor?" I point at her, making sure she gets the threat behind my words. Any other title will not do.

"You can pick it out. I won't even argue with you when you choose some nutty color like powder blue or bright yellow. And I'm thinking sometime next summer." She cocks an eyebrow at me and I know that look.

"Like I'd miss your wedding. I'll take whatever time off you need me to. Can I bring Jameson?" I ask and then I pause, realizing I'm assuming a lot about our relationship. I know we said 'I love you' this morning. I know we've become serious and despite our 'day-by-day rule,' we both want it to work out.

Regardless, the voice in the back of my head continues to ask, *how can it?* I've even talked to Robert about New York, but he won't hear of it. The office there is small and there are no studios. At least not ones meant for full record production. California is his home base.

I've been looking for other studios, making calls and sending emails, but so far, nothing else has come up.

"Of course, you can. But…"

I shake my head, shutting down the question instantly. I don't want to go there. I'm getting tired of obsessing over the perpetual ticking clock on my relationship with him.

"Come inside. Mom, Dad, and José are waiting on us. They let me have my moment, but I know they're dying to share it with you too."

Melody and I walk arm in arm into my parent's house. Melody can't stop talking. Her mouth moves a mile a minute. I've never seen her this happy, and in turn, that has me over the moon.

I hug José, my sister's new fiancé instantly. He's a tall, slender guy with dark brown hair, dark brown eyes, and gorgeous, tanned skin. José's father is originally from Cuba. He came over here for baseball and never went back after meeting his wife and having children.

"Lyric, my love," my father says with a huge smile. "We've missed you so much." He wraps me up in his tattooed arms, kissing the crown of my head. His blond hair is shorter than it was the last time I saw him, and I think I like it better like this. It fits him. My mother comes on the other side of us, holding me just as fiercely.

"How's your boy?" she asks in my ear. "We're so worried about him. About both of them," she adds.

They release me, taking my hand and leading me back into the sunroom. I love this house. It may be huge, but it's always felt intimate and cozy. It's always felt like home. My mother is also blonde, with big green eyes, and a smile that can stop your heart. She met my father when she was my age. They ran into each other after one of his shows. She went backstage with a friend, the two of them began talking, and that was it.

They married a year later and had Mel two years after that. My mother devoted her life to raising us and did a damn good job of it. I know how lucky I am to have a family like this. What it means to be loved and cared for to this degree. How special and rare what we have is.

I explain everything that happened with Jameson's father and how my Jameson is taking it. They listen with rapt attention, holding my hand, and looking as stricken as I feel.

"He can stay here with you," my mom asserts, looking to my father for confirmation. He nods like it's a done deal. "He doesn't have to stay in his dad's house with his stepmother. He's yours; that makes him ours, too."

"Thank you," I say, getting choked up for what feels like the millionth time today. We talk for a few more minutes, mostly about Melody and José's wedding plans. Then I excuse myself to shower so I can get back to Jameson. I have a feeling it's going to be a long couple of days.

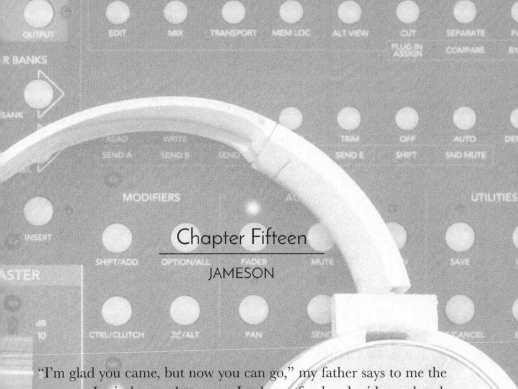

Chapter Fifteen

JAMESON

"I'm glad you came, but now you can go," my father says to me the moment Lyric leaves the room. I rub my forehead with my hand, trying to remain calm when his words just piss me off so much. My father looks about ten years older in this hospital bed. He's frail and sickly pale. I know he views this heart attack, this hospital bed, and the shit coming out of his body as some sort of emasculating assault. Like being sick is a weakness the world is just waiting to exploit.

"You're having surgery tomorrow. I'm not going anywhere."

"I'm having a procedure and I'm going to be fine. You have classes you're missing."

I stand up quickly, striding to the window that overlooks a courtyard, because if I don't leave my father's side I'm going to throttle him—and I think it's considered bad form to beat up a guy who just had a heart attack.

"I'm staying," I state firmly, staring out the window. I don't know why I'm so angry with him. Maybe because he's spent his life drinking alcohol, eating red meat with every meal, and smoking cigars. Maybe because I don't really feel like he appreciates that I flew out of bed in the middle of the night and came running up here for him. Or maybe because in this moment, I feel like a child and need him to just be my dad. Even if that's unfair given the circumstances.

But the last thing I can handle right now is the hard, tough-love routine he's been shoveling down my throat my entire life.

"She's special," he says, and I know he's talking about Lyric.

I nod my head, still blindly staring at nothing out the window. "Yes. She is."

"I hope it works out for you two. Not so easy when you both want big careers. Your mother was never all that into work. She was always happy to let me lead. I don't think your girl is like that."

"No. She's not."

"She's gonna have to learn if you want it to work out."

Shut up, Dad. Just shut the fuck up!

"It's why the divorce rate is so high in this country. Women want to have it all–big careers and a perfect home life. But men are simpler than that. We know we can't have it all and expect our women to take up the slack. When they don't because they're too busy with their own jobs to watch after their families, well, that's when couples break up."

I spin around on my heels and face him head-on. "You don't really believe that bullshit, do you?"

"No," he says with a tired grin. "I don't. I was just checking to see how invested you are with her. To see if you'll support her when she needs you to."

I laugh. It's slightly hysterical. I have no idea who this man is right now. My hands run through my hair, tugging on the ends. It doesn't help to ease the mounting pressure inside me.

Pressure.

That's all I ever have going on.

School. Sports. My father's expectations. This new company venture with Cane and Travers.

"I don't want to talk about Lyric. I want to talk about you."

"It's a heart attack, Jamie. No one's cutting off my balls. I'll be out of here in a few days and back to work by the end of next week."

I stare at my father, wondering if he'll ever quite understand. I don't think so. I think his stubbornness is so deeply ingrained in who he is that there is no seeing past it at this point. So why am I trying to fight him? Why do I feel like I can win when I've already lost?

And because he's like this, I can't show him any weakness. I can't tell him that he's all I've got, even though Lyric pointed out that he's not. It's different, though, and I know she understands that. I can't tell my father I'm scared for him. That if he doesn't change his lifestyle, there will be a next time and that the next time might not end so well.

I don't feel comfortable expressing emotion to my father, which hurts nearly as much as this situation does.

But there are some conversations people can't have with each other. Some words can never be spoken. Sometimes, you end up swallowing your tongue and part of your soul instead of your pride.

I turn back around, no longer able to look at him. "You win, Dad," I say. "You always do."

I think a part of me just died.

But ironically, it's not any part I want to possess anymore. It's the scared little boy I've been holding on to since my mother died. I am no longer afraid of my father, I realize. I no longer need his approval and praise. I have my own company. I have a beautiful girlfriend who loves me. In eight months, give or take, I'm going to have a degree.

Maybe then, I'll be able to breathe a little. I'll find some wiggleroom and space to maneuver. I won't feel like a weight is constantly pressing down on my chest. I may have always wanted to be like my father, and part of me still hopes I am to a certain degree, but I am so much more aware than he'll ever be. Accepting that we all have weaknesses makes us stronger...and admitting that simple fact to myself makes me stronger than him because he's never been able to face his own shortcomings.

"Good. Now go find that girl of yours. I'm tired and need my rest. Come back and see me later before you leave town."

"Did you know that I flew out of bed to get here? Dianne, who's not even here, called me at a quarter to four in the morning. I didn't hesitate. I packed a bag. Lyric and I drove an hour to the airport, and I got on a plane. Now here I am. And you're fucking kicking me out."

I drop my forehead to the window, wishing I were stronger in this minute. Wishing this wasn't so goddamn hard to say. Slapping my hand against the cool pane of glass, I right myself. I turn back around and march over to his bed, then drop down into the chair.

"Fuck you, Dad." His eyes widen at my outburst and I relish that small victory. "Fuck you for trying to get rid of me. Lyric and I are staying. You're going to shut up and accept our help. We'll leave when we're ready, and I'm satisfied that my father isn't going to die."

He stares me down and then smiles. "How's your business going?" A chuckle bursts out of my chest. Damn this man.

I slink back into the uncomfortable chair, run a frustrated hand through my hair and scrub it up and down my face. And then I blow out a breath and tell him everything that's going on with my business.

We talk. Well, I mostly talk, and he listens. Just when he starts to doze off, Dianne waltzes in like she hasn't been gone all day. Like her husband didn't just have a heart attack and is in the ICU. Bitch looks like she just came from the salon. I get up and leave his room, offering her no more than a nod, feeling more satisfied than I have in a long while. At least where my father is concerned.

Lyric is standing in the hallway, leaning against the wall with her foot propped up and her eyes on her phone, a soft smile pulling up the corner of her lips. "How long have you been standing there?"

Her head pops up and she shrugs when she finds me. "I didn't want to interrupt."

"How do you feel about going into the city for some dim sum?"

"Are you willing to go vegetarian?"

Shit. How on earth could I have forgotten that she's a goddamn vegetarian?

"Can I order shrimp fried rice?"

She nods, pushing off the wall and walking slowly toward me. "I know a really good place," she says, dragging her hands up my chest and around my neck, kissing my jaw.

"Then let's go. I'm starving."

"How is he?"

"The same. He's always going to be the same—and I think it's time to accept that."

She nods. Kisses my cheek. Runs her nose along the nape of my neck. Drives me wild in the middle of the freaking ICU.

"My sister got engaged."

"Yeah?" I ask with a smile, and she nods again, her smile double what mine is.

"Yeah. My parents are taking her and José out for a celebratory dinner. They invited us along, but I said we'd probably do our own thing." She winks at me, her smile turning into something else completely.

"You look like you've got ideas floating around in that pretty head of yours."

"I have to warn you," she says, reaching up on her tiptoes to whisper in my ear, "they're all dirty."

"Come with me then."

I take her hands from around my neck and intertwine our fingers. I lead her out of the hospital, telling the nurses to call me. We Uber back to my father's house, and I go into his garage to find my old car. He bought me my Jeep when I left for college, saying I needed a car there, but he didn't want me driving back and forth from Tennessee to Connecticut. I didn't argue. It was a new Jeep, after all.

But my old car is, in fact, old. It's a 1969 Ford Mustang. It was my grandfather's car. It's so goddamn cool. I took it when it was offered to me and slowly restored it over the years. It's black with smooth, black leather seats that are piped in white. There isn't any air conditioning, but it's late November in Connecticut, so we definitely don't need it, and the heat works just fine.

"You're not driving this is the city," she says, taking in the car, running her hands along the dash and seats.

"Fuck dim sum. I'm going to eat you for a snack, and then I'll take you out somewhere for dinner."

She looks over at me as I start the engine with a loud, powerful roar, thrilled that it actually started. Our seats vibrate with the horsepower, a surge of life spidering its way through my veins.

"You uh…sure?"

I laugh, taking her hand. "I'm sure, baby. Life is goddamn short, My father and I talked about a lot of things. Tomorrow, we'll wake up early and be at the hospital all day, but tonight is for us."

Lyric smiles at that, settling in for whatever I have in store for her. She doesn't ask where I'm taking her. I doubt she cares. She just wants to be with me, and I want to be with her. Nothing else matters.

I drive us down to a secluded area by the ocean. This part of the beach belongs to the yacht club, but my father is a member. You don't actually need a yacht to be a member, which is good for him since he doesn't have one. But I know for a fact no one will bother us over here. It's rarely patrolled, especially this late in the season.

I shift my car into park, turn off the headlights, find a station on the ancient radio and then tug Lyric into my lap. She smiles, her eyes locking on mine as she dips down and kisses me. My tongue invades her mouth, my hands cupping and squeezing her ass. Her arms wrap around my neck, toying with the ends of my hair as she deepens the kiss. She moans, rocking into my painfully hard cock that's already straining against the denim of my jeans and I squeeze her harder. Letting her know I have so many plans for us. For tonight. For her body.

"Get in the backseat and take off your pants and shirt," I command, but leave your bra and panties on.

She scurries over the bench seat so quickly that if I weren't so fucking turned on, I'd laugh. I watch her through the rearview mirror, our eyes locked in the glass as she pulls her blouse slowly over her head. I lick my lips as her hands glide down the smooth, taut expanse of her stomach until they dip out of range for my eyes.

With my heart racing in my chest, I reach behind my head and tug my own shirt over my head before I remove my jeans, pulling out a couple of condoms from my pocket as I do. I stroke my cock through my boxer briefs, already so ready for her I can hardly stand it.

I'm going to make Lyric come.

I'm going to make her come so hard and so loud, the windows will rattle.

A freaking Blind Tears song comes on the radio and we both laugh. But it's a good song, so I don't change it. Even if it's her father's voice coming through my speakers.

"If he only knew all the dirty things I'm about to do to you," I say, and I hear her suck in a deep breath.

I climb over the partition, the same as she did, and then we're both scrunched in the small backseat. This is not the best place for this, but I'm not going to touch her once we reach her father's house. I respect him and her too much for that.

She's wearing a lavender thong and matching bra, and her blonde hair is sprawled out across my seats. She's stunning. So crazy beautiful that my chest flutters. "I love you," I say to her, watching her eyes as I slowly peel her panties down her thighs. "I love you so fucking much."

She closes her eyes before they reopen to half-mast as my fingers glide along her slick, hot pussy. She moans when I slip one finger, followed by another, inside her tight heat. She's so wet. So fucking warm. She squirms, grinding against me when I add a third finger and my thumb finds her clit. I rub her g-spot from the inside, watching as my fingers fuck her over and over. The wet sounds are nothing short of erotic and god, no one has ever turned me on more than Lyric Rose.

My face drops—albeit at an awkward angle given the restraints of the car—and I kiss her pussy. I kiss her again and again, loving the way she moans. It's not her typical moan. It's slow and long and low.

"You want more, Lyric?"

"Yes," she breathes. "Please."

I love it when she begs. It doesn't happen often. Only when she's wound up, beyond needy. "Spread your legs wider for me, baby. Let me see all of you."

She moans even louder, her head falling back against the window as she complies. I remove my fingers from her pussy, and she growls in protest, which makes me chuckle. My lips take over, sucking her clit into my mouth and flicking it with my tongue, my wet finger gliding along her opening until I reach the tight bud of her ass.

"Oh," she cries, arching further into my face. "Jameson," she breathes. "I…"

"Shhh. If it's too much, I'll stop."

She nods, but I can tell I'm pushing her past her comfort zone. I'm good with that. In fact, I love it. My finger, still wet with her arousal, slips in just a little as my mouth continues to feast on her dripping pussy. Her hands find my hair, tugging and pulling and moving me this way and that. It drives me wild when she gets like that, when she becomes crazed, no longer able to hold back as she searches for the high she knows I'm going to deliver.

My finger goes in deeper. When I start to slide it back out, sucking on her harder, she comes, shattering into a million tiny pieces all over the back seat of my vintage Mustang. I've never had a girl in here, believe it or not. It's something I've always regretted, but now, I'm glad she's the only one.

I'm glad it's her who will always be a part of one of my prized possessions.

"Oh God," she hums when she's finally starting to come down. Lyric is not a talker while she's coming. She's not one of those girls who calls out names or swears. She just moans and whimpers and sighs and screams. "That was…" She shakes her head like she can't come up with the right words.

I kiss her lips, my finger leaving her ass. I can't wait for my cock to go there, but tonight is not the night for that fist. "Are you ready?" One hand grabs my face, kissing me harder. Her other hand grabs my cock, directing it to her entrance. "Control freak."

She smiles against my lips. "Don't ever forget it."

"Never," I say as I slide into her. So. Fucking. Good. I pump into her, groaning and picking up my pace, unable to hold back. Her legs wrap around me, drawing me in closer, taking my cock in deeper. It's only after a few minutes of losing my mind in my girl that I realize the reason this is better than anything has ever felt before.

I'm going bareback for the first time.

"Baby," I pant, my eyes practically in the back of my head. "I'm not wearing a condom."

"I've been on the pill for a million years, Jameson," she says with a small laugh to her strained voice. "You've known this. I think we're both safe, so we can stop with the condoms already."

Hell. "You sure?"

"Without a doubt."

"Thank God, because now that I've had you like this, there is no going back."

I hike her leg up over my shoulder, climbing onto my knees in the well of the back seat and I thrust in. Then pull back out slowly. She whimpers, her hands reaching out, grasping onto my shoulders, her nails digging in. Then I do it again, staring down at the way my wet dick looks sliding in and out of her.

"So goddamn pretty, Lee. Your pussy is so pretty. There is nothing better than being inside of you. So wet. So tight. Fuck, baby, you feel so good I can't hold off much longer."

"Then don't," she half-yells.

I grin as I reach in between us, finding her clit and circling it with my thumb. She screams out, rocking up into me, begging for more. Then

I start to pound into her, as much as I can, given the limited room we have to move. But still, I make it count. I screw her brains out while making love to her fiercely.

When I feel her body start to tremble around mine, I can no longer hold back, and I come, roaring out my release. Louder and harder than I've ever come before.

My sweaty forehead drops to hers, unable to draw in enough air. I think I nearly passed out. Lyric giggles and I realize I just said that out loud.

"When we're old, promise me we'll still slink off and have sex in this car," she jests, her words light and full of air, but they sink into me like lead.

"I promise," I say, hoping to hell I can keep that promise. I don't have the best track record with those where she's concerned.

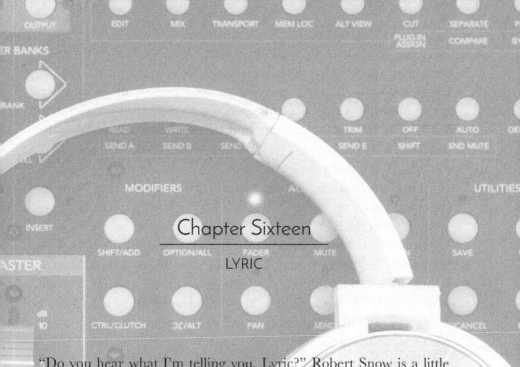

Chapter Sixteen

LYRIC

"Do you hear what I'm telling you, Lyric?" Robert Snow is a little hyper this morning. And considering it's eight-thirty in the morning Tennessee time and only six-thirty in California, I'd say he really needs to slow down on the coffee, because he sounds like he's about to run all the way here and shake me.

"I hear you, Robert." I'm smiling. Even though Robert is very hyper, he has an excellent reason to be. "I just don't know what to say."

"You're going to say yes. There is no other option. Cyber's Law asked for you specifically. They heard the albums you did last summer, and fucking called me up."

I'm walking across campus towards one of the few classes I have this semester. Turns out, I overdid it at NYU. I only need nine credits to graduate. Somehow, I talked my advisor and one of my music teachers into giving me credit for working with Robert and my father on an album. Seriously. Can you freaking believe that shit?

We have one more month left in school. One. Then we graduate. And now Robert is trying to mess with that piece of paper because Cyber's Law—a British alternative rock band that has taken the charts and the world by storm—has asked me to produce their next album. They finished a world tour in December, took a few months off, and are now ready to get going on album number three. They had a difference of opinion with their last producer and are looking for someone young and talented, who will collaborate instead of dictate.

Apparently, that's me.

But there's always a kicker, and that kicker is that they want to start immediately.

As in next week.

Honestly, I think I could make it work with my teachers. I'm pulling A's in the two other classes I'm forced to take. I have a feeling I could just show up for the final and do fine. That's not really what has me dragging my heels—and we all know it.

"I need to talk to Jameson," I say with a cringe because I know what's about to come next.

"What the fuck do you mean, *you need to talk to Jameson*?!" Yeah. Those two don't like each other all that much. "He's your boyfriend, not your keeper. This is the chance of a lifetime. This is the ability to write your own goddamn ticket. What sort of piece of shit fuck-stick would ever tell you no? This will make you a full-time producer. That means at the minimum you'll be worth seven figures a year. With no other offers. But you know there will be other offers! Lyric, you know I love you. You're like family to me. I like you more than I like my own children. So please, say yes. Take this contract. Make this album. This is your dream, honey."

I lower myself onto a bench just outside the business building where my class is. Believe it or not, Jameson and I actually have a class together this semester. He hasn't shown up for it yet and right now, I'm overwhelmingly grateful. He had an early baseball practice and seems to be running late. Good. I need to figure this out. "They won't do it in New York?" I ask, chewing on my nails that I've never chewed on before. That's how messed up I am with all of this. How conflicted and torn and excited and sick I am right now.

"No," he says slowly, quietly, which is so unlike him. "I asked. I know where your heart lies and because it's for you, I truly did ask, but they rented a house in LA, and its where they want to do the album."

I nod. I already figured that. Very few artists record entire albums in New York unless they're from the area or have places to live there. Studio apartments are nice, but not what these guys are used to, and albums take months to finish. I don't care who you are —no one likes living out of a hotel or an apartment that isn't theirs for that long.

"Okay. I'll let you know by the end of the day."

"Lyric," he sighs into the phone, but it's a resigned sigh. It's the sort that says he's not happy, but he understands. "If he loves you, he'd want this for you. And I don't know, maybe we can figure something out with New York in the next year or so. I like you here. The artists like you here. But I want you happy, and I want you to stay with my label, so we'll work on it."

I smile. I smile so goddamn big. Because, yeah, a year feels like a long time, but this also looks like light at the end of the tunnel. Even if I don't really love living in New York. Been there, tried that, but with Jameson, it would be different.

"Thank you, Robert. I love you. And don't badmouth your kids; they're just misunderstood."

He laughs, and I can picture him shaking his head with his hand on his lean hips. Robert looks so much like Michael Douglas in *Wall Street*, it's startling. Even his damn suits do. All that's missing from his side is that awesome massive eighties cell phone.

"Spoiled is more accurate, but that's my fault, so we'll leave it at misunderstood. I'm sure their shrinks would *love* that." He laughs again and then says, "You better call me before five California time. I have a dinner."

"Promise. And Robert?"

"Yeah?"

"Thanks. For everything."

"You got it, kid. Later."

He disconnects the call, and I set my phone down on my lap, staring straight at the building I'm supposed to be in. Robert wasn't lying when he said this was my dream. This is that moment. The one I feel not many people get or realize when it happens. The one where you want to scream and run up to a stranger and beg them to pinch you because it all feels like it's too good to possibly be real.

But Jameson is my dream, too, and I'm not ready to put distance between us.

Even though I know it's coming.

Things changed after his father's heart attack. Between them. Between us. We ended up spending the entire week up in Connecticut. His father had his procedure, and things went really well. But Jameson stayed because he wanted to talk to his dad more, and I stayed because I wanted to be with him and my family.

We went back for Thanksgiving a few weeks later. And then Christmas, too. His father is a different man now. Well, at least with Jameson. He hasn't changed his diet or lifestyle much. But he has talked Jameson into taking on both companies—the one Jameson and his friends are working on as well as his father's. It's stretching him thin already, and he hasn't even graduated yet.

Melody gets married in six weeks in Miami. It's where José's family is from, where his father settled when he came to America from Cuba. She wanted to incorporate his culture, and my family was one hundred percent on board with it. José doesn't play baseball the way his father did. At least not professionally. He's an accountant. How freaking adorable is that? I love that man and how happy he makes Melody. So, this wedding? It's going to be insane. If I take this contract, I'll have to boogie out for a few days for it.

"Why are you sitting out here instead of in class?" Jameson asks, standing over me. I didn't even see him approach. That's how lost in my thoughts I am. Typically I sense him before I see him. No joke. The damn hairs on the back of my neck stand at attention and my stomach does a swooshing thing. It's insanity and yet, I love it.

I look up, squinting against the sun that's directly behind him. "Just got off the phone."

He sits down next to me and takes my hand like he's afraid I got bad news or something. "Everything okay?"

I turn to look at him. Stare into his beautiful blue eyes. Absorb him feature by feature. He makes my chest hurt in the best possible way. I really had no idea love felt like this. I mean, you read it. You watch it in movies. I've experienced it growing up. But I really had no clue it was this...engrossing. Consuming. It has me questioning and challenging things I feel like I should never question or challenge.

Like my future.

"Yes," I say as I blow out a nervous breath. *I don't want to lose you, and I'm terrified I will.* "Cyber's Law asked me to produce their next album."

Jameson's eyes bug out of his head. "Holy shit," he gasps, wrapping me up in his arms so tightly I can hardly breathe. "That's incredible, baby. I'm so happy for you."

"They want me to start next week. In California."

He pulls back instantly, his eyes bouncing back and forth between mine as he tries to read...I don't even know what. "Next week?" I nod. "What about school?"

I shrug. "I'm pulling A's in two of my classes. I'm sure I can work something out, and my other class is an independent music study. I think this would cover me for the credits."

"So...you're doing this?" He stares at me, expression completely unreadable. I wish he would give me some indication of how he felt about this. Of what he's thinking.

"I told Robert I had to talk to you first."

Jameson stands up so abruptly, I start with the action. He walks off before turning back and marching to me, standing over me once again. His hands are running through his hair, and he's breathing hard. He looks like he doesn't know what to do or say. I'm sort of there with him because despite how freaking elated I am about the job, this *hurts.*

"You have to go," he says, and my eyes well up with tears at those words.

I don't want to cry. I hate crying. I love Jameson for those words —and yet, hearing those words from him makes me so angry at the same time.. It makes no sense.

"This is too big to turn down."

My face drops to my hands, my shoulders begin to shake as I

swallow and sniff and try to hold all the emotions inside me in. Jameson falls to the ground in front of me, his knees in the grass, his hands on my thighs, his breath fanning across my hands.

"Look at me, Lyric."

I can't. I need a second, so I shake my head. He laughs, pulling my hands away from my face and forcing my chin to meet his eyes.

"Are you upset because of me?"

I nod. I can't speak yet, or I know I'll lose my last shred of composure.

"When we started this, I knew things weren't going to be pretty with us. But the moment I told you I loved you, I knew there would come a time that I would be loving you from afar."

A sob breaches the dam, exploding its way through my protective barrier. Now my tears are coming and I can't stop them. They fall one after the other, running down my face and dripping off my chin.

"You'll come back for finals?"

I nod. At least, I hope I will.

"You're still going to Melody's wedding?"

I roll my eyes, swallowing and wiping at my eyes that are undoubtedly already red and puffy and lined in watery mascara. "Of course, I am."

"We'll make it work."

"It didn't last summer," I say and then regret it. That was almost a year ago. That was another relationship ago. But it's all I've thought about. I can't help it. Whenever I think about going back to California, I think about how I only saw him once in four months. And spoke to him only a few times a week. Last summer had a time limit, though. It was four months. This is indefinite. Yes, Robert says he'll try for New York, but what does that really mean? I'm scared that this separation will become permanent and we won't even see it coming in time to stop it.

"I know," he says, his tone cautious. "And I won't lie to you and tell you that it won't be harder than it was then. It really might be."

"Robert told me he'd try to get me to New York in the next year."

Jameson smiles, cupping my cheek and rubbing his thumb up and down, brushing away any remaining tears. "We can make it until then, right?" I can't tell who he's trying to convince more, himself or me.

"You're sure about this?"

Jameson leans in, kisses me softly before dropping his forehead to mine. "Yes. This is not something I can tell you not to do, Lee. It's not my place, but even if I was a dick and put my foot down, you'd never forgive me. I want you happy, baby. I want you to make this album because I know you will rock it. I'm so proud of you, Lyric. We knew this was coming. It's just sooner than expected."

I nod. I have no idea why I'm nodding when it feels like my life is simultaneously falling apart and coming together.

I don't want to lose you. I'm so terrified I will.

I kiss Jameson like I've never kissed him before. Right here on the bench in front of the business building in the middle of our campus. I kiss him with everything I've got, because somewhere, in the back of my head, in a dark hidden part that I continue to ignore, this feels like an ending instead of a beginning. This feels like goodbye.

We love each other, and we can make it through. We love each other, and we can hold on.

I'll get to New York. I'll find a way to be with him—one year. We can make it one year.

Chapter Seventeen

LYRIC

My eyes are closed, head bowed down, chest pressed against the edge of the mixer. My fingers aren't moving yet. I want them to play through this song without any adjustments from me. Once I hear the song, the one they insisted on adding to the album that's about seventy-percent produced, I'll have a better idea what we need to do with it.

"It's rough, Lyric." That's what Harry, the lead vocalist, said when he introduced it. We don't have time for rough. We've been working on this album for nearly five months. Five. Typically, it doesn't take that long. Typically, I get a band to finish recording in closer to two or three, and then it takes me another month, or so, to finish it up and get it out.

But these guys like to change shit. A lot. They've already scrapped two songs—two songs that were fully recorded—and replaced them with two others that needed a ton of work. Now this new song. Oh, and Harry has to take 'quiet time' to write or meditate or whatever the fuck he does, for like two hours a day.

I'm starting to understand why they had creative differences with their last producer. I feel like maybe I should have called him first to talk about what happened because Cyber's Law is very talented, but they're also making this newbie very stressed out. Especially when Robert continues to remind me about the December first release date he has in mind. It's freaking September. It's so ambitious I can't even think about it without wanting to vomit.

But they caught me on a good day. On a day where I'm probably willing to say yes to anything. That's how happy and excited I am. Jameson is scheduled to land at ten-thirty p.m. L.A. time. I cannot freaking wait. It's been so long since I've seen him. So. Goddamn. Long. And really, these last five months apart have been awful. So much worse than last summer.

My hours are a million times worse and I didn't even know that was possible. Because while Harry takes his 'mental kip' as he calls it, I've been working with an old childhood friend of mine, Naomi Kent as she and Florian Heart from Claw By Night work on a duet together. It's been amazing reconnecting with her after so long.

So there's that. That's my baggage and it's extensive. I won't even lie and say it's not.

Jameson's baggage is not that different from mine. He works psychotic hours. His business with Cane and Travers is going well. They're getting some clients and starting to have a decent revenue stream coming in. But he's also become a player in his dad's financial company. I think his father is grooming him to take over. At least, that's the impression Jameson has, even if his father hasn't said as much. So that means he's working two full-time jobs.

And much like last year, I try not to get angry when we don't talk or he cancels trips on me. I try not to let it eat at me, fester like a wound. But it does. It's always there in the back of my mind. The 'I knew its' and the 'I deserve betters,' and my personal favorite, 'can't he just try a little harder.' I hold it all back like a fire that can't spread unless I open the door and allow it to breathe.

When we do talk, I don't want to spend it fighting. So, I swallow a lot down. A lot. Because I really don't feel like he tries all that hard. Like he expects me to be the one to give in and go to him. Or be the one to always call and text first. I've gone to New York three times. And in the months we've been apart, that's the exact amount of times I've seen him. Three.

He's missed so much with me.

Like my sister's wedding, the bastard missed her wedding. He waited until the last minute to get a flight down to Miami because of work, and then there was a big rainstorm that came through the northeast, and his flight was canceled. And the five other times he canceled on me because he had too much work to do.

But none of that matters right now. He's coming tonight, and he promised me he would, and I can't wait to see him. I feel like a part of me isn't connected to my body when we're not together. I need him. I miss him. It's really that simple.

The door to the main part of the studio opens and shuts behind me. I don't pay any attention to whomever felt the need to interrupt this moment. Callum strums the last of the notes, ending on a C chord that makes him feel like he's a God for getting it right.

"Well?" Harry calls out, a bit impatient when I don't immediately praise their latest and possibly greatest.

"It's good," I say, taking off my cans and talking into the microphone. "It is rough, as you said, but I think we can do a lot with it. The lead guitar should be acoustic, not electric. Backup can be electric, but only to complement the sound of the acoustic. I think the drums during the chorus are too heavy on the high-hat cymbal. It's distracting. I'm feeling more of a low, steady beat that harmonizes with the vocals instead of alternating with them. The bass should be on point with that."

Harry's nodding. The other guys nod along with him as they talk to each other, but I can't hear them because I took my headphones off. I really should have them back on, but I'm mentally checked out at this point.

I put one of the headphones up to my right ear and listen as Harry says, "Right. We'll play around with it then." *Awesome. Just what I need to hear so far behind deadline.*

"Hey," a voice whispers from behind me. I spin around in my chair to find Ethan, a talented production assistant, and the man who has become one of my closest friends. "How's it going?"

I sit up, rolling my head back over my shoulder to peer into the sound booth, and ensure the mic is off from my side. "It's going," I state, turning back to face him. "It's a goddamn mess. This new song is going to take a lifetime to get together."

"Well, my dear," he says, placing his hand on my shoulder in a way that would be patronizing coming from anyone else, "if anyone can figure it out, it's you. Are you up for sushi, cocktails, and manhunting with Cassia and me tonight?" He holds his hand up as I open my mouth to protest. "I know, I know, no manhunting for you."

Cassia moved here shortly after graduation. She's in law school at UCLA. When I introduced her to Ethan, the two of them became instant best friends, which makes the three of us best friends. I love having Cass here. It's helped a lot, and Ethan is a very welcome addition to our little duo.

"Bad day?" I ask.

"Sometimes I look forward to bad days so I can have a drink. And I refuse to think too deeply on what that means."

I laugh, shaking my head. Fucking Ethan. "Can't," I say as a big grin erupts across my face. "Jameson is coming tonight."

"Pfft," Ethan scoffs with a dramatic roll of his eyes, crossing his arms over his muscular chest. I swear, the guy lives in the gym when he's not here. "I'll believe that when I see it. But if by some miracle, the man-candy does come, I expect cocktails with him tomorrow night. I need to meet him."

"We can try," I say with a wicked gleam in my eyes and an impish grin to match.

"Oh please. No one can screw for that many hours straight without a break. You can take an hour."

"An hour," I promise, and he laughs.

A banging on the glass of the sound booth pulls me back. "Your British invasion is waiting on you. Better get back to work before this shit takes another two months. I'm in studio eight if you need me."

"Bye, babe," I say, and he throws me a finger wave. Then he's gone with a swoosh of the door behind him. I spin around, put my cans back on and listen as they play it for me again, adjusting to some of the changes I've recommended. I haven't even gotten to them laying down their parts separately. That takes these guys forever. I sigh, rubbing my bleary eyes. I haven't slept in forever, and with Jameson coming, it's not going to get much better.

That has me smiling, though. It has me getting through the rest of the afternoon and the headache these guys give me. At six-thirty, we call it a day. We made some progress, but I think all of us are tapped out creatively at this point. Jameson's flight was scheduled to take off at six-thirty-six New York time, and as I walk into the Malibu house—that my father pretty much gave to me since he hates L.A.—my heart rate spikes when my phone rings with his number.

"Hello?" I answer tentatively, unsure of what this call could be since he's supposed to be flying over the heartland right about now.

"It's me," he says cautiously like he knows this call will launch me over the edge. I close my eyes for a second before reopening them, throwing my keys in the general direction of the entry table, followed by my purse. Then I'm storming past the great room, through the long hallway to the kitchen. I wrench open my fridge, pull out a bottle of water, open the cap and chug the whole thing down. Bastard hasn't said anything after that pathetic two-word sentence.

Coward.

"Let me guess: you're not coming."

"It's just not a good weekend."

I throw the empty plastic bottle across the room, hating how it bounces off the wall without a loud bang or a crack in the wall.

"I tried, okay? Before you go off on me, I tried."

"Bullshit," spews from my mouth before I can stop it. I don't think I've ever been this angry. And hurt. I'm definitely hurt. And God, so fucking let down. "You didn't try. If you tried, you would be on the goddamn plane instead of calling me hours after it was scheduled to take off. Did you even buy a ticket, Jameson?"

He's quiet. His silence has me pacing a circle around the island in my kitchen, running my hand along the smooth marble as I go, wondering what it would feel like to put my fist through it. Would it hurt more than this hurts? Somehow, I doubt it.

"I don't know what to say to you, Lee. I'm juggling two full-time jobs. This weekend is a big deal for our startup. I need to go to the Hamptons and meet with a potential client that could put us in the black instead of the red."

"And Cane and Travers can't handle that without you?"

"No. They can't," he snaps, and I have no idea why he's angry. Or maybe he's just defensive. Either way, I don't care. I don't want his excuses. I really don't.

"This makes what? Five times you've canceled on me? Six? Am I just that unimportant to you? That low a priority?" As the words tumble from my lips, I find myself stopping my incessant pacing, my eyes staring out at nothing. It's true. I'm not a priority for him. If I were, he'd try, just a little bit. "You're ending this," I say, that earth-shattering realization coming down on me like an avalanche.

He sighs…and that sigh has me dropping to the floor, my back pressing against a cabinet. "That's not what I want to do," he claims, but that doesn't mean that's not what he is doing. He's ending this, and he's doing it over the phone. "I love you. I love you so goddamn much, but I don't know how to do this anymore. How to juggle all these different balls and win."

"Are you seeing someone else?" I ask because I have to know.

"No," he says quickly with sharp indignation in his tone. "Absolutely not. I don't even have time to sleep, Lee. I can't remember the last time I had a day off. How can you even ask that?"

"Because I don't understand this," I half-yell.

"I need you here with me, and you're there. *Still*. And that doesn't seem to be changing anytime soon. Does it?" he accuses. "You left. You picked a job in California. I supported that. I support you and your dream, but what about me? What about what I need from you?"

"I told you, just give me a year."

"Right. And then it will be two. It's been more than five months, and you haven't even mentioned anything to me about moving here. You're just as busy as I am. You've only come here a few times. You hardly ever call. We never manage to fucking Facetime. I don't know, Lee. Tell me what to do. Because I seriously do not know anymore."

"So, you're ending this?" I ask again. "You're giving up on us just like that?"

"No," he growls, his voice growing flustered. "But I hate disappointing you. It eats me up inside. I hate knowing that when I don't pick up your calls or don't text you back for hours, I hurt you. I hate not seeing you every day, even if it's just for a few minutes at night or in the morning. I hate canceling on you time and time again because there isn't enough time to fly across the country and back and still get my shit done. I hate this relationship that is nowhere near a real relationship."

"I hate that, too," I admit, drawing my knees up to my chest and wrapping an arm around them, trying to make myself as small and unexposed as I can.

"I know you do, baby. You're just better at this stuff than I am. You battle your stress better. You're pure light—so bright, beautiful, and together. I'm the opposite of that. I feel like I'm drowning. Like I forgot how to swim and am stuck in the middle of the ocean."

"So, pick one job instead of doing two."

"I can't," he bites out harshly, his cadence shifting in an instant. We've had this conversation before. "I can't abandon my father or his company. I'm getting too much from it. Learning too much. He needs me and I like that. I like being important to him and the company he built. But I also can't leave Cane and Trav. They need me—I *love* what we're growing. It's incredible to watch and be a part of."

"That's it, right? Work over me."

"That's so goddamn unfair coming from you, but you're right. Our work is our main focus. Somewhere along the way, we've lost sight of each other. Of our relationship."

"I haven't," I whisper, my voice heavy with tears and heartbreak. "I haven't lost sight of you. Sure, I work my ass off, but I try to call you every day. I send you texts whenever I have a free minute. I come out to visit you even when I'm months behind on my production schedule. It's you, Jameson, who has lost sight. But honestly, I don't think you care enough to make the effort anymore."

"That's not true. I care so much about you. You're the love of my life. The woman I want to marry and spend my life with. But I can't give you what you need right now. I can't. I've tried and all I do is disappoint you."

Then why are you doing this?

I fall silent, unsure what to say next. Unable to ask the next series of questions. Unable to listen to his answers.

"I think I just need a break, baby. One small step back. Some time to figure all my shit out without the added pressure of trying to get out to California." *Without the added pressure of being with me, is really what you're saying.* "We'll still talk. We'll still be a part of each other's lives. Just not what we are now. It's not forever. In a few months, when you move here or things slow down for me, we'll try again. This isn't over. Or maybe if we stay together and slow down. I don't know."

I shake my head, knowing that will never happen. Knowing that this is an end and not a pause. Knowing that he's deluding himself if he genuinely thinks anything different. I knew this would happen eventually. It's what I always feared. It's what had me sitting on that bench outside the business building in terrified tears. He promised me forever. I want to tell him he was a fucking liar, but words suddenly fail me.

"I can't lose you completely," he says, and I just died. His words just killed me. Or maybe it was that one word. Completely. Meaning he *can* handle losing most of me. Or he doesn't want to be the asshole who just breaks this off over the phone with the girl he's been with for nearly two years. Jameson is the perpetual good guy. The dependable, reliable one. The one who tries to be everything for everyone.

And I'm the woman who tears that all apart for him.

"I can't keep you partially," I tell him, mustering up every last piece of strength before it leaves me completely. "I can't play the game where I love you, try to be in your life and not be with you. So, you need to make the call, Jameson. You have to be the one because I can't."

"I wish you understood what this is like for me."

"I do. That's the problem with this. I understand what's going on with your life. With your work. It's too much for you–having to come here or find time to talk to me is only adding to your daily pressure. Just be a man and tell me the truth. Tell me what you want."

I don't give up when things get tough, I think but don't say. I'm not about to beg him to be with me when he doesn't want to. When he so clearly wants to end it.

"It's just a break, Lee. It's not forever."

I end the call. I can't hear anymore. I can't hear him say anything else. Like goodbye. I'll die for sure if I hear that. He doesn't even call back. Not after five minutes or ten. I haven't moved. I've been sitting here on my kitchen floor, staring at my phone, begging for his name to light it up. I unlock my phone, scroll through until I find the number and then hit it. It rings a total of twice before he picks up.

"I need you to come over. Bring Cass."

Ethan clears his throat and then says, "We're on our way." Ethan is reliable. Cass, too. They're here with me when I need them. All Jameson had to do was come. Even for twenty-four hours. I get this situation is not ideal, and this outcome was probably inevitable, but still.

I can't take it.

"Thank you."

I disconnect the call, drop my phone to the floor and fall apart completely. Fuck you, life. Fuck you, distance and time. Fuck you, love. I hate you. I hate every single piece of you. I regret giving you power over me.

I shake my head at that. It's easy to regret something wonderful when it hurts like this. When the pain and longing feel like they're splitting you in two. Severing your heart from the rest of your body before smashing it to pieces with a wrecking ball. It's easy to look back and hate the perfection you had. To loathe its former existence because the now might just be the worst thing you've ever felt. Do I regret these last five months of trying to make it work? No. Because hope was seeing me through, but now hope is gone.

Chapter Eighteen

JAMESON

My head presses into the exposed brick wall of my apartment. The abrasive, unrelenting jagged edges digging into me do nothing to assuage my tormented thoughts. I hate everything. Seriously. That's not even an exaggeration.

"I finished the contract," Travers says from where he sits at my kitchen table, typing away on his computer. "I sent it to our lawyer to look over, but I think it's good."

"Awesome," I deadpan.

"I don't see why you're not more excited about this," Cane says, tossing a racquetball off my wall before he catches it, only to repeat the motion. Thwap. Catch. Thwap. Catch. "This is the moment, dude. The one we've been after. The one where we officially acknowledge that we kick ass."

I don't respond. I should be happy. I should be over the goddamn moon. My father made me a senior partner in his firm today. He also said he's planning on retiring in another six months, and he'd like to start merging his company with mine as part of the transition. When he retires, he's naming me as his successor. Translation? All of my father's clients will become ours in addition to the ones we already have. As in, we'll be a publicly-traded company with a business net worth in the billions.

He was even open to altering the name of the company to reflect both.

But instead of feeling like I won, all I can think about is how I lost. How I threw away the girl because I got a little overwhelmed. How I was angry at her for being angry at me. For not understanding my shit better and agreeing to just take a small step back. I wasn't ending it. I really wasn't. That was the last thing I wanted. But that's exactly how she took it.

And really, I can't blame her. I know it's how it sounded. But I just…shit, I couldn't think of anything else to do. All I was doing was hurting her, and that was like a perpetual knife to the gut. I thought if we went back to a place without expectations and demands on our time—like we had before—maybe we'd get through it. Maybe it wouldn't be so goddamn hard.

Day by day. That's all I wanted. Isn't that what I said to her? I honestly couldn't remember when I hung up. I was too damn indignant. To stubbornly prideful. Too fucking stupid.

"Just fly out to California already," Cane says, his tone indifferent and careless. Like the words he's saying don't have consequences that reach deeper than he knows. "Get on your hands and knees and crawl back to her. Tell her you were an idiot for breaking up with her, beg her for forgiveness, and move on with your goddamn life. Seriously. You've been a moping, wreck of a man for the last six months. It's getting hard to watch."

"Back off," Trav demands, not pulling his eyes away from the screen.

"No," Cane replies, catching the ball and holding on to it as he glares daggers into Travers in a way that makes me think they've had this conversation a time or two before. "Someone needs to finally say it."

"Yeah, but you don't need to be a clamgina when you do."

"Clamgina?"

"Yep," Trav says, twisting in his chair to face Cane with a big grin. He's trying to make me smile. He's trying to cheer me up.

Little does he know there is no light in my dark tunnel. If this is what depression or self-loathing—or a combination of both—feels like, then they can also go fuck themselves.

"That's pretty freaking nasty, bro," Cane says before he tosses the ball back against my wall. Thwap. Catch. Thwap. Catch.

Travers shrugs his shoulders. "I can't help it if that's exactly what you're being." Then he spins to me. "But the man does have a point. In all honesty, I'm shocked you've lasted this long."

"She doesn't want me anymore."

He rolls his eyes at me. "Right. Because she's suddenly fallen out of love with you."

"She changed her number." I look down at my hands, unable to watch as they exchange glances. Lyric did change her number. I texted her a few months after that horrible night, but she never texted back. And when I called, I got that automated recording thing that notifies dickheads like myself that the girl they're obsessed with changed her goddamn number. That the person you're trying to reach no longer wants anything to do with you.

"So, you're just going to be a pussy and eat that? She was pissed at you. Rightfully so, I might add."

I don't even bother to glare. He's right.

"Go to California. It's Friday, and you don't have to work tomorrow. For once. Just go."

It's not like that thought hasn't lived in my brain every day for the last six months. And really, at this point, what do I have to lose?

"All right. Fuck it. I'm going. Book me a flight while I pack a bag," I yell to Travers, who's still on the computer.

"On it, boss. And for the record, you owe us."

I flip them off and run into my bedroom to pack a bag. It's not late yet; I might be able to catch a ten-p.m. flight. I fly out the door not even ten minutes later. I'm impatient and restless the entire ride to the airport, which is only amplified when I get to the airport and have to wait through security, especially since my flight time is close.

But I make it just as they're calling final boarding. I take my aisle seat, relieved that it's not a middle, and settle in for the long flight. I try Lyric again. I get the same recording informing me that the

147

previous owner of this number has changed it. I sigh, leaning back into my small uncomfortable seat.

Goddammit, Lee. At least I know where you live.

That I know hasn't changed. She'd never leave her father's Malibu house. She loves it there. I haven't been there since that first summer we were apart. Every single time I was supposed to fly out to see her, I canceled. I put work, everything, before her. She stuck by me. Continued to love and support me. And what did I do to repay her for that unconditional love? I fucking told her I needed a break.

A sick knot of regret twists in my stomach. What a bastard I was. How arrogant to think she'd just keep taking the shit I was shoveling at her. That's she'd always be there for me when I wasn't there for her. I don't blame her for changing her number. I don't blame her for cutting me out of her life. And honestly, if she doesn't want to see me after all this time, six goddamn months, I won't blame her for that either.

How could I have been so callous with someone so precious?

I realize in this moment I might have genuinely blown it. It wasn't something I allowed myself to think before. I always believed we'd find our way back to each other, but now, sitting here on this plane with my heart in my hands, I wonder if I'm too late.

I somehow manage to fall asleep after I plugged in my earbuds and listened to the new Cyber's Law album she produced. It stayed at number one for six weeks and has been in the top ten for twelve. I was so unbelievably proud when it came out at number one. And when I called her to congratulate her, to tell her that I think she's the most incredible woman in the world, well, that's when I found out that she had changed her number.

I land around one in the morning California time, which means it feels like it's four for me. I rent a car and drive to her house, which takes me almost another hour. By the time I find her modern-style house in the private neighborhood I have no business being in, and park my car on the street, it's beyond late. And the house is completely dark.

Shutting off the engine so I don't draw attention to myself, I roll down the windows and listen to the sounds of the ocean that's on the other side of her house. I have no idea what homes like this go for in a neighborhood like this, but I know its mega millions. I'm about to get out and see if I can find my way down to the beach without getting the cops called on me when a sleek black car pulls into the small driveway, parking right in front of the double garage.

A tall, thin guy with features I'm unable to make out in the darkness gets out first before he runs around to the passenger side. He opens the door, and then I watch with rapt attention as he leans in and helps Lyric out of the car. They stand there for a moment, speaking, then he wraps his arms around her as she tucks her head into his chest.

I can't move. I can't speak. I can only watch as this man holds Lyric.

My Lyric.

They pull apart, but he maintains one arm around her, tucking her into his side as they walk up to her front door. Together. He doesn't release her, even as she's opening the door. She flips on some lights, bathing them both in a warm glow that gives me the perfect angle to see them. His hair is light brown and short. His clothes—a navy button-down and dark slacks—look expensive.

Lyric is smiling up at him. But it's more than a smile. It's the smile she gives the people she cares about. The people who mean something to her. They speak more words that I cannot hear. Then I watch as she laughs at something he's saying. He leans in and kisses her, whether it's her cheek or her lips, from here, I can't tell. She nods her head and then the door shuts.

Two minutes later, the light in one of the upstairs bedrooms clicks on, and I can't look anymore. I can't watch when that light shuts off knowing he's alone with her in the dark. I can't watch, knowing he's with her and I'm not.

That he's fucking my girl.

That it's him in there instead of me.

Jealousy roars through me, monstrously ugly and dangerously violent. My fists clench as my eyes water. I'm going to be sick.

How could she do this? How could she have moved on so fast? I haven't so much as looked at another woman since she came into my life and yet, not even a half a year apart, and she's already with someone else. Because that's how that moment looked. He wasn't some new guy she picked up at a bar. He held her tenderly. He touched her sweetly. He motherfucking made her laugh, and she gazed up at him like he's her everything.

My fists pound into the steering wheel over and over and over.

In all the ways I envisioned coming here to her, seeking her out and making her mine once more, I never once pictured her with another man. Never. I feel like I just went fifty rounds with a prize-fighter. I feel like nothing will ever be right again. How can it be when she's not with me? I did this. This is all on me.

I didn't just let her slip through my fingers; I pushed her away.

I get out of the car, slamming the door behind me and not even caring if the police come. I walk up to her driveway and stare up at the dark house. It's all glass balconies and sharp lines. I'm half tempted to scale up to one of the balconies. I don't hear any sounds coming from the house. It's dead quiet, but there is no comfort out here for me tonight.

"Lee," I whisper, feeling like a fool as the sound slips past my lips. I should get back into that car and go. Nothing can come from me slinking around her house like a creepy stalker. The sound of waves crashing on the shore pulls me along the narrow side of her house. The neighbor's house is only a few feet away, so I do my best to stay close to Lyric's as my sneakers crunch into the soft, smooth sand.

It's dark as hell out here. There are very few lights coming from the other houses, and the beach and ocean are black. I don't dare go any further than the raised pillar that holds the back of her house up and out of the sand. The February wind is cool, but not unpleasant. California is so very different from New York.

Then it hits me. Hard and fast like a racecar crashing into the wall of the track. Nothing has changed. I still live in New York and Lyric still lives in California. Even if she weren't upstairs with that douchebag, what would I have to say to her? Hey, let's give this long-distance crap another shot since it didn't work out so well the first or second time? Sure, I sorta kinda have more time now. I'm no longer going to be working two full-time jobs now that they're merging into one, but it would still mean regular cross-country treks. It would still mean missed phone calls and forgotten texts.

It would still mean Lyric and I are not together.

Do I want that for her? Can I even ask for something like that when I was so horrible at it before? I hate she's with someone else. Hate it to the depths of my soul, but I don't want her to be alone. I don't want her to be unhappy. And right now, I don't have anything new or special to offer her. I could leave my job. I could try and find something out here. I could do that. I've even looked a few times. But it won't hold a candle to what I have going on in New York.

Do I care about that? Yes and no.

She's found someone new, I remind myself.

I sigh, deep, long and loud, staring out into the abyss that is as black and bleak as my soul. I'm going to let her go. I'm going to let her be happy and have it all, and I'll go home to New York and try to tell myself this is for the best. That this pain and regret won't eat me alive from the inside out. That it won't become a permanent fixture in what now feels like an empty, meaningless existence. That I'll also meet someone else eventually and move on with my life.

I tell myself that over and over again as dawn slowly creeps across the sky and lights up the dark blue water. And before Lyric and her...guy have a chance to wake up and catch me here, I force myself to leave.

To walk away from the only woman I could ever imagine loving.

I drive to the airport on autopilot, my mind lost, and my chest empty.

And when I'm seated on the plane and the engine begins to hum and the doors are closing, locking me in tight, I tell myself this is not the last time I'm going to see Lyric Rose. That this is not the way we end. That at some point, I'll have one more chance with her.

One more chance. That's all I need.

Chapter Nineteen
LYRIC

Present Day

"FOR THE RECORD, I think this is a mistake," Cass tells me as I walk through JFK's baggage area.

"You're a lawyer, Cass. You think everything is a mistake."

"Not true. I fully supported you taking over after Robert died."

My eyes reflexively scroll through the crowds searching for John, my father's driver. "I need to do this."

"I agree, but did it have to happen on his terms? Why couldn't he come to you?"

I sigh, inwardly shaking my head. "Because his father had a stroke. And I was coming here anyway. I just made my flight two days earlier. That's all."

"It's not your place to run to his bedside or comfort his son."

I roll my eyes, knowing even in my own head, I'm using sarcasm and annoyance as a diversionary tactic. "Thanks, bitch. Not sure how I missed that one. Thank God I have you keep me in check."

A loud burst of air puffs into the phone, before Cass continues, "I don't want him to plow another hole through you. It took over a year before you even considered talking to another guy. Nearly two before you slept with one. None of them makes it longer than a month. Two tops. Jameson is your dark spot. The one you've compared everyone to, and when they automatically fail to live up to your memory of the bastard, you give up."

I realize I've stopped walking. Stopped searching for John. I'm just standing here, frozen in time and space. "I can't move on until I do this, Cass," I whisper after a quiet moment. "I've tried. I really, genuinely have, but I never got any closure. I need to finish what's always felt unfinished."

"I know," she says the words slowly, softly. "Just...do it quickly and then leave. Come back to California. I miss you. Ben and Josh miss you. Ben keeps asking when you're going to come over and play with him. You blow through here too fast lately."

I love California. I love my life there and the Malibu house. I love Cass's husband, Josh and their son, Ben. Yes, Cass decided she was more into team penis than team vagina after all. I love Ethan, my rock, the man who has been there for me through everything and then some. And I love the record company I inherited when Robert died of cancer four months ago.

I owe it to him to continue what we've been building over the last few years.

"I will," I promise her. "I'll be back soon, and I won't lose my head or heart this time. I'm going in with my eyes open."

"And your legs closed," she pushes, and I laugh.

"And my legs closed. At least where Jameson Woods the Third is concerned. I gotta go, Cass. I think I see John lurking over by the revolving wheel of bags."

"Okay. You better call me after you see the asshole. I'll talk Ethan off the ledge. I think he's taking the idea of you seeing Jameson harder than I am."

I would laugh at that if it wasn't so goddamn sad. "Thanks, babe. Love you."

"Love you, too."

I tuck my phone back into my oversized purse and meander my

way through the anxiously waiting people over to the tall bear I love so much.

"Ah," John gleams with a broad smile. "I was just starting to wonder if you'd had a change of heart."

More times than I can even begin to count. "Nope." I hug him tightly, expelling every last ounce of comfort I can without being creepy. "Thanks for coming to scoop me. Any chance you can drop me at Blue Elephant? I'm supposed to meet Melody there for dinner."

"Sure. I bet she's happy to get out of the house without the baby. Should I bring your stuff to your parents' house, or are you staying somewhere else?"

"I'm staying with them," I say with a smile that I do not feel. I haven't told my parents why I'm here. Honestly, other than the concern for potential homicide charges against my father if he knew Jameson was in town, there isn't anything to tell them. This is going to be a quick trip—a fly-by-night sort of gig. I'm going to see Jameson's father because I do care for that man even though I haven't seen him in a while. Then, at some point, I'll meet up with Jameson, in a very safe, neutral place and tell him he can never contact me again. That what we had all those years ago is over.

And once I've looked him in the eyes and told him that, I'll be able to move on with my life. I'll know unequivocally he's my past and not my future. Four years is too long to be hung up on the guy you hung up on. On the guy who never called you back. On the guy who threw you away like you were nothing to him after you gave every piece of yourself that ever meant anything to you.

I'm silent in the car. Contemplative. Nervous. My phone rings in my purse as we get to the outskirts of town, and I smile indulgently when I see it's Melody. "Am I eating dinner alone tonight?"

She laughs. "No. I'm just like, I don't know, fifteen minutes behind. Max just wouldn't get off my boobs. Now I smell like breastmilk and I think I might even have some on my pants. I need a quick shower, then I'll leave."

"Okay. I'm about ten minutes from the restaurant. Do you want me to order you something or wait?"

"Oh God," she moans. "Something alcoholic, please. I'll pump and dump. I don't even care if it's like throwing out liquid gold. I haven't had any alcohol in almost a year."

"And my beautiful nephew thanks you for it. But I believe I heard somewhere if you don't feel the effects of alcohol, the baby won't either."

Melody snorts into the phone. "A thousand says that sage, non-scientifically founded advice came from Cass."

"Yup," I pop the p. "And Ben has all his fingers and toes, one head and is already speaking in three-word sentences."

"Well, I'll still dump anyway. One can never be too careful. See you in a bit."

John pulls up in front of the chic Thai restaurant. I wave him off when he tries to get out to open the door for me. "Call me if you need me to pick you up later."

I shake my head. "I'll either Uber or have Mel drop me. You've already done enough for me tonight." I blow him a kiss and scurry out of the car before the coddling, overprotective man can argue with me.

Stepping inside the restaurant, I breathe in the enticingly spicy scent of garlic and peanuts. Dim lighting accented with the soft flicker of candlelight and crystal sconces set an intimate and slightly romantic tone. There's a soft, hypnotic beat in the background, and the bar off to my right is overly packed with after-work drinkers.

"May I help you?" the hostess asks with a pleasant smile.

"Yes." I step forward and around a couple who are perusing the menu. "I believe my sister made a reservation. Melody Diaz."

She lifts up her tablet, scrolls down the page and then nods. "Your table is ready if you'd like to sit, or you can wait in the bar for the rest of your party to arrive."

I glance over at the bar again, contemplating the choice. There is barely any room to stand over there, so I say, "I think I'll sit, please."

"Sure. Right this way."

I follow her through labyrinth of tables towards the back where she stops at a small two-person table. I sit down, taking my menu from her while wait on Melody, who better hurry up because my stomach is starting to growl. Someone comes over and fills my glass with water, and immediately after thanking them, my eyes return to the menu.

I'm reading through the various appetizers when I feel it. The hairs on the back of my neck stand at attention. My stomach swooshes in that familiar and forgotten way. Electricity hums in my blood.

Setting the menu down flat against my unnecessary place setting, my eyes slowly, reluctantly rise. Black shoes. Black slacks. White button-down that's barely able to hide the muscular definition beneath. Open collar. Smooth, chiseled jaw. Hint of a dimple. Cocky smirk. Wolfish, pale blue eyes. Ink black hair.

I blink. And blink once more, but it does nothing to expel him from my sightline. To delete the man I was not yet ready to see, walking steadily, confidently, toward me. Four years and not much has changed other than the length of his hair, which is shorter and more styled. He's still unmistakably the most gorgeous man I've ever seen.

My heart thrums wildly in my chest. My hands tremble in my lap. My stomach flutters to a nauseating degree.

The hostess, whom I haven't even noticed, waves her hand in an exaggerated fashion for him to sit. Once he smoothly slides into the seat directly across from me, she hands him his menu with a flourish, telling him that if he needs anything, not to hesitate to ask her.

As I pull my eyes away from his—scanning the restaurant for the traitor I affectionally refer to as a sister—I notice every ovary-carrying woman in this place is feasting on him with interest. Even the women whose ovaries have been closed for business for decades.

Melody is not here. Because Melody is not coming.

"I wondered how you got my number," I muse aloud, impressed by how calm and composed I am, considering I'm the total and complete opposite. "Good thing I didn't go with the scorpion bowl for two."

Jameson grins, his finger running across his lower lip. I cannot stand how I just fell for that bait and looked. *It didn't even take you one minute, Lyric.*

"I was concerned you might not forgive her, but she reminded me you're her baby sister and the godmother of her son, and that forgiveness is in your blood." He leans forward, pinning me with those magnetic baby blues of his. "It's what I'm counting on, actually."

I shake my head and lean back in my seat.

No. Just no. Like no motherfucking way, no.

"Can I get you anything to drink?" the waiter, who picked either the best time or the worst time to approach us, asks.

"The lady will have the scorpion bowl for two, and I'll have a vodka gimlet."

The waiter doesn't even flinch. He nods his head and tells us he'll be right back with our drinks and to go over the specials.

"What the hell are you doing?" I ask because I have to. I'm ambushed and I don't like the feeling that comes with it.

"I'm having dinner with you, Lee—"

"Don't," I snap so quickly I surprise even myself. Evidently, I am not going to be playing it cool tonight. "Do not call me Lee."

He's utterly unaffected and undeterred. "I'm having dinner with you, *Lyric*. I told you over the phone I wanted to talk to you, and this is the perfect place to do that."

I want to cry. The urge comes over me, burning like acid in my eyes and I hate it. I thought I was so much stronger. I swallow. Hard.

Ignore the way he watches my throat move as I do, and say, "Say whatever it is you want to say and then go."

Our goddamn intrusive waiter returns with our drinks—mine has two straws, more sliced fruit than is socially appropriate for garnish, and is in the most ridiculous Moana-esque South Pacific ceramic bowl. And before you judge, Ben—one of my godchildren —loves that freaking movie.

The waiter starts to go over the specials with an enthusiasm typically reserved for clowns at small children's birthday parties. I have no patience for this right now. Like none.

Jameson interrupts our waiter's rant and orders for both of us. The most infuriating part of that? He ordered exactly what I would have ordered for myself. And if I had to pick one dish he would order for himself, naturally it's the one he went with. I hate he just did that. I hate he *believes* he still knows me well enough to know my goddamn food preferences.

"Who's the guy?" he asks the moment our waiter is out of earshot.

"Pardon?" I ask, my eyebrows furrowing.

"I know you lied when you said you weren't seeing anyone. You've been seeing the same guy for years."

"What?" I half-laugh incredulously. "Have you taken to smoking crack instead of weed in the last four years?"

Jameson chuckles lightly. "Every time I see your pretty face at the Grammys—when you accept your multiple awards—you always have the same guy on your arm. Tall. Dark blond hair. Hollywood coiffed."

I burst into a fit of laughter, shaking my head. Closing my lips around one of the straws, I suck down a good third of my overly alcoholic beverage. I only know it's alcoholic because these things are toted to be deadly. But hell, it sure as shit doesn't taste anything but delicious.

"You mean Ethan?" I ask after I swallow down my multiple sips, amusement still dancing on my tongue.

Jameson sits back in his chair, lifting his pale green drink to his lips and taking a sip. "Ethan?" he echoes, lost in thought like he's searching the deepest recesses of his mind for something. "How do I know that name?"

I roll my eyes and cross my arms over my chest, staring him down and begging him to challenge me.

"Surely you remember me mentioning my very gay best friend, Ethan. I know it was a few years back, but I thought your memory would be better than this." Why did I just tell him this? Why didn't I let him stew? God, I really need to get to the point and get out of here. "Yes, he's been the main man in my life for the last four years. He's one of the best people I know."

His expression grows impossibly dark, his hand rakes through his hair in obvious agitation. He hisses something harsh and inaudible under his breath, but I don't care enough to decode what's going through his head. His other fist balls up, turning white and ferocious.

If I didn't know this man, I might be afraid he was about to kill someone with the amount of rage boiling under the surface of his not-so-calm exterior. I lean forward, pressing my stomach into the table and leveling this asshole with my most decisive stare.

"I have no idea why you wanted to talk to me after so many years, Jameson, and honestly, I don't care. You wanted a break from me, and you got one. So, ask me why I flew all the way out here."

His eyes return to mine only this time, in them, I see a world of differences. I see that this is not the same sexy, confident man who walked into the restaurant, hellbent on screwing up my world once again. This man looks wrecked. This man looks as if he's just had the crap beaten out of him. I would take some modicum of pleasure in that if this didn't hurt so much.

"Why did you come?" he finally asks, his voice soft and his tone dejected.

"For closure." His eyes close as he blows out a breath. "It's something I was never afforded the first go around. And it seems to be just what I need. So here it is. I'm going to lay it all out for you. Fuck you for texting me and trying to manipulate me by telling me your father would want to see me. Fuck you for telling me you miss me and asking me to come home. Just fuck you. I don't want to see you again. I don't want to talk to you again. I'm sorry about your father, and I will go see him because despite who you turned out to be, I still love him."

I take another sip of my drink, practically finishing it off with a loud slurp. I stand up, my legs numb, but my mind oddly focused. He finds me, his eyes scrolling around my face and my body before returning to mine for the last time.

"Take care of yourself, Jameson. I wish you every happiness."

I walk off, leaving him and the heart he broke behind. It's rebuilding time.

Chapter Twenty

LYRIC

I tap lightly on the front door, afraid I'm going to wake Max if I ring or knock too loudly. I may want to bang down the door and demand answers from my sister, but I love my nephew, even if my sister is a first-rate traitor.

The door swings open, and instead of it being Melody, it's José. "Coward," I mutter under my breath.

He laughs, stepping back and holding the door open for me to pass.

My father bought them a house as a wedding present. Homes in Greenwich are, well, they're freaking expensive. And José makes good money, but not Greenwich money, so my father bought them a house. He talked them into it by saying he gave me the Malibu house, which is worth more than three times what this house is worth.

"She's upstairs, hiding from you in Max's room."

"Why is he still awake?" I ask, and José just shrugs.

"He's two months old, Lyric. Two-month-olds don't sleep a lot, and just when you think you have them on a schedule, they show you just how wrong you are."

"Did you know about Jameson? About what Mel did?"

José looks away for a beat and then back to me. "She had her reasons for doing what she did. Go up and speak to her. *Listen* to her."

I roll my eyes. "Of course, I will, but I'm allowed to be pissed."

"I take it tonight didn't go well?" he asks, walking me through the foyer and over to the staircase.

I shake my head. "Nope. It was pretty freaking awful actually."

"Melody told me he begged her for your number. Like, actually begged."

"I'm done with him. We were over years ago."

José smirks knowingly. "Were you?"

I sigh, placing my hand on the banister and running my hand against the smooth dark wood. "It doesn't matter anymore. Coming here was a mistake. Agreeing to this was a mistake. Responding to his stupid text messages when I knew better was a mistake. That's all I do where Jameson is concerned. Make mistakes."

"If you really believed that, you wouldn't be here looking like someone just ran over your iPod with all your music on it. Go upstairs. She's waiting on you."

I leave José and ascend the steps in a jog, anxious to get to Melody. Because I know my sister, and while it feels like she betrayed me with the man who broke my heart, I appreciate that there's more to this story. Walking down the hall, I press my hand into the closed door of Max's room.

I don't knock. I don't enter. I just wait here, trying to breathe in and out past the tightness in my chest.

Because what if she tells me something? And that something changes everything?

I didn't listen to Jameson tonight. I didn't let him talk because I really don't want to hear whatever excuse he has. I don't want to hear him tell me he's sorry or that it was a big misunderstanding that's led to four years of just getting by. I don't want him to tell me he wants to try again or—and I seriously cannot decide if this is worse or not—say that he's after closure, too. I don't ever want to hear that from him the way I forced him to hear me say it tonight. I don't even care if that makes me a hypocrite. Bitterness is a bitch.

But I decided a long time ago, after months of tears and second guessing *myself,* wondering what *I* could have done differently, that I was done with him. That breakup was on him. Not on me. I hated him for making me feel like I'm less deserving than I am. That if I had done things differently, he wouldn't have ended it.

I promised myself that even if he came crawling back, I wouldn't give in. I wouldn't cave. That day on the phone, when he told me he wanted to take a step back? That was the day my heart turned to glass. Firm and unmovable. Cold and lifeless. But so easily shattered. And even when glued back together, there is always a crack. A fissure. A weak spot.

Jameson shattered my heart. And it took me months, if not years, to glue it back together. He is forever my weak spot. I may have told myself I was after closure. I may have told him the same. But it's that weak spot that really lured me in. The masochist who gets off on torturing herself where he's concerned. I'm forever pulled in his direction. We're like two bonded atoms when put together the right way, we spawn a chemical reaction.

Honestly, I was curious to see if it was still there after all this time.

He's a bastard who hurt you and left you behind without a backwards glance. Right. He did that.

He's going to hurt you again if given the chance.

"Stop lurking out there and get your ass in here," Melody calls out, and I find myself smiling.

Damn her.

Twisting the knob, I open the door to find Melody sitting in the light gray rocking chair in the corner of the room, nursing Max.

"When do you think he'll stop using me as a human binky? Every time I take him off my boobs, he cries. He's just like his father."

I snort, rolling my eyes as I walk over to them, sinking down onto the ottoman she has her feet propped up on. "Have you tried a real binky?"

She puffs out some air, her blonde bangs flying up before they fall back into her eyes. Melody needs a haircut. And to change her clothes and shower. Melody needs a break.

"I'm afraid to do that. I've read it's not good for their jaws, and they get attached them making it nearly impossible to get them to give them up."

"Yeah, but that won't be for a few years, and by that point, you'll have slept, and he'll have slept. And you can always get him braces and offer bribes to get him to give it up."

"Probably true. Okay, pass me that binky. The one with the stuffed giraffe hanging off it."

"That was easy."

"I'm fed up and exhausted. A little persuasion goes a long way with me right now."

I pick it up off the bookcase next to the rocking chair and hand it to her. I love this room. It's a little like Pottery Barn Baby threw up in here, but it's so great. There are wall decals of baby animals playing in a field with a giant tree, flowers, and a bright yellow sun. The furnishings are white with gray and blue fabrics and accents. My mother and José's mother had a really good time getting this room set up for Max.

Melody pulls Max from her breast and unsurprisingly, the little man goes nuts, instantly wailing at the top of his lungs and thrashing his ineffectual fists about. She shoves the pacifier in his mouth, holding it there for him, and after a few seconds, he starts to suckle and calms down.

"Ah," she says with a satisfied grin, "music to my ears. Now, if I could only get him to fall asleep without being in my arms, the world would be perfect."

"Why don't you swaddle him?"

"I'm afraid he'll suffocate."

"Christ, Mel. You bought all those expensive sleeping swaddle things. Try one out and keep the video monitor with you. You'll wear yourself out if you keep this up."

She shakes her head. "José helps."

"You know what I'm saying. Come on. We're going to swaddle

him and put him down in his bassinet thing. Then you and I are having a glass of wine and a long talk."

"Can't I just use the baby as a buffer? You're much less hostile when I'm holding him."

"No," I say, pointing a finger at her.

"Fine. Here. Take him." I lift Max out of her arms, his eyes already growing heavy as he sucks furiously on his binky. I bring him over to the changing area and set him down gently. God, he's so fragile and small.

Melody sets to work on changing his diaper and putting him in his pajamas. Then she begins tucking him into the swaddle thing that looks more like a blue straightjacket with white elephants.

"I ran into Jameson when I was bringing Max for his checkup," she starts, her eyes on her son. "He was there for his dad, and he saw me trying to get something to eat in the cafeteria while Max napped in his carrier. He wordlessly bought me lunch and sat with me, even though I told him to screw off." She pauses, glances in my direction and then back down to Max. "The first words out of his mouth were, 'I need to talk to her.'"

When she's finished with Max, she picks him up, holds him out for me to kiss his tiny, dark-haired head, and then sets him down in his bassinet with a kiss on both his cheeks and nose. We leave Max's room, head back downstairs and into her kitchen where the video monitor is. José is nowhere to be found. Even though I adore my brother-in-law, it's a relief.

"I know you think I set you up," she says, a sheepish grin on her face. "I guess I did, but I did it for a reason, and I think you need to hear me out."

"I know what you're going to say, Mel. It's the same thing Ethan and Cass have been saying. That I need to get over him. That facing him and getting the chance to say goodbye might be the only way to do that."

"Honestly, that's not what I was going to say. I get Cass and Ethan's thoughts on this. Part of me agrees, but a larger part doesn't."

I sit back in my seat, folding my arms protectively across my chest. I hate the look she's giving me right now. It makes me wish I had hopped a plane back to California immediately after I walked out of that restaurant, instead of marching over here.

"What I was going to say is everyone makes mistakes," I open my mouth to jump all over that, but she holds her hand up, stopping me. Max makes a few fussy noises from his room, and she turns her complete attention to the monitor, making sure her son is okay. He is and he quiets down after a beat, so she shifts back to me and says, "I know what he did was fucked up. I know he stopped trying and generally gave up on you. I know he ended things in the most bull-shit, asshole of ways. I know this. And I do not excuse that."

"Then what, Mel? I really don't get it."

Her eyes fix back on the monitor as she says, "José cheated on me." My eyes bug out of my head as my jaw hits the floor. "It was before we were married or even engaged. We had been dating for about a year, and he went to Vegas for a friend's bachelor party. Long story short, he cheated one very drunk night."

"Holy shit," I breathe, my hand covering my mouth in shock. "I had no idea."

"No one does. I didn't want you to hate him, so I never said anything. He regretted it, obviously. Hell, he was more of a mess than I was. It took a lot for me to forgive him. For us to work past it. And I'm not comparing the two, Lyric. I'm not."

She twists to me, staring me square in the eyes, her expression so severe I find it nearly impossible to maintain eye contact. I'm desperate to look away.

Anywhere but at her.

"But Jameson did make a mistake. A mistake he acknowledged to me over and over again. A mistake he regrets and wishes he could take back. A mistake he *hates* himself for." Melody reaches out, taking my hand away from my body and holding it between us as she squeezes it tight. "I'm not saying what he did was okay or right or just. I'm not even saying you should forgive him and take him back. I'm just saying you should hear what he has to say. That's all I was trying to do tonight."

"Did José come back to you and apologize?" She nods. "Did he beg for forgiveness?" Another nod. "Did he do everything he could to *get* you to forgive him?" A sigh this time and then a nod. "Jameson never did any of that."

Melody releases my hand as I stand up. She looks wrecked. I turn to walk away, and she stops me with, "You still love him, though."

I pause, my hands going to my hips, my chin hitting my chest. "Yes. But I don't want to. It's time I get on with my life. He certainly has."

"You don't know that. He wouldn't have called you if that were true."

I shake my head and walk toward the front door. So very done with this conversation. With Jameson.

"Let José drive you home."

"That's not—"

"Yes, it is," he says, suddenly appearing out of nowhere like a damn ghost. "Come on. Go get some sleep, Mel. You're exhausted. I just checked on Max. He's fast asleep and I'll be on baby duty tonight."

"I knew there was a reason I married you," Melody mumbles through a yawn, her exhaustion catching up her.

José and I reach his car, and we're silent until he says, "She told you? About what I did in Vegas?"

"Yes," I admit quietly, slightly embarrassed—both for him and for me.

"It's okay, you know. I told her she could. I was an idiot. I got blackout drunk and woke up naked next to some girl I couldn't remember. It was easily the worst moment of my life." He glances in my direction briefly, gauging my reaction before he turns back to the road. "I didn't tell her right away. I was afraid she'd leave me. I tried convincing myself what she didn't know wouldn't hurt her. It took me over a month until the guilt finally ate me alive and I fessed up."

"José—" I start because I know what he's doing.

"I worship your sister," he cuts me off, not letting me speak. "I've loved her from the first second I saw her. She is my goddamn universe, and I still did something I thought I would never ever do.

Sometimes people fuck up," he goes on, catching my eye briefly. "Sometimes people fuck up so bad they don't know how to fix it. They make excuses and rationalize things they know better than to rationalize. Sometimes we find ourselves in the deep end of a nightmare with no idea how to swim out of it and end up sinking in deeper. Drowning in our choices. I don't know if that's what happened with Jameson. I didn't talk to him, but Melody did. He told her something to convince your overprotective, adoring big sister to give him your number. To set up that dinner. That's all I'm saying."

I can't respond to any of that. My head feels like it's on a Tilt-a-Whirl. Or that Tea Cups ride at Disney World. Basically, I feel like my brain is being scrambled and I need to throw up. José pulls past the gates into my parent's house and I get out, thanking him for the ride and not mentioning the intense conversation we just had. My parents aren't home tonight. They drive home from Vermont tomorrow, and I've never been so grateful to have their mansion to myself.

Drowning in our choices, José said. Why do I have a feeling I'm about to know just what that feels like?

Chapter Twenty-One

JAMESON

I sat there in the restaurant much longer than I should have, just...
staring off. I heard her words. I listened to every single one with the
focus of a general going into battle. Closure. That's why she came.
She came for closure. And wow, that's like...shit. I have no words
for what that's like. I don't want her to have closure. I don't want her
to tell me she never wants to see me again.

I sat in that restaurant, didn't touch any of the food that was
brought out, paid the bill, and went home. A fucking mess of
a man.

But it's what I expected, so I can't exactly get too worked up yet.

What I didn't expect was for her to tell me the guy I've observed
her with—the one I saw at her Malibu house that fateful night when
I flew out to her; the one I've noticed with her in publicity shots;
and at the Grammys with—is her fucking gay friend, Ethan.

Gay.

As in, not interested in pussy.

As in, not interested in Lyric's pussy.

Jesus Christ. I can't even wrap my head around how stupid I
am. How so much of my life since then has been dictated by that
night. By that guy. By the notion Lyric was happy, even if I wasn't.

That thought got me through.

It's what stopped me from going completely insane whenever I saw those pictures. Whenever I saw him holding her hand at the Grammys as they smiled at each other.

Ethan.

How could I not have known?

Four. Years. For four years, I believed she was with him. I kept searching for a wedding notice. For something that would force me to once and for all let go of the Lyric Rose torch that continued to burn bright in my chest.

I never figured out how to extinguish it. There was no magic switch that would erase her. That would help me get over her. My love for her has not diminished. Maybe because she's right. We never had closure. We were always unfinished. And that's exactly the way I liked us. Unfinished.

I never moved on. Could barely tolerate other women. And believe me, Cane and Travers tried their best to find me someone new. But no. For four years, I have done nothing but work and pine away over one woman.

She's single. All. This. Fucking. Time. She's been single. It makes me want to simultaneously fist pump into the air and slam that fist into a brick wall. Melody told me she was single when I ran into her at the hospital, but I didn't fully believe her. Those pictures of her with Ethan were everywhere anytime I looked Lyric up. Which was embarrassingly often. I cornered Melody in the hospital cafeteria, averting my eyes while she nursed her tiny baby after I bought her lunch, all the while badgering and begging her relentlessly about Lyric. In truth, Melody didn't give me much to work with.

All she said was that Lyric is single and that if I go after her and hurt her again, she'd have their father use every connection he has and have me eliminated. Doesn't worry me, I told her. I have no intention of ever hurting Lyric again. All that hurt she threw at me last night is old hurt. It's festered hurt. It's why she says she needs closure.

Because she hasn't been happy.

All this time, she's missed me as much as I missed her. So yeah, I promised Melody I wouldn't give Lyric any new hurt and I meant that. I no longer make promises I don't know I can keep, and I know I can keep this one.

Four years in between then and now and look at us. It would be comical if it weren't so goddamn tragic. And ironic. Yeah. It's that, too. But I have plans for Lyric. She just doesn't know it yet.

Sighing out, I clear my throat. "So, now what?" I ask the neurologist as I sit back into one of the uncomfortable chairs in the waiting room. It's annoyingly reminiscent of the last time we did this. Only this time, the right side of his body is weak. And the right side of his face droops a little. And he doesn't have as many words directed my way, and whatever he does say is slightly garbled.

I hate seeing my father like this. It's so much worse than when he had the heart attack. Now he just looks beaten by life. By his poor health.

"He goes to rehab," Dianne says, even though I wasn't asking her. She's been standing by the window and staring down at her nails or out at the crap scenery every time she's here, which isn't often and isn't for very long. The waiting room evidently isn't any different than my father's room. I don't say anything about it. I accepted the last time my father had a major health incident that some people are not strong enough to handle things like this. That's Dianne. She loves my father, and that's all I care about.

"Right now, Mr. Woods is stable and doing very well with the treatment plan we've set up for him. We should be able to discharge him in two days to the rehab you chose. It's a great facility and he'll have the very best care. With enough diligence and proper lifestyle changes, we're very hopeful about his recovery."

I love that. Doctor language. What that actually means is we have no fucking clue if he'll be a limping, drooling, slurring mess for the rest of his life. And I get it. There are no guarantees with this. My father never changed the things he was supposed to change after his heart attack. He figured having a stent placed in his artery was enough. And since no one appreciates it when someone says I told you so, I've kept my mouth shut about that.

I had that talk with him multiple times and it didn't do dick.

"Okay. Sounds good, I guess." Because really, what am I supposed to say? I seriously have no idea. If something like this is going to happen every five years, I need to develop a better way to cope.

"If you have any further questions, I'm on call tonight and my colleague, Dr. Guhan, will be here tomorrow."

I stand up, and the doctor follows suit before we shake hands. "Thank you," I say to him. He throws Dianne a cursory glance, though she doesn't turn or say anything, then he's gone. "I'm heading back in," I tell her.

"I'm going to go, but I'll be back tomorrow."

"Sure." I walk toward the door without so much as a backwards glance. I'd love to say that over the years our relationship has improved. It hasn't. The only thing about me she likes is the fact that I'm very good at what I do. Which is exactly what my father used to do before he retired and left everything to me. Which means our stock is doing well, and she will never have any financial worries for as long as she lives.

I hate hospitals. I hate the smell of chemical disinfectants and sick people. I hate the way everything looks sterile and yet contaminated at the same time. I hate the way everything takes hours instead of minutes to get done.

Walking down the center of the hall because I can't stand the idea of touching even the walls. I round the corner, smile at the nurses behind their station, and then find my father's room, all the way down at the end of the opposite hall.

But before I can even reach the door, my chest clenches, and a smile inadvertently curls up the corner of my lips.

Lee.

She came. And I bet the adorable girl thinks she's getting away with something right now because I wasn't there when she arrived. I do my best to listen in to catch some of their conversation before I make myself known, but it's tough to do. Lyric isn't speaking all that loud. and my father's speech is difficult to understand. Plus, he practically whispers now because he's so weak.

"It's going very well. Better than Robert or I ever envisioned," she says, and even though I have no idea what she's referring to, I can't help but hurt for her. She lost Robert. I knew that. I tried to reach out, but finding her number was like trying to get in touch with the Pope directly. She doesn't have any personal social media accounts. Her number is unlisted, and her cell phone number was an enigma.

I tried to steal my father's phone once to get it, only to discover the bastard had it memorized because she wasn't listed anywhere in his contacts. When you call her at work, you have to go through twenty different people, and then her assistant chronically tells you she'll leave a message for Lyric.

I even said I was family once and that it was an emergency. She hung up on me.

It's why when I saw Melody, I went a little nuts. It was like the perfect storm, though. I had hit the peak of my desperation, and then there she was.

"No," she laughs, and I didn't hear anything my father said to elicit that laugh. I love that they talk like this. That they have a relationship. That my father still calls her and that they keep up. Even if I hate it. Even if it makes me angry that my father keeps her a secret from me.

"She made me promise never to tell you anything about her or her life and I honor my promises," he'd said when I asked him for some morsel of information on Lyric. Bastard. I'm his freaking son.

"I have the Rainbow Ball. After that, we'll see."

Rainbow Ball? I've heard of that. It's in New York and it raises money for various cancer research charities. It's exclusive. A-list only.

Another laugh. "I'd love you to be my date, but I think that will have to wait until next year."

My grin turns into a full smile. This girl…wow. She's just… everything. Everything I threw away. Stupid life. If only one of us could get through unscathed. Without wanting to go back and fix everything we've done wrong.

Checking my smile at the door, I knock twice, just to give her the proper warning she deserves, the one I didn't afford her last night, and then I enter. Lyric glances up with an apprehensive start. When she sees that it is, in fact me, she slowly rises.

"I should get going," she says, her eyes only on my father.

"Stay," he whispers slowly, trying to reach out a hand to her and then one to me. But he's not our olive branch. This is something only I can fix.

"I'm sorry," she says. "I'll try to come again before I leave." Lyric bends down and kisses his forehead, brushing some of his black hair from his face. "Go easy on the nurses," she teases. "Your looks and charm will only get you so far."

My father gives her a lopsided smile. But the moment Lyric rights her body and focuses on the doorway just beyond me, he gives me a look. A look that says don't let her get away. I return his look, except mine says, I'm on it.

"I'll walk you out."

She shakes her head and adds, "I can manage." She won't even meet my eyes. She won't even glance in my general direction.

I don't give her the option; I turn on my heels and walk with her. Next to her. Close enough that it's nearly impossible for her to ignore me. "Thank you for coming to see him," I say and she nods. That's it. "Come have coffee with me?"

"No."

"Yes." I spin to stand directly in front of her, stopping her in her tracks before we reach the elevator. "Yes. Because you're here. You're right in front of me, and I can't let you go back. Not without telling you everything."

"It's not going to change anything, Jameson. The past is what it is. There is no turning back."

I nod, stepping into her and staring intently into her beautiful eyes, taking in the ever-changing pattern of green, brown, and gray. Oh, how I've missed these eyes. Missed every single thing about her.

"You're right. There is no turning back. I can't change what I did or how things turned out for us. I can't fix the past. But I've got all this future, Lee. All this future that could be our future."

Lyric swallows hard, the sound audible and the sentiment heavy.

The hospital is too busy. There are too many people around. I need quiet with Lyric. I need a moment that is just her and I.

But before I can do anything about that, she says, "I need to go." Her voice is weak and lacks conviction. Her pulse is thrumming at the base of her throat. Her breaths are coming out just a little shorter and faster. "Please, just let me go." The heartbreak in her eyes stops me dead in my tracks. Fractures me into a million tiny pieces.

She pushes open the door to the stairwell, needing to run from me faster than the elevator will allow her to go. I watch her go, her head swiveling back over her shoulder to find me, to check if I'm following before the door shuts behind her. This is the moment that I feel so helpless. So freaking lost as to what to do next.

Shit!

None of this is going as planned.

Do I follow her? Push her harder and faster than she might be ready for?

I honestly don't know. There is no manual with this woman. It's been four years without her, but the moment I saw her, sitting there in that restaurant, it was like no time had passed. Every single thing I've ever felt for her came rushing back to me like it was never gone in the first place. And it wasn't. I've always held on to her. Was never able to let her go.

But now it's back in the forefront of my mind.

All I know is that she came. She got on an airplane and flew across the country. For me. She might say it's for closure, but she could have told me all of that on the phone. She could have called me and told me to fuck off then and there. But she didn't. She came out here. And it has to be for more than to see my father. It has to.

Spinning around, I kick the wall, my frustration and indecision waging a war inside me. I need to find her. I need to talk to her. I need to do whatever it takes to show her this time is different. I have no more time to waste.

Chapter Twenty-Two

JAMESON

I ask the nurses to inform my father that I have to leave. He'll understand. He knows what I'm trying to do. I run down the stairs as fast as my legs will take me, but the moment I hit the main floor of the hospital, I realize I have no idea where Lyric parked. Or what car she's driving—if she's even driving—and it's been more than five minutes since she walked away from me, so she's no doubt already gone.

I could try her phone, but I know she won't pick up for me. Even if she did, I doubt she'd tell me how to find her. I could call her sister, Melody, but I figure I've pushed my luck with her as far as it can go. Sprinting to the garage, I hit the clicker to unlock my car, the lights flashing as it makes that boop-boop sound. Slamming the door behind me, I blow out a heavy breath as I start it up with the push of a button. And then I freeze. *Where are you, Lyric? Where did you go?*

Maybe she went home? Seems like the most logical place, so that's where I'll start. Pulling out of the garage, I fly through town, my eyes searching everywhere while trying to focus on driving and not crashing my car or hitting a pedestrian. Ten minutes later, I'm rolling up to the gate of her house and pressing the buzzer. No answer. Not even their housekeeper. I get out, my car still idling as I peer through the heavy metal gate, trying to catch a glimpse of the house toward the back. It looks dark so I'm going to go with she's not here. Or she's hiding.

Shit. Motherfucking shit.

A growl passes my lips. Dammit, Lee. Where. Are. You?

Getting back in the car, I head over to her sister's house, but when I get there, right before I turn the corner, I catch sight of Melody leaving the house with José and their baby. They're both laughing at something as they set the carrier into the backseat. And Lyric is not with them. I sigh, leaning against the headrest, running a hand across my forehead and down my face. I have no idea where she could have gone.

Flipping the car around, I spend the next half hour driving through town. Going every place I can possibly think of. Coffee shops. Random stores. Our old high school. The park near her house. The freaking ice cream shop. No Lyric to be found.

And then it hits me. Like a slap to the face. The beach at the yacht club. Our beach. The one I took her to when my father had his heart attack all those years ago. It's the only place left I can come up with.

When I pull up to the secluded spot, I realize I was right. A black Jaguar that must be her father's is parked, and when I look down to the shoreline, I see her sitting in the sand, her blonde hair whipping behind her in the breeze.

She came here. Of all the places she could have gone, she came here. To *our* spot.

Filled with a new surge of confidence that this is not over, I get out of the car and make my way down to the sand and over to her. If she hears me approaching, she doesn't let on. Even when I sink down next to her, she never moves her eyes from the chopping blue-gray water slapping against the rocky shore. The salty brine of the air is tinted with the sour note of seaweed that you only seem to get in New England.

"Not as nice, or as warm as California, I imagine." It's May, but that doesn't mean it's all that warm down here on the water. Lyric is wearing a long-sleeved shirt, but her arms are wrapped around her knees that are tucked into her chest, and her body is stiff, and I have to wonder if she's cold. Shucking out of my leather jacket, I place it around her shoulders. "Better?"

She nods. That's it. But I do notice her body relaxes.

"I'm sorry about Robert," I start after a quiet pause of staring at the water. "I know how hard that must have been for you. I tried to get in touch with you after he died, but you're not an easy lady to do that with."

"Not when I don't want to be found, no." *Touché, but wow, that stings.* "Thank you, though, for saying that, I mean. It was a very hard time."

"You're running it now, right? Turn Records?"

"Yes," she replies but doesn't comment further on that.

"I know you're still furious with me, and you have every right to be, but I'm glad you came. Not only to see my father but because I asked you to."

"I told you why I came."

"And yet, you're here at our beach."

"I needed to think, and the ocean always helps me do that." But there are plenty of other beaches she could have gone to for that. Public beaches. As it is, we're technically trespassing on private property. Luckily, my father is still a member of the yacht club, so if anyone challenges us, I have a small card I can play.

"I hate that I thought you were with Ethan all this time. You have no idea the mind fuck that is."

She snorts, the corner of lips pulling up into a small, reluctant grin. "And I'm sure you've been a monk these past four years. Chaste and virtuous."

I nudge her with my shoulder. Unable to fight my grin, I look away for a beat before turning back to her. She's looking at me, and it's the first time she's really done that since last night at dinner when she told me she never wanted to see me again. But this look is entirely different than the one she gave me last night, or even an hour ago at the hospital.

"Most definitely. It's a relief we've been saving ourselves for each other all these years. Really helps with the whole jealousy thing I've been rocking all this time."

She laughs, and the sound makes my heart clench, my stomach dip, and my cock thicken. All at once. From just that one small giggle.

She thinks I'm kidding. But I'm not. I might as well be a monk for all the action I've seen in the last four years. Three girls. Three completely drunken, trashed-out-of-my-mind, one-night stands that I hardly remember. Three encounters where I spent the entire time wishing they were her.

They weren't Lyric. No one is.

I want to ask her if she's missed me like I've missed her. If she's thought about me the way I've thought about her. If she still loves me the way I love her.

But I don't.

I may not be a lawyer, but I know better than to ask a question I don't want the answer to.

Instead, I move closer to her, my body gently brushing hers. She breathes in. Breathes out. Looks away but doesn't move. The atmosphere shifts. The earth beneath our feet slips away. I'm touching her, not skin to skin, but it's enough to feel her heat. To catch the scent of her perfume as the breeze carries it in my direction. For the mounting tension swirling around us to become electrified.

I reach over and cup her jaw, her eyes skating everywhere else they can reach. Everywhere other than on me. But the moment I turn her face to mine, caressing her smooth, warm skin, her gaze finds mine and she holds on.

"Do you feel it?" I ask, my thumb skating up and down against her cheek. "This electricity between us that makes everything in our bodies feel awake and alive? This current tethering us together? It's pulsing between us. It's always there. Like an excited heartbeat. Constant. Steady. I've never felt this with anyone else, and I know you haven't either. We let time make us its fools. We let confusion and misunderstanding lead. We let stubborn pride direct us, and now we're here, four years later."

She shakes her head violently, trying to get my hand to fall. It does. I let my hand drop and lean back. Her eyes narrow, harden. Anger seethes from her pores, coloring the air with a red haze.

"*We* didn't do all of those things," she bites out. "*You* did. But really, it doesn't matter. None of this matters. Sometimes things don't work out. Sometimes two people aren't meant to be together and life reminds them of that. You can't tell me you regret the last four years?"

I shake my head, because how does she not get it? I can't tell if this is just her defense mechanism or if she really believes the shit she's spewing. I'm inclined to go with the former. Because there was no one before her and there hasn't been anyone after. There never could be again. Not like her. Not anywhere close to what we had together.

Screw this. Getting up onto my knees in the sand, I shift so that I'm facing her full on, hovering over her and crowding that personal space she seems so determined to maintain. I lean in, placing my hands on either side of her body, bracketing her in so she has no choice but to see me. To hear me.

"Move back," she hisses, but she doesn't do much to try and get away. Doesn't push me off or get up and move.

Ah, Lyric, it's been four years, but your body hasn't forgotten me.

I ignore her half-hearted plea. I have things to say and she needs to hear them. "I don't regret these last four years. Professionally, I've gotten everything I've ever wanted out of them. I got my father's company and merged it with the one Cane, Travers, and I created. We've made Fortune's list of most profitable companies. We're kicking ass and taking names. But none of it is complete, baby."

She blinks slowly, her face only inches from mine as I tower over her, holding her captive without touching her. And all that fight she had in her moments ago is gone. It's just her and it's just me, and we're right back where we started all those years ago.

"I've had everything I could have wanted. Except you, Lee. I didn't have you. I regret the last four years without *you*."

Her face drops, her chin hitting her chest, unable to take the way those words feel. It hurts. And it feels good. And it *hurts*. It's all those things for me. Everything with this woman hurts and yet feels so amazing that I'm willing to endure just about anything if it gets me this with her.

"Lyric Rose, I fucked up." The magnitude of speaking the words out loud to her slams into me like an earthquake, shaking my very foundation. A piece of my soul slowly begins to release, like air leaking from a balloon. Only instead of deflating, I feel like I'm expanding. Like those are the words my body has been waiting for me to say. To let go of. "I fucked up so bad." The wind howls past us, interrupting me, the temperature dipping further as the sky becomes cloud-covered and angry. "Let's get out of here. Please come with me so I can try and explain."

"Tell me now," she demands. "Tell me now because I don't want to walk anywhere. I don't want to sit in a restaurant or a quaint little coffee shop or in your fucking car. I need you tell me, and I need you to tell me now. But I need you to back off. I can't think with you like this. Give me space and give me your words, and then be done with me."

A humorless laugh passes my lips. "I'll never be done with you."

She's staring me down, waiting for my move. Space. She wants space. So, I push off, out of the sand and away from her body. I sit back, dusting my hands off as I go and placing them on my thighs.

"I'm sorry," I start because those words are long overdue, and I need to say them.

Her knees are back up, her arms wrapped around them like that's all that's holding her together. But I don't think that's true. I think Lyric is as strong and self-possessed as she ever was. Maybe more so. She's watching me. Patiently waiting for me to say something that will undo everything I've done, only I just don't have that for her. Sometimes we make mistakes that are so big they cannot be undone. They can only be learned from.

"We like to believe we choose our lives, Lee. That we choose our path. But sometimes life, or maybe fate, steps in. It takes all of our best laid plans and flips them upside down...and then runs away like a small child, leaving us to try and navigate through the mess they left us with. I had plans for you, Lyric Rose. I had so many plans for us. And then life stepped in and things got so fucking complicated. I was trying to make everyone happy, but I was failing. Especially with you," I point at her as I attempt to tell her everything I've had in my head for the last four years. "I knew you were unhappy. I knew I was the cause of it. I was continually letting you down. Believe me when I tell you there are few things in this world that are worse than knowing you're letting the woman you love down. But I didn't know how to change that. How to fix it. There just weren't enough hours in the day. I genuinely believed if we just took a step back, if you didn't have the expectations of a girlfriend, then I wouldn't hurt you so much. That I could buy more time to get control of things."

"Well, you succeeded. You ended it with me," she says, a bitter note to her tone.

I shake my head, clawing my fingers into the sand. "I didn't want to end it. That was not my intention. That was not my thought process. All I knew was that I couldn't breathe. I was being pulled in so many different directions, and I was ill-equipped. I was outmanned and outgunned, and I failed. When you hung up on me, after misconstruing everything I was trying to say, trying to ask for, I was so angry. I felt like you didn't get me. Like you didn't even try to understand what I was going through.

"I didn't call you back because I was a petulant asshole. And I let months go by hating myself and being angry at you. What I was really angry at was myself...and being so much more miserable with my life than I was before I even asked for that step back. By the time I called you, your number was different. You changed your number on me, which felt like you were dismissing me completely, and so my cycle of anger and self-loathing began again."

Lyric's cheeks color and she looks down. "I was angry, too," she says, but her tone is guilty. Contrite. "You didn't call me back, and I was heartbroken. I felt like I was always waiting for your call that never came. For you to come to your senses, and when you never did..." she trails off, blowing out a breath. "I changed my number because I was sick of obsessing over you not calling."

"I don't blame you for that, Lee. I just hate that you did it. Hate that you felt like you needed to." I inch forward, pulling her chin up until she's staring right at me. "It was my mistakes that got us there. Not yours." I lean in and press my lips to her forehead, allowing myself to breathe her in for the first time in four years. It's everything and yet not nearly enough. "Things got worse instead of better, at least for me. Professionally, everything was going great. Then, a couple months after that, Cane and Travers gave me the push I needed, and I hopped a flight. And what I witnessed was you and a man—who I now know was Ethan—driving you home, holding and kissing you before he stayed the night in your house. It killed me, Lee. Seeing you smiling and laughing and kissing another man was one of the worst moments of my life. I left because I didn't know what else to do. I told myself you were happy, and ultimately, that's all I wanted for you."

"Jesus," she says, her eyes turning glassy from the tears she refuses to let fall. "I can't believe..." Then she laughs. Loud and mirthlessly. Rancorous and so achingly sad that another piece of me breaks. She shakes her head, running her fingers through her windswept hair and staring off into the ocean.

"I stalked you pretty hard after that. I won't even lie about it. Every public picture of you, every award show you attended, the guy was there with you, referred to as either your date or friend. So, I stayed away. Bided my time. Until my father had a stroke and I ran into Melody."

"I don't know what to say," she admits, her features incredulous, wracked with indecision as she tries to come to terms with everything I just told her. "I don't know what to think or do or feel."

"I've told you everything I've got. I made mistakes, Lyric. So many mistakes. I screwed up epically."

A tear falls from her left eye, followed by her right. But those are the only two, and she does nothing to wipe them away as they glide down her face, leaving a wet trail behind.

"I'm hoping you will forgive me. I'm praying you will give me another chance."

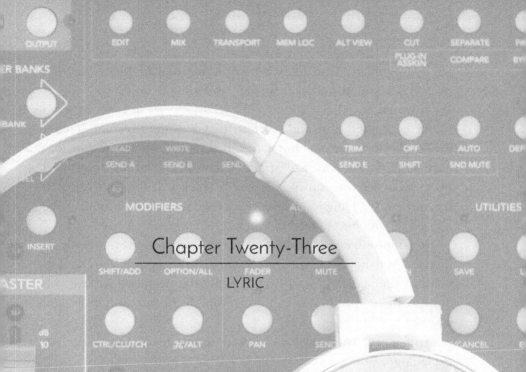

Chapter Twenty-Three
LYRIC

I left Jameson sitting there on the beach. I just got up and walked away. He was stunned, I think. Truthfully, so I was I. I said something like, 'it's not always that simple,' and then I left. I ran through the sand, ignoring the way the granules felt in my shoes, and up the wood plank bridge. By the time I reached my car, I was panting and sweating and yes, crying. But just a little.

Not even a lot, and maybe that's what surprised me most.

Four years. It's been four years since Jameson was mine and I was his. But really, it's been longer than that, because he was right. We weren't a couple while we were away. We were a stitched-up, patched-together, half-assed, look-alike. Our relationship ended the moment I left school and didn't come back. I took my finals online. I didn't even come back for graduation.

And then he missed Melody's wedding, things just spiraled out of control from there.

So yeah, retrospect. Hindsight being 20/20 and all that, right?

He didn't cheat on me. He didn't betray me. He just asked for a step back —a way to regroup. But hell, I was so hurt we had hit that point. That we couldn't find a way to make it all work out the way we had planned. That he was even asking that of me in the first place. I was young, and heartbroken, and so incredibly angry.

It would have been almost too easy to say yes to him. To wrap my arms around him and tell him that I do forgive him. That I would like to try again. But I meant it. Some things are not that easy. Why does the idea of trying again, of loving him again, feel like a weakness instead of a strength? Like a failure instead of a triumph? Like giving in. Admitting defeat. Why do I always feel like I'm losing with him instead of winning?

It's impossible to rebuild trust when your heart is not ready to forgive. And how can you forgive when it's impossible to forget? Getting your heart broken by the man who promised to love you always makes you wary. It makes you distrustful. It makes you cautious.

His story was exactly what I needed. An apology. An explanation.

But I need more than words. I need more than apologies.

I slide into the two-door Jag that belongs to my father and speed home. I'm expected to be in New York tomorrow night for the Rainbow Ball. And as that thought flitters through my head, my phone rings. Ethan. The man that Jameson thought I was in a relationship with. I have no words on that one. Like none. I don't even think I have the heart to tell Ethan.

"Hey," I say, answering the phone and trying to navigate my way around town.

"I cannot wait for you to come to the city tomorrow," he says, his tone so excited I can practically see his white teeth gleaming from here. "The building is gorgeous. The facilities are perfect. I've already had six calls from agents about booking time. You are going to shit a kitten when you see it, Lyric. I am not even exaggerating here. Motherfucking gorgeous."

I smile. Probably just as big as I imagine his smile is because wow. It's actually happening. Years of planning and hard work, and it's finally come together.

"I wish Robert could see it," I mumble, more to myself than to Ethan.

"I know," he agrees, his tone somber. "He would have liked the view."

"I'll be in by two tomorrow to see it."

"Perfect. How's it going there? Or do I not want to know?"

"I…" I let out a humorless laugh. "I have no idea how to answer that, Ethan. I honestly don't."

"Did you see him?" he asks, almost accusatorily.

I tap my nails on the steering wheel as I wait for the light to turn green, my attention fixed on the pedestrians as they go about their day.

"Yes. I saw him."

"Oh, Lyric. If you tell me you fucked him, I'm going to kill you, hide your body in his garage and pin the whole thing on him."

A burst of laughter flies out of my chest. "At least you don't have it all planned out."

"Lyric!" he yells, losing his patience.

"No, Ethan. I did not fuck him. Christ, give me some credit. We talked, okay? We talked. Well, more like he talked, and I listened."

"*And?*"

"And don't use your motherly tone with me, bitch. I seem to recall you doing something very similar when Harrison came back into your life." He blows out some air, and I can hear him deflating with it. The light turns green, and I continue on heading toward my parents' house. "I have a lot to think about."

"Because he's trying to get you back."

It's not a question. It's a statement, but I still say, "No." It's automatic. But I'm not totally sold on that because I think Jameson really might be after that. I know he said it, but it wasn't even that. It was the way he was looking at me. The way he was seeing through me. "Yes," I say after a quiet beat. "He might be."

"Do you still love him?"

"Don't ask me that. That question is off-limits."

"Fine. But for the record, I think it's a mistake. Whatever you decide, it's a mistake."

I laugh again, shaking my head. "Good to know. Your support means everything to me."

He laughs. "That's what best friends are for."

As I pull into the driveway, we end the call with promises of tomorrow in New York. Entering the garage, I shut off the ignition and then I just…sit here. My father has a lot of cars. The man likes his machinery. Foreign ones. Domestic ones. Old ones. New ones. My mind drifts to Jameson's Mustang, and a smile spreads across my face as I think about that night. It was a good night, despite the circumstances of our visit.

If you had asked me that night if I would have ever slept with another man again, my answer would have been no. And not a small no, either. It would have been more along the lines of a hell no.

Tethered together. Those were the words he used today. But do I still want to be tethered to him? Do I want to break free of his spell or succumb to it once again? I don't know. There is too much in my head right now to make that call.

The passenger side of the door clicks open, and then my father is there, sliding his long, lithe body in and sitting next to me with a happy-to-see me smile. I look like my father. Blonde hair and hazel eyes. I love my mother. She's an incredible mom, but my father and I have always had that special other thing between us.

"Mom send you out here?"

He laughs and nods. "Yup. We saw you drive in and when you didn't come inside, well, she got worried."

I roll my eyes. "Did she think I was asphyxiating myself on carbon monoxide? I'm not that screwed up."

"No. But she spoke to Melody."

"God," I groan, dropping my head back against the soft leather of the headrest. "That girl has a big mouth."

He grins, reaching across to brush some of my hair back from my face. "She does. She and your mother are a lot alike. Wanna talk about it?"

"Not really. I saw him. I listened to him. I left."

"Did he tell you the things you wanted to hear?"

My head rolls along the seat until I'm partially facing him. I shrug a shoulder. "I lost trust in the one person I loved the most and it tore me apart. Now he's back. Or trying to be. I'm honestly not sure what to do about it. About him."

My father nods, leaning back in his seat like he's getting comfortable for a long chat. Like he's about to get real with me. I'm not sure if I'm ready for his brand of honesty.

"If words could erase time, I wouldn't be sitting here in the car with you while you question if you can forgive him, and while I question how to show you that trust is earned slowly, especially after it's been broken."

I roll my eyes at that. "What's that supposed to mean?"

He laughs, propping his ankle up on his opposite knee. This car is small and my father is tall, but he somehow looks at ease anywhere. I don't think I've ever seen my father discomposed once. On anyone else, it would be unsettling, but on my father, it's comforting.

"Love's a funny thing, Lyric. We expect so much out of it. We relinquish ourselves to it, and when it fails us, we let it break us apart."

I stare at my father as he stares out the front windshield into the garage. I don't know if we fail love or if we fail ourselves. Each other. But either way, I'm not sure it matters all that much.

"Do you want my advice?"

"Sure," I shrug because I know he'll give it to me anyway.

"Let go." A startled laugh pushes out of my chest. "No," he says, peeking over at me with that warm smile he only gives me. "I'm very serious. Just let go, Lyric. You're all thoughts and immediate expectations. Your mind is always going. You constantly have to have everything figured out. What would happen if, for once in your life, you didn't? What would happen if you just went with the flow? Went about your business, about your life, step by step, moment by moment?"

Moment by moment. Did he have to use those exact words? The same ones that Jameson and I lived by for much longer than we should have. I think on that, my fingers running along the thick seam of leather stitching on the wheel as my father waits me out. Evidently, his questions were not rhetorical.

"I don't know, Dad. I'm not very good at that sort of thing."

"Most people who have had their hearts broken aren't so anxious to go out and do it again. Especially with the guy who ran them through the first time. Not every love is meant to last a lifetime."

I have no words for that. None. I stare out the driver's side window, no longer able to look at my father. Those words just gutted me. Made me feel so exposed and...pathetic. Yes. I feel unbelievably pathetic right now.

He laughs, his hand finding my knee as he squeezes me, forcing my eyes back to his. "I think I have my answer on that." I glare at him and that only seems to make him laugh harder. "Lyric, you'll find the answers you're searching for come to you on their own. Life will do that for you naturally. Just let go. Give all this bullshit with Jameson time and distance. Don't force things upon either of you. Go to the ball tomorrow night. Get things set up for yourself, for the new venture that you and Robert were planning and see where you end up."

"It's not always that simple."

"It is always that simple. We're the ones who complicate things."

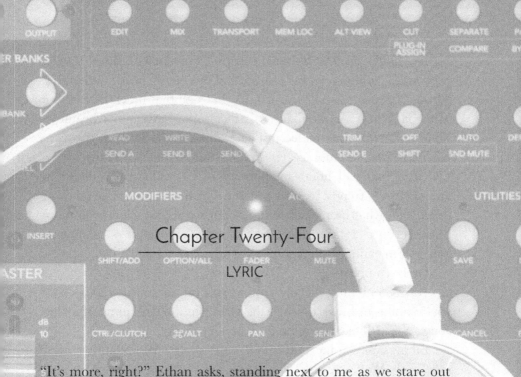

Chapter Twenty-Four

LYRIC

"It's more, right?" Ethan asks, standing next to me as we stare out the window of my office. His voice is so hyper, I'm surprised he isn't bouncing off the walls like a pinball in one of those arcade machines. "Like so much more than you ever possibly envisioned more?"

I laugh, nudging him with my elbow, but I can't look over at him to show him just how big my smile is. My eyes are stuck on the view of the New York City skyline. A view I never in a million years thought I'd have. A view that sort of screams, you did it. You made it. You rocked this and now you're a player. "It's definitely more. I mean, wow. Just wow. This view is—"

"Worth every penny."

I nod. And laugh, possibly a bit hysterically. Maybe even as hysterically as Ethan. I don't want to think about the cost, but looking at this place completed, and this view that lives up to the price tag... "Yeah. I'd say it was." Now I do look over at him because I can't tell if he's shaking, vibrating with enthusiasm, or bouncing up and down on the balls of his feet. "How much caffeine have you had today?"

He holds up his Starbucks cup. "This makes three double expressos." I think my eyes just bugged out of my head. "Whatever. This is New York, and I don't think that's all that much here. If we were back in L.A., I'd have to drink some goddamn wheatgrass slime in between my coffee just so I didn't get kicked out of town, but here, people embrace consuming things that are bad for you. Like it's a badge of honor to abuse your body as long as you do it in an expensive, trendy way." I just stare at him because somehow, I think I get what he means, and he's not wrong, which is even more disconcerting. "I can drink Diet Coke and smoke an e-cigarette as long as I'm eating a fifteen-dollar organic kale salad with it."

He has a point.

"Okay, but I'm officially cutting you off the espressos, because you're about to break through the glass window and jump, thinking you can fly. It's like you're on PCP or something."

Ethan smiles at me, and I return that smile. "We did it, Lyric."

"Yeah. We really did."

And then we both do the girl-squeal, complete with jumping up and down and holding hands. We revel in our moment because you don't get too many of these in your lifetime. It's a beautiful moment, but so bittersweet, I both ache and feel incredible everywhere.

"Madam CEO, now that you've seen your beautiful—and perfectly decorated, I might add—office, would you like me to take you down to the studio floor?"

"Why yes," I say, looping my arm through his, "I would be delighted."

Two years ago, before Robert was diagnosed with pancreatic cancer, there was a label in Brooklyn that had some big-name talent, mainly hip-hop, but was struggling to put out albums, and get good producers, and pay the way they should have been paying. An artist who jumped ship because of all the uncertainty filled Robert in on this. Then, Robert decided he wanted to buy the label.

I was still busy with the production side of things and not so much the business. And I had given up on ever moving to New York long before that. But Robert brought me in on this deal. We worked it so that all the artists stayed and the previous owner, Kaplan Ross, is now the talent director since that's where his strength lies.

It was also contingent on moving to Manhattan because even though Brooklyn is considered super chic and the 'it' place to be if you're a millennial or a hipster, it's not really the place to run a billion-dollar, high-profile record studio. At least that's what Robert believed. Personally, I've always been a fan of Brooklyn, but it was his call and not mine. And seriously, the cost of real estate is just as expensive there as it is here.

Robert was diagnosed with cancer three months after the deal went through, and then he died a little more than a year later. Finding and putting together the New York office was put on hold. I was focusing on running the label while he focused on fighting cancer.

I think part of him had always wanted his children to be more involved in his business, but they were more content with spending their father's money while ignoring his business. They're nice people. I really like Tamara, a part-time yoga instructor living in a beach-front condo in Venice Beach. His son Milo, I don't think does much of anything other than go out to clubs and occasionally gets arrested for fighting with the paparazzi.

Two months before he died, Robert stepped down, and I was named CEO. I knew it was coming. He told me that's how he wanted it. We discussed it. His family was on board with it as long as their money still came in. But it was still a shock to me. And after he died, I got started on the space in New York and have worked tire-lessly to make it just as big and impressive as our offices in LA.

Ethan was my main guy on it, and I have to say, he's blown away every expectation I've ever had. Not surprising, though. I wouldn't have survived the last four years without him, both person-ally and professionally.

We hit the elevator and go down three floors to forty-one. We own five total floors in this building, although most of them are administrative. But we have an entire floor for our studios.

Ten studios in total. Some large enough to accommodate an

entire band, including drums and other instruments. Some smaller for just putting down vocals.

We step off the elevator, to the smell of new carpet, sawdust, and heaven. He opens the door to one of the first studios that happens to be one of the larger ones. There are two couches, two large reclining chairs that appear incredibly comfortable, and a huge soundboard, or mixing deck as it's often called, complete with dual screens and a laptop. Some producers want to do everything digitally, be entirely computer based. Some are old school and like the feeling of the board. Some, like me, use both.

"Wow," I breathe, running my fingers lovingly over the knobs, buttons, and slides of the board. "I'm in love. Is it wrong if I ditch the ball tonight and hang out here?"

"Nope," Ethan says, fully reclined in one of the chairs, his arms propped behind his head, and his eyes are closed. "This might just be my favorite place in the entire building. It's dark, quiet and oh-so-comfortable." He wiggles around just to prove his point. "My office is pretty dope too, though."

I sit down behind the board. I don't turn anything on, but I seriously cannot wait to get going in one of these rooms. "Is it weird that I'm pissed Jasper Diamond and the guys from Wild Minds aren't working on their album here in New York instead of in LA?"

"Considering all the drama that happened with the band the last time they were in New York I'd be shocked if Wild Minds ever stepped foot in this city again."

"I know." I sigh. "And truth, that was some serious drama."

"I still can't believe all that went down with Jasper, his daughter, and Viola. While on tour no less."

"Right?" I snort.

"Still," Ethan muses. "I wouldn't mind being stuck with Jasper Diamond. Broody asshole or not he is one seriously hot man."

"Freaking for real," I laugh, my hands running along the soundboard.

I have two albums that I'm going to be starting in the next couple of weeks here. One is with Dax Star, a rapper who occasionally likes to mix in a ballad or two onto his albums and another with

Cyber's Law. Yes, that Cyber's Law. The one I swore I'd never work with again after the first time.

Then again, this is going to be the third album of theirs I'll be producing. They're still a creative pain in my ass, but I can't get enough of their sound, and we seem to have a thing now. A way of communicating what our respective needs and wants are without killing each other.

I don't ever mix business with pleasure. That is my hard rule and it's one I've never broken. Not even with the hot men of Wild Minds.

That doesn't mean I don't get flirted with. Even if I *am* the boss now. I'm still a pretty young woman in her mid-twenties. I work long hours, one-on-one with a lot of famous, gorgeous musicians. Attraction happens. Flirtations happen. I know what goes on in some of the studios. I'm not stupid. I know that occasionally people have sex in some of these booths.

I've just never been one of them.

But the lead singer, Harry, from Cyber's Law? Yeah. He makes it known that he wants to change that for me. It's going to make the next several months with him a challenge. Then something else, something I've refused to think about since the advent of this takeover and this building and these studios comes rushing in.

"I'm going to be living in New York."

"Doesn't mean you have to see him," Ethan says, clearly reading my thoughts. "It's a big city out there and he works downtown. He might even live down there. You," I turn, and he points at me with a stern finger, his posture still completely reclined in the chair, "work in midtown and will be living ten blocks north and two blocks west of here."

"Different worlds," I say, and he nods.

"Different worlds." He sits up now, the feet of the chair dropping with a thud that reverberates through the room. Leaning forward, he pins me with that stare of his. The one he gives when he's not taking any crappy excuses from anyone. "Because that is what you want. *Right?*"

"Right," I confirm, but I can't meet his eyes. My fingers are still playing with one of the channels on the mixer.

"I think love should be one of the seven deadly sins. Not lust. Lust can be the best thing in the world when done right. It's love that gets everyone in trouble."

"I wouldn't change love. I'd just make it easier to get over when it's done and have it hurt less. It's not fair when the heartache lasts longer than the love that gave it to you."

"Just because he shows up now, after all this time, doesn't mean you need to give into that. Just because you haven't found someone better to replace him yet, doesn't mean that person doesn't exist. You've come so far, Lyric. You're such a strong, successful woman, and you don't need a man for that. Men are a luxury, not a requirement. They're like an added bonus. Friends and family keep you from being lonely, a good vibrator keeps you from being unsatisfied, and work keeps you fulfilled."

I spin in my chair to face him. Sometimes it would be easier if the people we love didn't know us so well. Couldn't read us like the open book we try so hard not to be.

"I agree with all of that. I genuinely do. I never felt I needed Jameson, or any man for that matter, to make me a whole person. I am that on my own. It would be poetic to say I've made something out of my heartbreak. That I turned it into art or used it to reach a higher plane of existence. Or that I've been gifted with an over-abundance of bullshit prose that inspires people. But that would be a lie." I lean forward, dropping my elbows to my thighs and leveling my friend so that he can understand this, even if I'm not sure I fully do. "At the end of the day, I'm still me. The girl who fell for the guy she knew better than to love and lost. And I still wear my heartache on my sleeve because I don't know how to keep it in without it taking more of me than it already has."

"Then let it out, and eventually, it won't own you. Honestly, I think you've been holding on to it, and him, afraid to let go and fully move on."

I can't deny that, so I don't even bother. Instead, I stand up and Ethan does too. "I need to get ready for the ball tonight."

"I do as well," he says, taking my hand and leading me back into the empty hallway. It won't be like this on Monday. Monday, it's going to be crazy busy. That has me smiling as I take one final look at the floor that will be my new home away from home for the next several months. I just hope I can survive living in New York again. Especially after the last few days with Jameson.

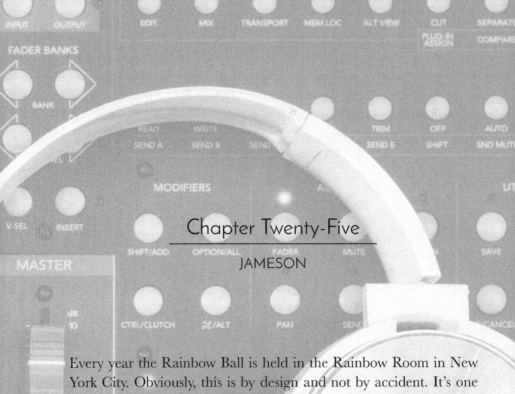

Chapter Twenty-Five

JAMESON

Every year the Rainbow Ball is held in the Rainbow Room in New York City. Obviously, this is by design and not by accident. It's one of the largest cancer events in the country. It raises over a million dollars in just one night, and then that money is divided into three different cancer charities. Those three charities change annually and are literally picked out at random as long as they meet certain organizational criteria and were not given money from the event in the last three years.

It's an A-list event. I think I already mentioned that. And I knew it was difficult to get in to, but I didn't realize it would be nearly impossible. I called every single person in New York I know, and no one could pull any strings to get me a ticket. Sold out is what everyone had said.

Then I called Cane. And Cane spoke to his wife, Greta. I probably should have gone to her first, but I didn't really want to involve my best friend or his wife on my voyage to win my ex back. Mostly because I didn't want to hear the bullshit from Cane. But desperate times, right? Cane, with his built-in gold-digger alarm met Greta, the daughter of a third-generation shipping mogul.

Born and raised in New York, she's the epitome of a socialite.

She knows everyone who is anyone in this city. She's also the biggest ballbuster in the world. She'd have to be to live with Cane. "I expect you to come over every night for nanny duty starting immediately after the baby is born," she orders, rubbing her large round belly in a way that appears both adoring and speaks to her level of discomfort. "I'm going to need a lot of sleep because I haven't gotten any in this last trimester. I swear, this baby does crazy gymnastics all night, which probably means you'll be up all night with her. You'll be required to feed the baby from a bottle, obviously," she says with an eye roll. "As well as diaper her and generally keep her quiet while Cane and I get our much-needed rest."

It would be amusing if she didn't look so damn serious.

"Why don't you just hire a nanny?"

"I believe we just did," she says to me with a smug grin.

She turns to Cane for confirmation, and because the bastard loves his wife more than he loves me, he says, "You'll have your own room directly next to the nursery, but if by some miracle of nature this thing with Lyric works out, you're not allowed to bring her with you. When you're here to work, you're here to work. She can come visit when you're off-duty."

All I can do is stare at them blankly and pray to God they're joking. Greta hands me the invitation she acquired from her mother, who decided not to attend this year and I leave. As fast as I can, as a matter of fact. Cane did wish me luck, though he followed that up with, "You're going to need it to win her back."

Yeah, yeah. Tell me something I don't know.

The glamorous and elegantly appointed room with the floor-to-ceiling windows overlooking the Empire State Building and the city in all its glory beyond is teaming with women in colorful gowns and men in tuxedos. I know most everyone in here simply by sight. Actors. Singers. Socialites. Models. Directors. Producers. They're mingling, drinking expensive alcohol from expensive glasses as they bid on the items that are part of the silent auction.

Things like Hawaiian vacations, a guitar signed by Gabriel Rose —Lyric's father—hotel stays at the Four Seasons, spa getaways at Canyon Ranch, bottles of wine, trips on private jets and week vacations on private yachts. A week at a Malibu beach house that just so happens to look identical to Lyric's. The list goes on and on.

And as I peruse over everything and everyone, I cannot find my girl anywhere. But I spot her name on the sheet of paper next to the Canyon Ranch getaway. And then again on one of the bottles of wine. And then again on the Hawaiian vacation. They're starting bids, I realize, but they're not lowball offers, either. She's trying to raise money for her cause, and I love that she's doing it in this passive-aggressive, fuck-you-rich-ass-people, way.

I put down a fortune for the Malibu beach house that I know is hers and move on.

Heading toward the bar on the opposite side of the room, I freeze when I spot a flash of sparkling color and flesh. Lyric. My breath catches in my chest, unable to be expelled. My heart rate jacks up, and my cock becomes unbearably hard as I take her in from head to toe.

Her dress is entirely made up of multicolored sequins or beads that sparkle, glowing rainbow fire whenever they catch just the smallest hint of light from one of the crystal chandeliers or candles. The bodice is skin-tight, hugging every single gorgeous curve on her body. It has long sleeves and is floor-length with a slit that climbs completely up the side of her right thigh all the way to her hip bone.

And if that wasn't enticing enough, the entire back of her dress is open down to the cleft above her ass. Her long, blonde hair is pinned up and off to the side, revealing the tattoo she has on her back in between her shoulder blades. The tattoo I watched inked on her body.

That was the moment I fell in love with her.

Even if I refused to admit it at the time.

Lyric turns around, a glass of champagne in her hand. She's talking to that guy, Ethan. The bane of my fucking existence, Ethan. Lyric's lips are red, and her eyes are shimmery, and I don't think I've ever seen her look more beautiful in my life. Or maybe it's a tie between this and when I held her sleeping in my arms in my bed that very first night over Christmas.

My focus is singular: Get Lyric back.

It's become my mantra. The steady beat of my heart. The pulsation of blood in my veins.

That is until Harry Evans, lead singer of Cyber's Law, approaches her. That is until he takes her hand and leads her out to the middle of the dance floor. That is until he draws her into his arms, brings my girl into his chest, and begins to dance with her like he's staking his claim.

"You look like you could use this," a voice says off to my right. My head whips over to find Ethan standing beside me, holding out a glass of something that looks and smells like scotch. I wordlessly take the glass and down the entire thing in one large gulp. "That help?"

"Not even a little."

"Good," he says, and I can't stop my sardonic laugh as I redirect my attention to Lyric. Does she have to smile like that? Ethan shifts so he's facing me, his hand outstretched in my direction. "Ethan Simons, but I think you already knew that."

I nod, being magnanimous and shaking the prick's hand. "You're the man in my girl's life."

"I am," he confirms with a wry grin. "Just not the way you thought."

I eye him with an irrational anger I cannot control. I know it's not Ethan's fault. I know it's mine. But that doesn't stop my possessive jealousy where he's concerned. Because for the last four years he's had her and I haven't. Even if, like he said, it's not the way I thought.

"How did you get in here? I know you weren't on the invitation list. I made sure of it."

"Wow," I muse. "You really don't hold back."

He shakes his head. "Not where Lyric is concerned, no."

I shift my eyes back to her, unable to look away for very long. "So, what? You came over here, introduced yourself, and gave me a drink. What's next? You planning on kicking my ass?"

"I think we both know you deserve it, and I'd be doing Lyric a favor if I did, but no, that's not why I'm here."

He falls silent, and I realize this guy is not going to give me anything without my asking for it. And normally, I wouldn't take that. I'd roll all over him and never think twice about it on my quest to win Lyric back. But Ethan here is not just any guy, and if I want to get Lyric back, it seems I have to go through him first. So, I turn to him. Give him my undivided attention even though it's pisses me off to the tenth degree to avert my attention from Lyric and the asshat dancing with her. Touching her bare skin. *Motherfucker*!

"Here's the thing, best friend—"

"Shut your mouth and listen up, pretty boy. I'm tall and built, and I fight fucking dirty."

My eyes narrow, my fists clench, and I stand up straight. We're eye to eye and about the same weight too. He might fight dirty, but I am damn positive that I'll fight dirtier.

We do the stare-down thing with each other and slowly, through the haze of anger-fueled male testosterone, awareness creeps in. I know he's just trying to protect Lyric. Even from me. And as much as I hate this guy on principle, I can't help but love that he's in her life.

"Speak," I grind out through clenched teeth.

He doesn't gloat, and he doesn't grin. Instead, he jumps right into it without any pretense. "Lyric lost a piece of herself when you ended things." I open my mouth to explain, but he holds up his hand and shuts me down quickly. "She loved your stupid, undeserving ass, and you threw her away. She's the most amazing goddamn person I've ever met. She chronically sees the best in people. Always wants to help them. But she never helps herself, and that's where I come in. I pick her up when she stumbles and never let her fall. It's what I've been doing for the last four years, and it's what I'll be doing in another ten." He pauses. Leans into me. And levels me with a ferocity I can't help but match and respect. "In another ten years, I'll still be here. Where will you be?"

"If you weren't her best friend, and I wasn't the guy who fucked it all up with her, I'd kick your presumptuous ass." He doesn't flinch at my statement, nor does that *try me* grin of his waver. "Loving Lyric was never the problem. Life was. I don't owe you an explanation for that. She's the only one who gets answers from me. And I'm certainly not about to ask your permission. But I will tell you this, best friend, if for no other reason than to use you to pass along my message. I love Lyric. I've loved her since the moment I walked into that damn finance class in college. Since she sat next to me in Spanish our junior year of high school and refused to be called by the Spanish version of her name because she thought it was ugly. Since she was my sixth-grade lab partner in science and thought dissecting frogs was cool instead of gross. Since she walked into my kindergarten class wearing a Rolling Stones shirt, a sunshine yellow skirt, and fucking pigtails. She was born, put on this earth, to be mine. And yeah, I might have lost sight of that. I might have let shit get in my way. But that's a mistake I'll never make again. You wanna know where I'll be in ten years? With Lyric. Killing myself to make sure *my* girl gets her happily ever after, because like I said, she. Is. Mine."

Ethan stares me down for another long minute. Then he straightens up and steps back, a satisfied smile slowly peeling up the corners of his lips.

"Then what are you waiting for?"

A small relieved—and slightly shocked—chuckle escapes my lips. I extend my hand and Ethan shakes it firmly. "Thank you, Ethan. For being there for her when I wasn't. For making sure she never fell."

"My pleasure. Now, go get her before Harry Evans makes his move. And if you fuck this up again, I'll make sure they never find your body. There is no such thing as third chances in this world."

I give him a nod and turn around to go get my girl. No way I'll need a third chance. No way.

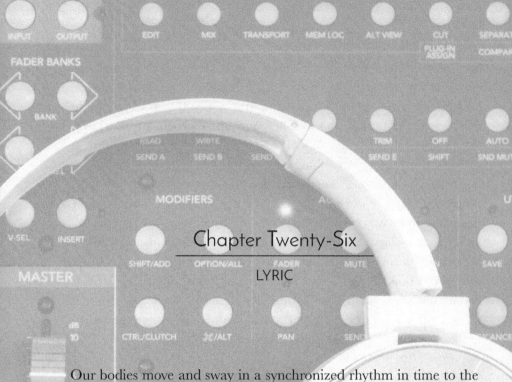

Chapter Twenty-Six

LYRIC

Our bodies move and sway in a synchronized rhythm in time to the music the band is playing, and in harmony with the other dancers surrounding us. Harry is talking to me about a song he wrote, that's —wait for it—not part of the original tracks we're starting from. He's humming it to me as we dance close, his hands on my lower back, just above the fabric line of my dress where they, ever-so-slightly, run across my bare skin. My arms are on his shoulders, trying to maintain awkward distance from an overeager guy like I'm at an eighth-grade dance.

His voice tickles into my skin, and when he hits the chorus, he sings the words directly into my ear. If I wasn't so focused on his physical proximity and how to disentangle myself from it without causing an issue, I would say I like the song. That it has potential. I think it might, but I'm not entirely sure.

He presses me closer, and I inwardly cringe, about to open my mouth and put a stop to this once and for all when I catch movement out of the corner of my eye. That familiar electrifying feeling lifts the hairs at the back of my neck. My stomach does that same goddamn swoosh. My body knows who's headed for me with focused determination before my eyes can even catch up. Jameson's pale eyes are an eloquent mixture of dark and dangerous as they smolder with lust and fury.

My breath hitches as nervous energy fills me, making it difficult to keep the giddy laughter from bubbling past my lips. I cannot believe he came. I have no idea how he got a ticket, but evidently, the man is resourceful when determined. Drunken butterflies take flight in my stomach, bouncing around and making me sick with their uncoordinated flutters.

Jameson smirks, stalking toward me like an animal about to pounce on his prey. Harry says something to me, but I can't tell what it is past the blood rushing through my ears. My body hums with nervous anticipation. I know Jameson is here for me. I know he must have gone to great lengths to get a ticket. I know I should still run in the opposite direction, but when he looks at me like this, I can't help but draw closer instead of farther away.

I used to love the way Jameson would see me. The way he was able to look past what everyone else saw on the outside and find me hidden beneath. He made reality better than any dream, and he did all that simply by smiling into my eyes or watching me from across the room. That's what he's doing to me now. Reminding me that he knows me. That he owns me. That this is so much more than simple attraction or a need to reconquer what was lost. This is soul-searching, depth-scouring, primal recognition of your other half.

My knees weaken, and my resolve turns to mush.

"May I cut in?" It's a demand, not a question, and Harry stops his half-baked dancing and turns to face him, ensuring he doesn't release my body from his grasp even the slightest amount.

Harry's smile doesn't touch his eyes as he replies, "The lady and I were in the middle of something."

"And that something is over."

Harry shakes his head, more into the fight than I would have imagined. "Sorry there, mate. Not gonna happen." He shifts his position, allowing his posture to dictate the message that he's not afraid to fight for what he wants.

I'm almost tempted to interject, but I'm dying to see where this little standoff is headed.

"Come now, Harry," Jameson patronizes with a small tsk of his tongue. "I can't imagine you want to start something at the Rainbow Ball. Especially considering you're just coming off your DUI incident a few months back."

I don't smile, and I hold in my snicker. Mostly because I'm shocked Jameson even knows, a) who Harry is, and b) that he was arrested for a DUI.

Harry's back straightens like a rod, and this is the moment I need to get over my morbid voyeuristic enjoyment at watching these two square off.

"Harry," I say, touching his shoulder so he'll turn his attention back to me and away from Jameson. "He's an old friend from college." I have no idea why I just said. The words flowed out of my mouth like a burst pipe. "Why don't you go speak to Ethan about which studio you want for Monday, and he'll make it happen."

Harry's eyes search mine as he weighs the situation at hand. "I always do as my lady requests," he says with a flourish that has me suppressing my eye roll. "I'll catch up to you later, beautiful." He leans in and plants a kiss on my cheek and then walks off, intentionally bumping into Jameson in the universal way that says: you didn't win; I ceded the victory.

Jameson doesn't waste time. In the next second, his arms wrap around me, pulling me into his warm body. The scent of his enticing cologne disarming my better judgment. His fingers glide up my bare back, running lovingly over my tattoo, as if to remind me he's as much a part of me as this ink is. I shudder, chills running up my arms as he presses my head to his chest directly over his heart. His heart that is beating wildly, betraying his cool, confident exterior.

"Home at last," he murmurs into my ear, his voice soft and his tone so sincere I can't help but mimic his sentiment. Because nothing has ever felt as right as it does in Jameson's arms. I close my eyes, sink into him, and then my eyes snap open wide.

What am I doing? Why am I giving into this so easily?

Four years, Lyric!

Four years with not so much as a peep out of him. His story

about seeing me with Ethan and thinking that I was with him and that I was happy feels like bullshit. It all feels like bullshit. Because at the end of the day, he didn't fight for me. He didn't fight for us or what we had. Which means I wasn't special to him. I wasn't important. And now? Now I don't know what this is. Regret? Nostalgia? Quarter-life crisis over his father's poor health?

I can't say, but it's like a cold hard slap on my underused and overzealous libido.

I realize I've stopped moving when he says, "Dance with me, Lyric. Let me hold you in my arms and press you against me. Let me remind you what it feels like to be touched by someone who knows every inch of you better than you do." He draws back and meets my eyes, the glitter in them spreading warm tingles through my body. "Come on, baby, let's make the world around us disappear the way only we know how."

"And what happens when it comes back into focus, Jameson? What then?" He silently stares at me, almost like he doesn't quite know how to answer. And wow, that's just...shit, I don't even have words. "You've missed so much. Four years is not an insignificant amount of time. In fact, it's a hell of a lot longer than we were together."

He shakes his head at me like I'm not getting it. And maybe I'm not. I feel too lost to understand much beyond my own sense of this. "I was reckless. Reckless with your time. With your heart. With your love. I was reckless, Lee, and I don't know how to express my regret in terms you could understand. It goes beyond words or even emotions. It's inside of me. It's a part of me. I was reckless, and I let the love of my life get away."

"That's the thing," I say, staring straight into his eyes, "I never went anywhere. I was still there. The whole fucking time. I hadn't moved. Not houses. Not jobs. I was there, Jameson, waiting on the guy who never showed up. For the guy who was too *reckless* to even call me back. I know it was a no-win situation, but we should have never ended like that. That's on me, too. I know it is. But I don't know how to forgive you. I honestly don't. Even if I could find a way, I don't know how to trust you. I'm not sure my heart could sustain another blow like the one you gave it."

He stares at me helplessly as he imagines up the magic potion. The one that erases time and memories. The one that makes all of this better and allows us to try again. And when he comes up empty, he just pulls me back against him, holding me so close, knowing this moment is fleeting. That our expiration date on this dance is just about up.

"Inevitably, we're forced to make sacrifices. It's when we sacrifice the ones we love for the things we shouldn't that change us. That's what I did, Lee. I sacrificed you for something that wasn't anywhere near as important to me as you were. As you still are. It's not something I would ever do again. *Could* ever do again. Yours is a forgiving heart. It's the biggest, most beautiful heart I've ever had the pleasure of holding. But I get it. You need more than just my words or promises." He moves back, only now he's grinning like he's got it all figured out. Like he just had that ah-ha moment, and it's all coming together for him. "When you've screwed up so bad that you're at the bottom, there is no place else to go but up. I'm gonna fight for you, Lyric Rose. I'm gonna fight like crazy. Because I love you and I know deep down, you still love me and we're it. We're meant to be. Fucking kismet and all that bullshit, but no less true. This is it, baby. So yeah, you're not done with me yet."

And then his mouth finds mine. No, it devours mine. In the middle of the dance floor in front of New York society. This kiss says: I dare you to contradict me.

One hand is in my hair, holding my head as he controls the kiss, his other on my lower back as he toys with the line of my dress. He sweeps his tongue against mine, tasting me. I taste him, too. I can't stop it, so why try? Scotch, mint, and Jameson. That last one so good I'm high, dizzy, and weak in the knees as he kisses me unlike any man has never kissed me before. Like his world starts and stops inside my mouth. Inside my soul.

And when he pulls back, he cups my face in both hands, his thumbs brushing along the crest of my cheeks.

"Don't give up on our forever. It's just getting started." He searches my eyes, vacillating between each one as he tries to read me. "Are you really working with that Harry guy on Monday?"

"Yes," I say softly, still stunned by the kiss, though my voice is steadier than I would have thought.

Jameson's eyes close slowly as he releases a breath. And when he reopens them, they're filled with fiery determination. "When do you leave for California?"

He doesn't know about the studio here in New York.

"Tomorrow," I lie. And I can't even explain the lie. I have no idea where it comes from, but I don't retract it. I don't try to change it. I need the time the lie buys me. I need its security. All of this is happening so fast, and I feel like I can't get my bearings.

"What time is your flight?"

"Ten in the morning."

"Then, I don't want to waste another minute." Jameson takes my hand and leads me away from the dance floor.

"I can't leave," I protest, trying to pull away.

He gives me a sideways glance and a smirk to go along with it. "We're not. We're just going somewhere more private." He guides me out of the main room and over to the outdoor garden that overlooks St. Patrick's Cathedral and Fifth Avenue. The lawn and gardens are beautiful. Perfectly manicured hedges lined with small flower beds and short trees make up the majority of the refuge high above the city. The air is cool and crisp, and the sounds of the city below are muted by the elevation. In fact, it's surprisingly quiet and romantic out here with only the glow of the cathedral to light our way.

The outer hedge that lines the stone perimeter has breaks every few feet and it's to one of those breaks that Jameson leads me. Leaning forward, our forearms rest on the cold, rough stone as we stare down at the street below.

"It's lovely up here," I whisper reverently. "In all the years I've been coming to the ball, I've never been out here. Do you like living in New York?"

"Yes," he says quickly, his gaze focused on the cars flying south on Fifth Avenue. "I wasn't sure I would, to be honest. But it grows on you."

"Like a rash," I mutter under my breath. I don't hate New York. But I'm mad at it, if that makes any sense. I realize I'm going to become a temporary resident over the next few months, but that doesn't mean I'm fully resigned to it. I think I have more a love/hate relationship with it actually.

"If New York is a rash, LA is a disease."

I nod my head. "I do not disagree with that. I love my house in Malibu, but there is a lot about the city I could do without. The smog. The traffic. The congestion. The fakeness of the people. It eats at you, but I imagine that's like anything else—after a while, you just…acclimate."

"I'm proud of you, Lyric."

My head swivels in his direction, my eyes wide and mouth slightly agape.

"Don't look at me like that. I am. You're one of the leaders in your field. You run your own record label and have the respect of people more than twice your age."

"Look who's talking," I laugh, nudging him with my shoulder. He smiles. He likes that I just initiated physical contact while I sort of wish I hadn't. Mostly because I liked it, too. I lose sight of my anger when I'm with him for any length of time. I fall into old, familiar patterns quickly. It's impossible not to.

I still like talking to him. I still want to know about him. I still *care* about him. And worst of all, I can't do anything to stop it. I'm torn in two. Half of me wants to throw myself into his arms and never look back. Half of me wants to slap him and run in the other direction. I love him and I hate him. I care about him and I want to kill him. But I guess that's just love, right? It's not known for being the most rational.

Love. You make smart women so very stupid.

"I guess," he says modestly, inching a little closer to me. A cool breeze brushes across my face, momentarily stealing my breath. Or maybe it's the man next to me doing that. "We've been busy," he says, but I don't miss the somber note to his tone. "Do you still like making music?"

I grin, just thinking about that question. About the meaning behind it.

"Music is the passion of my life." A crooked smile graces the lines of his perfect lips as he stares at me. I'm not looking at him, my gaze is locked on the cathedral across the way, but I see him all the same.

I always see him.

"Not the *love* of your life?" Ah, so that's the smile.

I shrug, unwilling to explain further. He knows. I know he knows, and he knows that I know he knows, and so goes the game.

"What is it you love so much about music, Lyric? I think in all our time, I've never asked you that directly and it's something I've always wanted to know." Lyric. He called me Lyric, which indicates this is a serious question that demands a serious answer.

I like his question. Or maybe I like the way it makes me feel.

"Music is universal. It defies borders, language, race, ethnicity, age, and gender. Everyone out there has a song they can connect with, even if they don't 'like' music." I put air quotes around the word. "People all over the world, with virtually nothing in common, may like the same song. It unifies in a way nothing else can. I also love the power it can wield. The way it can both heal and tear down. The way it can make you smile, cry, sing, and dance. Or all at once, sometimes. People feel music in a way they allow themselves to feel little else."

He stares at my profile, but this stare is different than any before it. This stare says I make him feel everything. That I'm his version of music.

"Lyric Rose…," he pauses here. Waits for me to find him. To match his intensity. "You make it impossible not to love you. And just when I think I couldn't love you any more, you prove me dead ass wrong."

I turn away at that. It's too…*much*.

Because it's exactly how I feel about him.

Even after four years apart.

"Thank you for flying across the country to see my father. It meant a lot to him…and me. Especially me."

I don't know what to say to that. My pleasure, or it was nothing, doesn't really fit with this. I came because I care about his father a lot. But I also came because I was searching for closure. A closure I clearly never received. A closure I'm not all that interested in anymore, and that might scare me the most out of everything.

His fingers brush across my cheek at my silence, and he forces my face to his. His lips caress mine once. Twice. And then again. It's whisper soft and elegantly sweet and heartbreakingly beautiful. It's everything I need and yet not nearly enough. I pull back and stand up, desperate to clear my muddled mind of the man who is making it harder and harder to know what the right thing to do is.

"I need to get back."

"Then let's get back. And maybe tonight, you'll let me take you home." He gives me an impish grin, stepping into me and bouncing his eyebrows suggestively. "Whosever home that may be."

"Stop flirting with me, Jameson."

"Then stop being the most stunning woman I've ever seen, Lyric."

I roll my eyes. "I don't like charming, either."

"I'll work on being less charming. But you should know it's my natural state, so it won't come easily to me to give all that up." His arm snakes around my waist, pulling me firmly against his chest. I lean back and stare up into his eyes. "Let's get you back in. I want to dance with you again. If I only have tonight, I'm going to give it everything I've got."

Chapter Twenty-Seven

JAMESON

Sunday mornings in New York are for running along the river, expensive alcohol-infused brunch, or sleeping in. Or all three. Typically, it's all three for me. It's the day my friends and I relax. The day where we just get to hang out without the pressures of work or women or families. Today, even after last night, is no exception.

I'm walking up Park Avenue toward the restaurant Travers picked for today. We typically try to mix it up, and today the guy picked Upland, a California-inspired place. Or so the website says. California. It's like the bastard is mocking me or something.

After Lyric and I went back inside, we were immediately ushered to our respective tables to eat the four-course dinner that was beginning to make its rounds. When I negotiated my invitation out of Greta's manipulative hands, I didn't consider table assignments. Not sure I would have had a choice so last minute anyway. It turns out I was across the damn room from Lyric at a table of old-school New York socialites. All friends of Greta's mother who were not happy to have me there.

Lyric, on the other hand, was seated next to Ethan—okay, obviously I'm cool with that one now—and fucking Harry Evans. Clearly, the bastard is a better player than I thought, or maybe more interested because I'm sure he had to work some magic to be at her table.

I spent the rest of the evening watching her from afar, loving how every few minutes, her eyes would find mine. Occasionally she'd blush like she was embarrassed I busted her or—and this might be wishful thinking on my part—like she was having dirty thoughts about me.

I sure as shit was about her.

I ate my dinner like a good little boy, barely tasting any of it when douchetard Harry felt the need to put his arm along the back of her chair. I had one more drink than I should have, and by the time dinner was over, it was time for the silent auction. The woman on my right kept trying to engage me in conversation about her son, who she was convinced I knew—I didn't—and by the time I got back to Lyric, she was gone.

At least, I couldn't find her anywhere. Ethan was also gone, so I assume she ran out early with him. And yeah, that stung. I wish she had stayed. I wish I had gotten to gloat to her face that I won her Malibu house for a week. I wish she had let me dance with her again and take her home. Even if I knew there wasn't a snowball's chance in hell I was going to sleep with her.

I have plans for Lyric Rose. Big plans. And her not saying goodbye to me last night was not part of that. But maybe there are no more goodbyes for us. If I have to move to California, I will. If I have to open a branch of my company there, I will. I will do what-ever it takes for her. The moment my father is fully out of the woods and back home with whatever care he needs, I'm on the next plane out there for good. And in the interim, I plan to make it impossible for her to push me aside. Even if she might try to.

It's with that thought that I nearly drop my phone on the ground when I see her name blowing up my phone. I smile, pausing on the sidewalk and shifting off to the side of a building since I'm only a half a block from the restaurant.

"Good morning, beautiful Lee," I say, unable to hold back my playful tone.

I have an itching feeling what this call is about, and when she screams, "What have you done, you bastard?" in my ear, I know I'm right.

"Could you be a bit more specific on that, baby? I have done a lot of things to be called a bastard over."

She growls, clearly not as amused as I am. "You bid and won the week at my house in Malibu."

It's not a question, but I feel the need to answer her all the same. "Of course, I did, crazy girl. It was for charity. And I couldn't resist the opportunity to spend a week with you."

I hear her scoff into the phone. "Clearly, you didn't read the fine print all that well then. It's for the week of Fourth of July. I won't be there. So even though you were very generous, I'm sorry to tell you that you'll be staying there without me."

Leaning my head back against the stone edifice of the building, I prop my foot up and think about what she just said. July fourth is like two months from now, and if she's starting a new album with twat-lick Harry and his band of assholes, then why wouldn't she be in her house? And now that I think on it, isn't she supposed to be on an airplane back to California at this very moment?

I check my watch, and sure enough, it's just about noon. She told me her flight left at ten a.m. And now that I listen closely, I can hear the sounds of the city—my city—in the background through the phone. Which means she lied when she said she was leaving town this morning.

And if she was lying about that, and is not planning on being home the week of July fourth—which I believe, since it was part of the auction—then maybe she's not recording that album in California after all? Or she could just be on vacation that week, and I'm completely misreading this.

Ah, Lyric Rose. Now I have a lot more digging to do on you.

"That's a shame, but honestly, it's not why I bid on your house. I did it to get your attention." She growls again, but she doesn't hang up. "What are you doing today, baby? I'm having brunch with the guys, but after that, I was planning on going out to see my father. Wanna come with me? I mean, since you're clearly not on an airplane heading back to LA?"

She hisses out a slew of curses under her breath, and now my smile is so big, my goddamn cheeks hurt with it. "I have to go." And then she hangs up on me.

In this moment, I am seriously regretting I did not get that guy Ethan's number. I need more information and I need it now, so I do what everyone does when they're trying to stalk someone. I google her. But instead of just her name, I google the name of her label. And sure as death and taxes, Google comes through for me.

It makes me question how I missed this. Actually, I'm insanely pissed at myself for this one because not only did her label take over another New York based label a few years ago, she just finished a midtown office and recording studio. Which means my girl is staying in the city. *My* city. As in, here with me.

Tucking my phone back into my pocket, I start walking toward the restaurant. A freaking hop in my step and a stupid grin on my face, but I don't care. I can't remember the last time I was filled with this sort of triumphant joy. I open the door to the restaurant, look around for my friends, and catch Travers when he throws a hand up in the air to signal me.

The moment I approach them, my two best friends exchange glances. Knowing glances at that. I ignore them. There isn't a goddam thing that can dampen my mood. Cane slides his phone across the smooth light-wood table, his back pressed against the forest-green padding of the booth.

Except this.

This can definitely dampen my mood.

Because what the motherfuck?

I stare at the phone in disbelief.

"It's bullshit," I say automatically, though a part of me is not entirely sure. They were dancing together last night. He was sitting next to her at dinner. His arm was slung over his chair, and he made a point to comment on seeing her on Monday. And she told me she was leaving for California today even though she wasn't. And she hung up on me after yelling at me about bidding on her house. *Shit.*

"We figured," Travers concurs, looking to Cane for backup on that. Cane stays silent, and sometimes, I wish the guy wasn't so freaking honest. Wish he gave more fucks than he typically does. "It's at a distance and an angle. And these paparazzi guys are paid to make nothing look like something."

Something indeed. Because Harry Evans has his arms around Lyric. *My* Lyric. Not only that, it looks like she's smiling up at him as he stares lovingly into her eyes. My chest tightens, and my fists clench, and I'm so sick with this.

"Maybe you're too late after all," Cane deadpans with a shrug, and in one minute, my clenched fist is going to end up breaking his nose.

The headline reads, "Love at the Rainbow Ball." Not all that original if you ask me. Below that, it says that the two have been working together for years and are about to start their third collaborative project together at her new studio in New York.

Damn, everyone knows this shit but me.

"Doesn't matter," I say both to them and to myself, sliding the phone with the picture that just stole my appetite, away. Because it doesn't matter. Lyric is mine. She kissed me last night. Or at least she kissed me back. Right? I didn't misread that. No way.

"Go find her," Cane suggests, taking a sip of his Bloody Mary and looking around the room aimlessly. "Stalk her ass down and show up at her building."

"Definitely," Travers agrees. "You can't let that prick Harry get her. She's ours. Well, yours, I guess. But she always felt like ours."

"I have no idea how to do that."

Travers shakes his head like he's disappointed in me, and silence descends upon us as our waiter takes this bleak moment to interrupt us with specials. I order the first one he says. I don't even know what it is. I also order myself a Bloody Mary because I think I need one.

"My assistant is gay," Cane states out of absolutely nowhere. Travers glances at me, and then we both look to him with equally puzzled expressions. "Ethan, right? Her BFF. He's gay."

"And?" I draw out, wondering what one has to do with the other.

"If you're about to say all gay people know each other, I'm

going to punch you on behalf of gay people everywhere," Travers says.

"It's worth an ask." I don't know how to argue with that. Even if it's somehow offensive and makes little sense. He shoots his PA a text anyway. Because that's Cane for you. "Do you guys know what hypnobirthing is?"

Travers and I just stare at him. Cane takes a large pull of his Bloody Mary. When he sets it down, he leans forward, pressing his chest against the table and leveling us both with the most serious expression I've ever seen on him.

"Greta says she doesn't want an epidural. She wants to do this child-birthing thing au natural. She thinks if we take a hypno-birthing class, she won't feel the pain of pushing a watermelon out of her lemon because that's how it looked in the YouTube videos. Those mothers were barely making a noise and looked all placid and shit. It's a freaking racket."

"Okay," I say slowly because I have no idea how to react to that. Birthing babies is way out of my jurisdiction.

"It's not okay," he protests, slapping his palm on the table just as my drink is delivered. Our waiter scurries away, a little afraid, I think. "Drugs were invented for a reason. So that smart, sane women can take them during the birth of their children. But there is no arguing with her. I don't know if it's hormones or she's genuinely trying to bust my balls or what. But we've been taking this class, and it's all about deep breathing and finding a rainbow of colors, or some crap. I don't know because I end up falling asleep during the meditation or hypnosis part or whatever. And then she gets angry at me because I'm supposed to be learning how to help guide her to find her relaxation color and giving touch massage. I feel like I'm going to fail at this child-birthing thing."

"When did we become an episode of *Sex and the City*?" Travers asks, twisting back and forth between both of us, a little freaked out by the conversation at hand.

Honestly, I'm not too far off. Actually, I'm wondering how I got to this point in my life when I'm only twenty-six. We're talking birthing babies and hypnobirthing at brunch when we should be talking about weekend pussy, and which bar we hit up last night. But we're not. I'm broken up about my ex possibly being with a famous rock star, and my friend is talking about his wife's vagina. Obscurely, I'll give you that, but let's call a spade a spade here.

"Yeah, I was sorta wondering the same thing," I admit.

"Screw you both, this is serious," Cane growls, losing the last shred of his composure. Clearly, this is a real issue for him.

This would almost be amusing if he weren't so worked up about it. Women were like an endless bowl of peanut M&Ms to us once upon a time. Each one just a little different, and once you had one, it was impossible not to pick up another and eat it.

Now, Travers is the only one who regularly indulges in the variety life has to offer. But I don't miss the variety. I miss the girl who makes all the other M&Ms look like Pez or Smarties or some other candy that you really liked as a kid, but once you grew up, realized weren't all that great.

"You're the support system, right?" I ask, bringing my mind back to Cane's dilemma.

"I can't handle my wife being in pain," he says, and I can't stop my resulting smile. "Stop looking at me like that, dude. I'm not playing around. We're getting scarily close to go time, and she's talking about deep breathing instead of drugs."

"Then you let her squeeze your hand until it breaks," Travers tells him with a shrug that indicates the situation is not nearly as dire as Cane is making it out to be. "It's childbirth, not open-heart surgery. Women have been doing it forever."

Cane opens his mouth to protest when his phone dings on the table, and the three of us jump forward simultaneously. "Ah," he says with a smug grin, "will you look at that. Who's the asshole now?" He leans back once more in his seat, his arms crossed over his chest. "My boy knows your boy, bitch."

And then my phone rings. I suppress my hopeful thoughts in thinking it's either Ethan or Lyric, but it's not. It's some odd California number. I look cautiously between my two friends before I slide my finger across the phone to accept the call.

"You need to remember something, Jameson Woods," the very

familiar female voice barks into the phone before I can even say hello. I blink, my brain a few seconds behind, and then a startled laugh passes my lips.

"Cassia?"

She sighs heavily like she doesn't have the patience to deal with me. "I will gut you like a fish if you hurt her. I will cut you up piece by piece, and I will start with your penis. My husband is LAPD, and in case you miss the national news, those people do not care. You hear me, douchebag? They do. Not. Care."

"Um. Okay?"

"No. It's not okay. Because you have my high-school friend texting Ethan about Lyric."

My eyebrows knit together, my head shaking in total bewilderment. "It's like you're speaking in encrypted Chinese to me, doll. I'm about ten paces behind."

She does that heavy sigh thing again. If we weren't in a crowded restaurant on Park Avenue waiting for a meal and drinks that cost more than some people's weekly paychecks, I'd put this on speaker. As is it, both Cane and Travers are laughing. They think it's freaking hysterical that Cassia is calling me. I do, too, if I'm being honest.

"Not surprising. But here's the thing, gumdrop, your friend's assistant is a guy I went to high school with. Small world and all that crap. When Ethan moved to New York, I gave them each other's numbers. You know, so they could connect and shit. Anyway, Howard just sent me a text that Cane sent him about getting Lyric's address. I assume it's because you saw the tabloids, and I assume it's because you're uber pissed about it."

"Cassia," I say, my grin still intact. "I miss you, too. It's been ages. I'm doing great. Glad to hear you are, too. Now that we have formalities out of the way…" She bites out a sarcastic laugh. "Yes, I've seen the tabloids, but that's not why I want to find her. If you need my declaration of undying love for Lee while I'm at brunch with Cane and Travers, I'll do it. I'm just that sort of man. But the truth is, she loves me back and you know it. Ethan knows it, and Cane and Travers know it. It's happening, Cass. So please, help an old college friend out, and text me my girl's address so we can just skip three steps ahead, and avoid a lot of back and forth."

Silence. She's silent, but I know that means she's thinking this through. I give her those few seconds as I sip on my unfortunately not-very-alcoholic drink and take a bite of my...steak and eggs with some sort of sauce? Yeah, I think that's what this is. Anyway, I wait, and the guys wait, both quiet as they eat and watch me, waiting for the verdict.

"What sort of guy gets a crepe?" Travers questions Cane, and Cane just shrugs as he shovels another bite of the delicate pastry into his mouth. This deliberation is taking too damn long.

"Tell Howard the Duck I'll fire his ass if he doesn't help out," Cane yells, with a nodding grin like that will seal the deal. We get looks from the people on either side of us, but they back off quickly after Cane throws them a few menacing glances.

"God, I forgot how much Cane sucks," Cass mutters into the phone, and I laugh because fucking Cass, right? She's everywhere, even when she's not. "Fine. I'll text you her New York address. But I meant what I said about my husband and the LAPD and the zero fucks they give."

"Got it," I assure her.

"And you're going to have to give this your all, Jameson. She's been trying to talk herself out of you since she got your first text. Hell, for the last four years."

"Noted," I reply even though *that* hurts. "Thanks for sugar coating it for me."

"I'm hanging up now."

"Okay. I appreciate the help."

"Just so you know, she cannot stand Harry Evans."

The phone disconnects and five seconds later, it pings with a text that shows an upper west side address. I grin like the happy bastard I am, and as I eat my delicious brunch, life is good once again.

"Eat up, boys," I say. "Time to go and win my girl back. And I know just how to do it."

Chapter Twenty-Eight

LYRIC

"You do realize it looks like he's snagging your ass, right?" Melody asks as I stare out the window of my apartment, half-afraid to go out since that stupid tabloid posted that stupid picture of Harry and me at the Rainbow Ball, where I was thanking him for his generous bid on my father's autographed guitar. "And your dress is super sexy so that only adds to this whole thing."

"Yep," I agree, not even caring that my answers have been nothing but short with her. She's undeterred and seems to be eating up the gossip with a spoon. I can practically hear her clicking on websites through the phone.

"I bet his PR people are loving this," she muses with a small laugh. "I mean, you're the daughter of Gabriel Rose, and you're his producer. It's all so publicly perfect for him. CEO and producer with an impeccably clean history. Harry was getting a lot of backlash after that DUI. He lost a few endorsements because of it. I'd be willing to bet this is all just one big set up."

I nod. I'd thought of that. Harry plays like he's interested, but I have to wonder if it's genuine or not. He's certainly turned up the charm since the arrest.

"Do I make a comment?" I ask, chewing on the corner of my lip. "Deny it?"

"Why would you? There is no benefit to you or to him. If the world thinks this is happening between the two of you, it will only drive up sales." She has a point. But I can't help think about Jameson and what he must think of this. Or the fact that he now knows I'm living here in the city for an indeterminate amount of time. The dumbass bid on my house, thinking I'd be in it when he came to collect on his prize. I secretly love that.

And I secretly hope he's insanely jealous of these pictures. And not even in a malicious way. I want his interest. I want his obsession. I want him to come crawling on his hands and knees. I want him to give me a real reason to say yes other than because he asked and said it would never happen again.

"What do I tell my publicist?"

"Tell her whatever you want, but I'd make her keep her mouth shut about it. Everything we do and say matters. Is indelible. There is no eraser. No delete button, especially with social media. You can go the whole, we're just good friends, route. People won't believe it, but at least you're saying it."

"Yeah. I think I have to. I can't just let it ride silently." I sigh, twisting my bottom lip between my thumb and pointer finger. "Tomorrow is going to be hell. You know that, right? The studio is going to be swarmed with the 'razzi."

"No such thing as bad publicity."

"And why aren't you a publicist again?"

"Because Max sucks the lifeblood from my body. I have no time for anything other than laundry, changing diapers, nursing, and occasionally sleeping, and if I'm really lucky, sex with my husband. And because I'm totally lazy."

I laugh at that. "Sounds like it. Clearly, taking care of an infant is for the inherently lazy." My phone makes that beeping noise that indicates another call coming in, and as I pull it away from my ear to check who it is, I groan. "I gotta go, Mel. It's my doorman. Kiss the little bloodsucker for me. Love you."

"Love you, too."

I hit the button to switch over to the other call. "Hello?"

"Sorry to bother you, Miss Rose," the doorman says, a nervous edge to his voice. "I had to step out to help a resident get a taxi. When I returned to my post, there was a package waiting for you."

"You didn't see who delivered it?"

"No ma'am. I'm sorry. Would you like me to bring it up?"

"Uh, sure," I shrug to myself.

"Be right up."

I set my phone down on the coffee table and head over to my front door, not-so-patiently waiting for my mystery package. I have no idea what it could be. I know I'm not expecting anything, and it's Sunday, so I doubt it was delivered by UPS or the mailman or anything. A few minutes later, there's a knock at my door, and I open it up—a little too anxiously probably—to find the doorman holding a large white box with a pink bow tied around it.

"Oh," I say because this is not what I was expecting. I expected one of those brown boxes covered in tape and stickers like you get from Amazon. This is most definitely not one of those. This is not a package. It's a present. "Thank you, Parker."

"My pleasure," he says, handing me the light box.

I shut the door and immediately drop down to the floor so I can open it up. I pull off the pretty ribbon with gusto, and when I lift the lid off, I gasp. It's just a bunch of random things, but it's not. On top is a chewed-up pen that's resting on one of my old sleeping t-shirts. I pull it out, setting the gnarled pen on the floor and bringing the t-shirt up to my nose. Jameson. It smells like Jameson and not me.

And this pen. Now that I look at it, it's not just any old pen that Jameson chewed into nothing. It's a pen from the tattoo shop we went to when I got my tattoo.

Tears burn the backs of my eyes, a lump forming in my throat that I force back down with a hard swallow. Under the t-shirt is other things—all things he must have saved from our time together. Concert ticket stubs, handwritten notes we used to pass back and forth to each other in class because we were caught texting too many times, presents I had bought for him, a tube of my old flavored lip gloss, and pictures. Dozens and dozens of pictures.

I dump the box upside down, running my fingers along the contents as I splay them out on the hardwood in front of me, my tears falling freely now. I pick up a random picture, and the strangled sob I was desperate to tamper down escapes with a vengeance. It's a selfie I took of us when we were snuggled up in bed one night, our smiling faces pressed together. The next one is a candid of me walking across the quad at school, my eyes fixed on the horizon beyond. I didn't even know he took this picture. More selfies of us. More candids. Posed pictures. Kissing pictures. Hugging pictures. Christmas pictures. Day trips and a million other moments we shared. Our entire relationship. So much love and happiness together.

He had them all printed out.

He saved all of them.

I pour through each one before I come to a picture all the way at the bottom that I don't recognize. It's a man's forearm and on it is a new tattoo, red and angry. A rose. It's a goddamn tattoo of a rose and above it is my name in beautiful script. He tattooed me on his body. Not just the rose but my actual name. His words from the day I got my tattoo back when we were in college echo through my head. *I doubt I'll ever get one. Your song feels different because it's timeless and was written for you by your father. Nothing in my life feels like forever, and the things that could aren't worth making permanent.*

He tattooed me on his arm. He made me permanent.

The photo slips through my fingers, cascading down to the others still scattered on the floor. My hands come up to my face and I let go. I cry. And I can't tell if this cry is heartbreak or forgiveness or healing, or some miserable combination of all three. Heartbreak is a wound that never fully heals, even with the passage of time. But maybe I don't need it to heal. Maybe that's not what this is about. Maybe it's about letting yourself love again, even in the wake of that heartbreak, because the ride is worth the fall.

My phone pings a text from the coffee table where I left it. Reluctantly, I pry myself up and off the floor, wiping away at my tears, only to have them start again when I read the message from Jameson.

Take a chance on me. Let go, Lee. I promise I'll catch you. I'll never let you hit the ground again.

Let go and you'll find your answers. It's what my father had said to me in the car after I left Jameson at the beach?

Before I can text back or even form a coherent thought in my brain, another text comes in.

I'm downstairs at the back entrance—black town car. Please come to me.

I do. This time I don't hesitate. Because Jameson kept our entire relationship, and he just gave it to me in a box with a pretty bow. Because he had me permanently inked on his body. Because he still loves me, and I still love him, and at the end of the day, that's what life is all about. Loving and being loved. It's too short for anything else.

I grab my purse, stuff my keys and phone into it, check the mirror quickly to make sure I don't have mascara all over my face, and then I'm out the door. Vibrating impatiently in the elevator as it descends. The doors open and instead of looking left toward Central Park West, I head right, the direction that will lead me out to 74th street. I try not to run. I really do, but it feels nearly impossible. The moment I hit the street, looking left then right, I spot the car. It's double parked because this is New York and street parking is impossible.

The window rolls down and there he is, smiling at me with that barely-there dimple and those perfect white teeth and those blue eyes I love so much. His hair looks windswept and perfect. He gets out of the car and walks toward me, tall and gorgeous in a black sweater and jeans. My heart. Oh God, my heart is beating so fast I'm tempted to place my hand over my chest to try and slow it down. I smile, doing my best to stop my giddy laughter from bubbling at my lips.

His arms wrap around my body, and before I know it, I'm tucked into his chest as he buries his face in my neck, inhaling deeply like he hasn't seen me in decades and not hours. He pulls back, cups my face with both hands and stares into my eyes the way he did last night.

"I choose you. Above everything and everyone. I'll choose you over and over again. Every minute. Every second. With every piece of me, I'll choose you. And you'll never even have to think about it. It won't be a question in your mind because our love is like that. I choose you because I've made the other choice before and can speak from experience when I say it's not a mistake I would ever make again. For the rest of my life, it's only you, Lee. There is nothing else."

Tears leak from my eyes, one after another. His lips capture them, taking them in and kissing them away.

"I love you," he whispers against me, his lips still kissing me everywhere. My eyes. My cheeks. My forehead. My nose. My lips. "I'm absolutely crazy, insane, turned upside down in love with you. I know I'm the man, and therefore by definition, I'm supposed to be strong. But you make me so goddamn weak. You leave me raw and vulnerable. Barefoot and exposed. You tear down my defensives one by one. And I'm okay with that. I'll gladly walk around the world and back like that if it means you're there at the end waiting for me."

His eyes catch mine and I see it. I see that raw vulnerability. That question. That love. I see it all over him. I feel it flowing from him. The amount of times he's turned my talkative mouth mute is staggering.

No more doubts.

No more second guessing.

Because for the last six years, I've loved this man. Even when he broke my heart. Even when he hurt me. Love doesn't shut off in the face of pain. And even though I've fought him, fought this, there is no other place I want to be right now than here with him. Even if it's scary. Even if it's downright terrifying.

I don't know if this is forgiveness or acceptance. But I'm not sure it matters anymore. All of my arguments that felt so important, so vital, are now rendered insignificant. Like a switch has been turned on. Like that present, those keepsakes washed away the last of my doubt. Eliminated the last of my fears that were weighing me down. And now I feel...free. Light.

Maybe that's stupid and maybe it's not, but I can't find the part of me that cares enough to stop.

"Love me back, Lyric," he says at my silence, his voice frenzied, anxious. "Love me back forever. Please, baby. I'll do whatever I have to do to prove to you that I'm not going anywhere. That we're in this together. That you can trust me. I'll never hurt you again. I swear to God, I won't."

My gaze drops to his left arm that's annoyingly covered with black cashmere. Taking his arm in my hand, I tug up the fabric until I see the tattoo that is so much more beautiful in person. Especially since it is very healed.

"When did you get this?" I ask, running my fingers reverently over the rose and my name. His forearm is soft and smooth and warm.

"Three and a half years ago."

I look up at him, my fingers still touching, unable to stop their ministrations.

"After I flew out to see you in California only to find you with Ethan. I told myself you were happy. That you deserved a happiness I was clearly incapable of giving you. But I also told myself that the guy whose arms you were in wasn't your forever. That I was. That I was going to bide my time. That I'd get another chance. And until then, I wanted you with me."

I lean up on the tip of my toes and kiss him. I practically maul him in the middle of the street, not even caring who's around us. My fingers thread into his hair, my body presses against his, and I kiss him. I kiss him because I cannot speak. I have no words. It's all too much. Too perfect.

"I love you," I whisper into his mouth, and he swallows it down, altering the gravity our kiss as his tongue sweeps against mine. It becomes a promise. A vow that he means everything he says. That he's never going to hurt me again. That I can trust him.

Maybe it's that Jameson and I were never complicated. We were easy. Effortless. It was everything else that got in our way.

"Come with me?" he asks, pulling his lips from mine, pressing our foreheads together.

"Where are we going?"

"To see my dad," he laughs. "I have to. He's being moved into rehab today. But I want to spend the day with you. I want to spend every day with you, and I really can't wait anymore."

I peer beyond him at the waiting town car. "Is there a partition in that thing?"

He nods, his eyes glowing with fire.

"Can we put it up?"

Jameson growls, his mouth finding my neck, nipping and kissing and licking. "You want to get it on in the back of a town car? Have we become that cliché?"

"There is nothing cliché about it. But I don't think I can wait all day to kiss you more, and it's a long drive to Connecticut in Sunday traffic."

He nods against me. "It can be. Let's go."

I giggle at his eagerness, letting him take my hand and lead me to the car. The driver is there, opening the door for us, and I slip inside the warm cab, a swarm of butterflies taking flight inside my chest. My stomach does crazy somersaults. Jameson slides in beside me, raising that partition and then drawing me onto his lap until I'm straddling him, looking into his darkening blue eyes that are filled with so much love my breath hitches.

His hand runs through my hair, brushing it back and off my shoulders. The car begins to move as we silently stare into each other. I never thought I'd get here again. Never thought I could.

"You're so beautiful," he says softly. "And now that you're mine again, I'm never letting you go."

I not only want to believe him, I need to. If I'm going to take this leap of faith, jump back into the pit feet first and plow on full steam ahead, then I have to. There is no other alternative. And where the quiet voice in the back of my mind is still trying to remind me about the last four years, the much louder voice in the forefront of my mind is telling me that my heart is safe with him. That's he's going to protect it. Cherish it.

So, I do the only thing left to do. I let go. I fall blindly, kissing him with vigor. Reacquainting myself with his touch. His taste. His smell. With the sensation of his body against mine. His hand slides up the back of my blouse, pulling it up and over my head.

"So beautiful," he says again, his eyes feasting on my breasts before he buries his face in my cleavage, both hands coming up to cup and squeeze me through my bra. "This isn't how I pictured our first time back together. I never planned on making love to you in the back of a car on the way to see my father. I hoped I'd spend the day in tortured agony, and then after I took you to a romantic dinner, I'd beg you to come back to my place."

"Tortured agony, huh?"

He draws back with a grin. "Yup. The best sort."

"What if I don't want to wait?" I ask, tilting my head to the side, rolling my hips into his hard cock that's straining against the rigid fabric of his jeans.

He groans, his head dropping back against the seat. "Then I guess I have no choice but to give you exactly what you want."

"Good. Because all I want is you."

A smile lights up his face. "All I want is you, too. Always."

Our lips meet, and our clothes find their way to the floor of the car. When he slides inside of me, our bodies become one and our souls reunite in the back of a car driving from New York to Connecticut, I know beyond a shadow of a doubt that nothing has ever felt so right.

We get halfway to Connecticut only to have Dianne call me and tell us not to come. Evidently, the rehab my father has only been in for less than a day worked him to the point of exhaustion.

"He's sleeping and I don't foresee him waking anytime soon," she said. "Come tomorrow. He should be awake by then." I wanted to roll my eyes at that. God, this woman has no give in her when it comes to me.

But all I said was, "Okay. If he wakes up, tell him Lyric and I will be there tomorrow."

Lyric's eyes widened when I said that, and I realize what I intimated. I know she has a full day of recording tomorrow with the douchetard Harry.

But then she calmed down and said, "I'll be there." That's why I love this woman. And I do love her. Don't for a second believe that I take her giving herself back over to me for granted. Because I don't. I know what it means to have her trust replaced back in my hands. I covet it, dammit.

And really, it's so much more than I ever expected.

Lucky bastard 101: Don't fuck up. And this time, I don't need her to tutor me to get an A.

We make it back into the city and drive by her apartment under the pretenses of having her shower and change for the romantic dinner I'm so desperate to take her to. But when we drive along Central Park West, the sidewalk in front of her building is lined with the press.

"What the hell?" she whispers, clearly as bewildered as I am.

I slide my phone out of my pocket and punch in her name. Sure as shit, Harry Evans's press agent referred to him and Lyric as 'special friends.'

Awesome.

Looking over my shoulder, she spots the newest headline and does that heavy sigh thing she does when shit gets to be just a bit too much for her.

"I don't know, baby. But really, it's not something we have to handle tonight. Come home with me. We'll order take-out. Something yummy and meat-free, and we'll sit in front of my fireplace and drink delicious wine, and I'll go down on you for hours."

She laughs at that last part, but I'm not joking. That actually sounds like the definition of my perfect night. "I want veggie tacos—"

"With cooked onions, the guacamole on the side, and no sour cream. I know."

She grins at me. And I feel that grin everywhere. "I know you do. You know me."

I nod. "I know you."

And then I kiss her because I can. I can kiss her whenever I want. And that might be the best thing of all.

"I have to come back here tomorrow morning to get ready for work."

"I can have—" My phone blares out an annoyingly loud and persistent ring. Cane. "Hello?" I answer.

"She's in labor," he bursts out, his tone slightly hysterical. "Greta's water broke, and she's already in full-blown labor, and it's too soon, dude. She's only thirty-six weeks. I'm freaking the motherfuck out, and she's all Zen and shit, and I can't do this. I cannot have a baby tonight. What if something is wrong with it? What if it's sick and that's why it's coming out early?"

Lyric grabs the phone from me, bringing it to her ear as she points to the driver with a look that indicates I should tell him to head directly to the hospital.

"Hey asshole," she says into the phone, and I can't stop my small laugh. "We're on our way. And don't worry, thirty-six weeks isn't all that early. My sister Melody had her son at thirty-five, and he's the healthiest, sweetest boy in the world."

"I'm scared," I hear him admit, and I think he's only saying that because it's Lyric talking to him and not me.

"I know," she says with the most empathetic, nurturing tone ever. "But we're on our way. You're not alone, Cane. I swear. Whatever happens with you and Greta and this baby, you're not alone."

He blows out a breath like he's relieved and believes everything Lyric is telling him. I can hear it from here even though she has the phone and I don't.

"For the record, I've always loved you with him. I'm really glad you finally realized you two belong together. Even if he was a total twat for letting you go."

Lyric grins, laughs a little, her eyes flashing up to mine. "Me too," she says, and I lean in and kiss her because I absolutely have to. The call disconnects, and the driver takes us to the hospital.

We hop out of the car and I tip the man like I'm God and money is eternal and no object. He deserves it and I don't care because Greta is in early labor, Cane is freaking out, and Lyric is with me. This suddenly becomes one of those life moments. The ones that you hopefully look back on with smiles over drinks.

Travers comes bursting through the doors of the ED almost immediately after Lyric and I get there. He enfolds Lyric in a hug that seems to last forever. Those two always had an easy friendship, and I know he's missed her. I accept it, even if I want to beat my friend's ass for so much as touching her. They hug, but it's more than that. They hold each other. And I let them because I know what this moment means to each of them.

We go upstairs to the labor and delivery floor. *Jesus.* I'm scared out of my goddamn mind. What if this baby is not okay like Cane said? What if something goes wrong? Lyric takes my hand like she's reading my secret thoughts, and I glance over at her, suddenly choked up with emotion. I feel like a pussy for being this easily over-come, but I don't care enough to stop it or hold it at bay.

"This will be us one day," I say out of nowhere. "I'm going to marry you and get you so very pregnant. And then we'll make phone calls to all the people we love in a panic. But really, I cannot wait to see your big, beautiful belly with my child in it."

She blinks at me, her hazel eyes swirling more green than brown or gray. They do that when she's crying or they grow glassy. Which is exactly what they're doing this very minute.

"Not yet," she tells me, and I agree. I need to get through Cane having a baby first. Which brings me back to this waiting room. And the fact that our friends are somewhere else, delivering a slightly premature baby.

"Not yet," I echo, but now it's all I can think about. I cannot begin to fathom how drop-dead gorgeous Lyric will look with my baby growing in her body. I smile because it's going to happen. I'm going to marry Lyric one day, and she's going to carry my children. I'm going to buy her a house, and we're going to live somewhere awesome, and shit is going to be fucking perfect. Because that's how you always envision life—perfect.

Travers is pacing, Lyric is wandering around the on-floor baby gift shop, and I can't move. I'm just sitting here, my ass glued to this seat. An hour—a motherfucking hour—later, a woman with black hair and aqua eyes walks out. She's wearing scrubs and an exhausted but satisfied smile.

"Are you part of the Vandelay party?" she asks, and all of us freeze, turning our rapt attention to her. "My name is Gia Bianchi. I'm a midwife here at the hospital. Greta and Cane Vandelay wanted me to inform you that they delivered a healthy baby girl. They're all doing very well, and dad will be out to update you more in a few minutes."

I blink. And then I blow out a breath I didn't realize I was hold-ing. Travers and I exchange looks, and then Lyric breaks down into tears, thanking this Gia woman like they've known each other for years—complete with hugs and laughs and more tears. A baby girl. Holy God, Cane has a baby girl. He's going to be permanently strapped with a shotgun on his back once that poor thing hits twelve.

"A girl," Travers says, slightly in awe. I'm in awe as well. What the hell are we going to do with a baby girl? We are not men equipped to handle that. "I'm an uncle."

And now I laugh, because yeah, we're uncles. And this is one of those incredible moments that I spoke of earlier. And yeah, we're going to share this over drinks one day when we're all old as hell, life is good, and our kids are running around a backyard together.

Twenty minutes later, a glowing and bewildered-looking Cane comes out to greet us. He brings us back after hugging Lyric a bit longer than I would like and whispering shit into her ear, which cannot be good. But man, this baby. She's small. And so goddamn beautiful. Like holy shit beautiful. She has this soft-knit pink hat on her bald head, her eyes are this dark gray-blue, and her skin is red and sort of irritated, but she's perfect. Absolutely perfect.

Lyric and Greta hit it off instantly, talking about things that only women know, and I hold my new niece by friendship in my arms. She weighs nothing but smells incredible, and when she peers up at me with those big eyes, I realize I'm done.

"I want one," I say aloud, though I'm really only talking to Lyric. Even if we just got back together tonight.

"No," she says again, and I relent because it's only been a few hours. "What's her name?"

"Elena."

"Welcome to the world, Elena." Lyric joins me on the couch and quickly steals the little bundle from me, holding her close in a way I wouldn't understand. We don't linger. Greta, Cane, and Elena need time to themselves. On our way out, I ask Lyric once again, "Spend the night with me?"

"Yes," she says with a caveat. "I have to be at work by eight tomorrow, which means I need to go home first to change."

"That's fine. I'm planning on heading to see my dad early. I have some meetings in the afternoon."

She opens her mouth to say something else when we're bombarded by bright, flashing lights. Cameras and press are everywhere, and for a moment, I think there must be a celebrity behind us. Or that they have the wrong people. But then I hear them yell Lyric's name. They're asking her about Harry. About me. About a million different things all in rapid succession.

"How did they know I was here?" she asks, drawing into my side nervously. I shake my head, at a total loss until I spot our driver from earlier today off to the side, standing by the building. That motherfucker! He must have recognized Lyric and thought he could make some fast cash. I always forget who Lyric is. What world she grew up in. Mostly because we grew up in the same town and I've never thought of her as a rock star's daughter. As a celebrity in her own right. After the bullshit picture with Harry that's been spreading like wildfire, that status has only grown.

I had ordered us an Uber from inside the hospital, and as I check my phone, I see that it's here. But there is no way I can find it with all these people around us, clamoring for a photo and a sound-bite. Wrapping my arm around Lyric, I tuck her tighter into my side and begin to push through, anxious to get my girl out of here. The questions keep coming. The flashes of light relentless. Lyric stays quiet and finally, I find the car I ordered.

After slipping inside—with some difficulty because these assholes are no joke—I tell the driver to go and we speed off into the city. "Jesus," I whisper, running a hand through my hair before twisting my head to peer out the back window.

"It was one picture," she says softly, shaking her head like none of this makes sense. "They've photographed me with Ethan a million times. I've been seen walking through the streets of LA with other male artists. And yeah, some of those pics end up in magazines or on the internet, but it's never been like this before. I don't understand." She looks to me, her eyes wide. "Why are they suddenly so nuts over this Harry crap?"

"I don't know, baby." I take her hand in mine, give it a squeeze of reassurance. "But now that they got pictures of us, maybe it will die down."

"God, I hope so. It's going to make tomorrow at work very awkward. I'm also going to have to speak to Harry about this, but I don't want him to pull his album away."

"I doubt he will. He's worked with you before, and you've earned him a lot of money and awards."

Lyric just shakes her head and falls silent, still out of sorts from everything that just transpired. We reach my apartment, and mercifully, it's camera free. The moment the door shuts and locks behind us, she spins around to face me with an unreadable expression.

"I never thought we'd be back here," she says, waving her finger back and forth between us. "I'm nervous, Jameson. I'm scared that tomorrow when I wake up, something is going to happen that will pull us back apart. That I'll have to go back to California, or your work demands will change or—"

I silence her with a kiss before I cup her face in my hands. "If you go back to California, I go with you." She blinks, surprised by how quickly and effortlessly I said it. "My work is my work, and whatever it demands, it will always come second to you. To us. I was stupid, Lee. So reckless and stupid. I swear I'll never be that again. I just need you to try with me. To place just the smallest amount of faith in me and allow it to grow as I prove myself to you." I search her eyes. "Can you do that?"

"Yes," she says. "I love you, and I want to take this leap of faith with you."

"Thank God, because there is no going back for me now. You're mine and I'm never letting you go."

I sweep her up into my arms and carry her over to my sofa. I set her down gently, kiss her sweet, delectable mouth, and leave her to turn on the gas fireplace and order her those veggie tacos we never had. I return with a glass of wine for both of us. The way she looks, sprawled out on my couch, her blonde hair fanned out in every direction, her eyes sexy and sleepy, has my chest tightening as my heart beats wildly against the constraint it's not placed in.

God, this woman. She's breathed life back into me.

Reawaken my half-dead soul.

Her eyes have been locked on the dancing flames in my hearth, but when she feels me watching her, she turns to find me. She smiles and that tightness in my chest turns into a hummed electricity that pulses through my entire body.

"I've been locked on autopilot for so long. Wake up. Work out. Go to work. Sleep. That's been my life for the last four years, Lee. Automatic. Thoughtless. Dead. But now, here, looking at you?" I shake my head and smile. "I don't want to sleepwalk through anything ever again."

Her beautiful hazel eyes light up. Her hand lifting as she crooks a finger at me. Setting the glasses of wine on the coffee table, I get on top of her, propping myself up on my elbows, so I don't crush her and can simultaneously continue to gaze at her.

"We never have to. Because the world has picked us up and spun us around, but we finally managed to get it to turn in our favor. And I cannot wait until tomorrow and the day after that and the day after that, because no matter what, I get to spend them with you."

"How about you start by being inside me."

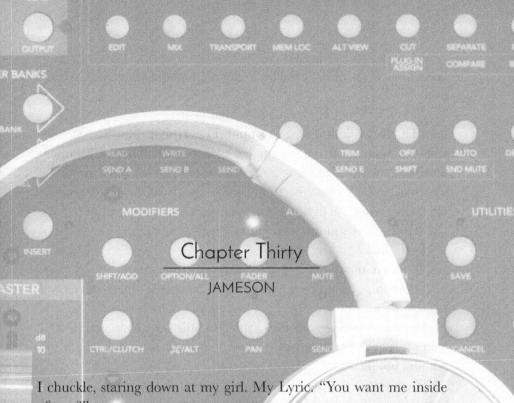

Chapter Thirty

JAMESON

I chuckle, staring down at my girl. My Lyric. "You want me inside of you?"

"Any time now would be great."

My hand sweeps across her cheek, up through her hair. I stare into her eyes. "You know, all my special plans for today have been ruined."

She smirks, titling her head on the couch and mussing her hair up. "How so?"

"Well, we were supposed to go see my father. That didn't happen. I wasn't supposed to have sex with you in a car. That did happen. I was supposed to bring you back here for a romantic dinner. Then Cane and Greta had their baby. I wanted tonight to be romantic as hell and I don't feel like I've done it any justice."

"How did you see this amazing romantic night going?" she questions, her hands coming up, her fingers running through my hair. It feels so good when she does that. I dip down, rubbing my nose along hers, stealing a kiss.

"I don't know. What were we talking about? I got distracted." She smiles up into my lips and I kiss her again. Unable to stop. "It's been four years. You feel like a dream I never want to wake up from."

"Then let's not. It's been a long four years."

"That's my fault. I was so stupid, Lee. How I thought you were with that guy…," I trail off, unable to finish that thought. So much time wasted. So many moments we missed out on. "It'll never be like that again. I swear it. You're mine and I will never let you go. No matter what. I'll fight the world for you."

"How about you just start with a kiss."

I grin into her. "*Just* a kiss?"

"I believe the phrasing I used was *start* with a kiss."

"Hmmm." I dip down and kiss her. But I don't linger the way I know she wants me to. "Do I get to pick where I kiss you?"

Her eyes sparkle with fire. With lust. It's been four years and I plan on spending the rest of my life giving this woman beneath me nothing but pleasure.

"Gentleman's choice," she rasps on a shaky breath, already knowing exactly where I intend to kiss her.

I give her a wicked grin, sliding down her body. And fuck. Her body. My god. Everything about her is my fantasy. My lips meet the crook of her neck, my tongue sweeping out to taste her sweet skin. I take my time. There is nothing about this moment I want to rush.

Fucking her in the car is exactly what we did.

We fucked.

Quick and dirty with only the partition and tinted windows to give us privacy. But now. Now is when I'm going to make her mine.

I slide up the hem of her shirt, cupping and squeezing her breasts over her bra. Lyric leans forward, helping me along by removing her shirt and bra. Normally I wouldn't let her do that, but my desire to see her bare is taking over everything.

Lyric's tits bounce free and my mouth instantly swoops in, needing a taste of these pretty pink nipples I've missed so much. Her skin is flushed, her chest rising and falling in quick, shallow breaths. I suck one peaked nipple into my mouth, my hand playing with the other, then switching it up.

"So goddamn gorgeous," I murmur into her chest, loving how

she makes that humming noise that drives me absolutely insane. My mouth comes back up to hers, stealing a fevered kiss. Something messy and wet as I work on the button and zipper of her pants.

I manage them halfway down her legs before I abandon her mouth, my lips skating down the valley between her breasts, along the smooth slope of her belly, down to her black, satin covered pussy. I stare at her panties for a moment, my cock straining in my pants, and I know I'm a lucky bastard.

I remove her jeans, running my finger up and down her panties, right over her already wet pussy. I can smell how aroused she is, her body squirming beneath my touch. "Jameson," she begs on a low, soft moan. She gasps as I run my fingertips up her inner thighs, spreading them wider for me.

I'm debating between removing her panties or simply sliding them to the side, but decide fuck it, and grasp the thin strings on either side of her slender hips and rip. The material doesn't stand a chance, and I grin up at her, loving how her eyes narrow and her lips part.

I shrug, smirking at her aggravated expression. "They were in my way."

"Now I'm going to have to go commando until I go home in the morning to get changed."

"Good. I like you commando. In fact, I think you should wear a dress tomorrow and no panties. Because when I come to get you after work, I plan to eat your pussy again and I'd hate to have to ruin another pair of your sexy panties."

She emits a harsh laugh. "I'll think about it. But until then how about you give me that kiss you promised me."

"Whatever my girl wants."

Bending down, I place a soft, wet kiss directly over her clit. Her hands fly down to my hair like she has no control over the action. I inhale deeply, closing my eyes and getting high on her smell. Being with Lyric again is like coming out of a coma. Everything is familiar and new all that the same time.

I suck her clit into my mouth, loving how her hips thrust up, searching for more. Lyric whimpers, her grip tightening in my hair

239

as I flick her bundle of nerves with my tongue. My finger slides into her opening, toying with it and she cries out, "Oh God."

"Does that feel good?"

Her eyes spring open, her chin dropping to look at me, my eyes peering up from between her thighs. "I can't tell if you're being ironic or not."

I grin, blowing air over her and watching as she shudders. "I just want to make sure what I'm doing feels good."

"Jameson," she warns. "I swear to god..."

"Oh, you're about to," I promise, kissing her clit as I thrust two fingers inside her. I roll my wrist until I hit the spot that I know will drive her over the edge. Slipping my fingers in and out, I suck on her harder, making out with her pussy like a goddamn teenager.

Starving. Without mercy.

"Jesus, hell," she whispers harshly, her neck arched back. One hand abandons my hair, going up cup and play with her tits. It's so sexy watching her touch herself, that I grind against my couch, so desperate to get inside of her. I alternate between kisses and licks, my tongue swirling as my fingers continue to pump harder and faster. Her legs start to tremble, her sounds growing louder, more urgent as she gets closer to the edge.

I increase the pressure of my mouth and then she's coming, the orgasm tearing through her, lighting her body up. She yanks on my hair, moaning and whimpering as her body rocks into me. And when I've wrenched every last ounce of her orgasm from her, her body sags back down into the couch, an arm tossed loosely over her chest.

I plant one last kiss over her sensitive clit and climb back up her, kissing her mouth as she pants into mine.

"I forgot how good you taste. How sweet your pussy is when it comes in my mouth."

"I think I saw stars with that one."

"Multicolored or just silver?"

One eye perks opens. "Silver."

"Room for improvement." I kiss her again and remove my sweater, my eyes staying on hers, brimming with raw need. I stand up quickly, staring down at my naked girl, her legs still spread and her pussy glistening. Lyric's cheeks are the most stunning rose color. The flesh on her chest too and mine clenches.

"I love you," I tell her, my eyes locked on hers. "More than anything, Lyric."

Her hand skims up along my now bare thighs, cupping me and dragging me back closer to her. "Come here," she whispers. I bend down and kiss her, my tongue sweeping into her mouth, my hand cupping her face. "I love you too, Jameson. Make love to me."

"With all my heart."

Lowering my body back over hers, I wrap one leg around my waist and sink into her all the way to the hilt. A growl gnashes past my lips, the sensation of Lyric's tight, wet heat almost my immediate undoing. My hands find her hair, my elbows bracketing her head, digging into the plush fabric of the sofa, and I start to move.

I go slow. I slide in and out of her, savoring every breath of pleasure she sets free in my body. Our eyes are one, our noses kissing. "Lyric," I moan into her, my forehead dropping down to hers as I adjust my hips and hit her at a new angle.

"More, Jameson. I need more."

My lips capture hers as I give her what she needs, tossing her other leg up and over my shoulder. My hips piston into her, over and over, harder, deeper, but never losing those eyes I love so much.

"You feel so good. *Fuck.* So good."

"Yes," she cries, her hands gripping my shoulders. "Yes. Like that."

I start to lose control, my body going wild as her pussy clenches my cock. My hand reaches between us, finding her clit and rubbing it while I start to pound into her. "Come Lee. I want to watch you come, baby." I rub her harder until she can't take it any longer. Her body explodes around me, a scream ripping from her chest. I follow her, coming along with her, our eyes open, staring into the other's.

My body sags into hers, rolling us so she's on top of me, her head on my chest over my racing heart. My fingers glide through her hair, holding her so close to me, our bodies still one.

That's the moment the doorbell rings with our food. Lyric gives out some combination of a giggle and a growl. "I'm hungry, but I don't want to move."

I kiss the crown of her head. "I'll get the food. You stay here. And then after we eat, I'm tucking you into bed."

"Okay," she says on a sleepy sigh. "Sounds perfect."

"You're perfect." My lips meet hers and I kiss her. I kiss her because I can. Because Lyric Rose is finally mine. Forever.

Epilogue

One year later

THE SOUND of the waves crashing on the beach creates a steady rhythm of background noise as the California evening sun seeps into my skin, warming me from within. In the distance, surfers sit on their boards, waiting for the perfect wave that seems to be coming with stubborn infrequency.

The sun is getting close to setting, and in Southern California, it's a sight that never grows old. An orb of orange fire as it lights up the sky, reflecting off all it touches.

This moment would be perfect, but it's missing one very important element. Jameson. He's been inside for most of the afternoon, working. Or so he told me. But I think I've also heard him making dinner, so I won't complain too much about that working-while-on-vacation stuff.

The past year together has flown by. Seriously, I cannot fathom where the time went. Last summer was spent in my new office in New York, in my new recording studio making music non-stop.

I finished Cyber's Law's album in record time, pun intended.

Well, record for them. It wasn't awkward with Harry the way I anticipated. In fact, when I came in that next morning after the whole paparazzi tabloid buzz, he wrapped me up in a friendly hug and laughed the whole thing off.

"Media," he said with a dramatic eye roll like they had run away with themselves without any help from a third party.

In truth, the photographs of Jameson and I leaving the hospital stormed the internet. My PR agent went nuts over it, and when she texted me late that night, I told her to tell the world Jameson and I were a couple and that Harry Evans was just a close friend. It was left at that, and since that time, Harry has been nothing but professional with me.

After I finished the two albums I was working on, I had to fly out to California. Gus Diamond from Wild Minds needed my spin on a song they were recording with Naomi Kent, another artist I've nurtured for the last several years. Plus, the band had more drama and fires that needed putting out.

I spent two full months out here with them, and though I was wary about how that time would go with Jameson and me on opposite ends of the country, I didn't need to be.

He was a man of his word.

I was his priority.

He flew out here three times during those two months, and every single night, he Facetimed me. He even sent me lingerie he wanted me to wear during some of our calls.

It was fun. It was sexy. And it kept the whole absence-makes-the-heart-grow-fonder thing going.

I knew that if we could make it through those two months, then we could make it through anything.

Something crashes inside the house, from my kitchen I presume, and I try my best to suppress my grin. Some men can cook, and some can't, and some are in between. Jameson is the latter, I'm afraid. He can make four or five things really well and the rest is just a disaster. I hear him growl under his breath, and seconds later, the back door slides open and shuts, his bare feet slapping against the wood of the deck as he makes his way over to me.

"You break my kitchen?"

"No," he grouses, his voice equally weary and irritated. "I was trying to be romantic and make you dinner since I was working all day while you were basking in the California sun."

Now I smile. "I know." Rolling my neck against my lounger, I gaze up at him through my sunglasses. Because that's his thing now. Trying to be romantic. He's insanely good at it.

His eyes are fixed on the ocean beyond the beach, staring off at the view I was just admiring. We've been back at my Malibu house for only a few days. It was his idea to take advantage of it for a little R & R, but he hasn't done much of that yet.

Me? Yeah, I've been taking advantage of all that California has to offer me, including seeing Cass, her husband, and my godson, Ben. Ethan decided he liked New York better than LA and has made it his permanent residence. No complaints from me.

And even though I miss it out here, this house and this beach and this sunset, my world is now in New York.

"Do you have to be a vegetarian?" he teases without bothering to avert his eyes from the horizon. "It makes everything so difficult."

"I've been that way since I was seven. Hard to change now."

"And since I wouldn't change a thing about you, I guess I'm stuck with meatless food."

"I don't mind you eating meat. It's sort of cute in a caveman way."

He chuckles lightly, turning to face me. "Scoot," he commands, climbing onto my lounger without waiting for me to follow his instructions. He wraps his arms around me, kissing his way up my neck to my ear, eliciting delicious tingles in his wake.

He's wearing a pale blue t-shirt, which makes his eyes look almost colorless in the bright sun and khaki shorts. His face has two-days' worth of black stubble, and I decide that I like vacation Jameson as much as Wall Street office Jameson.

My fingers run along the tattoo on his inner forearm. My tattoo. It might be my favorite thing on him, though that is a very difficult call to make as it has some stiff competition. Stiff competition that is pushing into my hip at this very moment.

"Why did you put the tattoo here?" I ask. I've always been curious.

"Because the flow of blood from the left hand goes directly up to the heart."

I smile, unable to stop my reaction to his words. He shifts our position, bringing me in front of him, my head resting on his chest as we watch that glowing ball of fire slowly descend into the ocean. The beach on the other side of the deck is private, but it's still crowded. It always is this time of day, as everyone stops whatever they're doing to watch the show.

"Too bad we can't bring this back to New York. Maybe we really should move back here."

I jab him in the stomach, and he laughs, squeezing me tighter against him. "I like our new place in the city."

"Me too," he whispers in my ear, kissing along the sensitive skin.

We bought a place in Chelsea a few months ago. We had been living separately but together, and with him being downtown and me being more uptown, it was aggravating. And inconvenient. So, we compromised and got something in between our respective workplaces. I like the neighborhood and the building we're in is very nice, and our apartment has a beautiful view and lots of natural light.

"But this is pretty spectacular."

I nod against him, enjoying his warmth as the sun sets, and wondering if life could get any better when he says, "I got you an anniversary present."

"What?" I laugh the word, twisting around and giving him a sideways glance. "It's not our anniversary."

"You sure about that, baby?"

I open my mouth to say that I am sure, but then I realize that I have no idea what our actual anniversary would be.

"Today is Elena's birthday." It is. We got her this really cool riding pony thing that I saw with her in the store and eventually had to drag her off of to get her to leave. They're in Sweden right now, because that's where Greta's father is from. Otherwise, I think we would have delayed our trip out here until after her party. "One

246

year ago, today, we got back together. That makes it our anniversary."

"Yeah," I muse, a little lost in that. "I never really thought about it. Christmas Eve was always the day I associated with us getting together."

He kisses the side of my head, shifting his weight so he can pull something out of his pocket and hand it to me. "I know it is, which is why I won't be upset that you didn't get me anything." I laugh, elbowing him once again. "Hey, quit that already and open your present."

He hands me a small, square black velvet box, and my heart picks up a few extra beats. He's silent. No getting onto one knee or offering professions of love, so I don't think this is *the box*.

And when I pry it open, I feel both disappointed that it's not and bemused with what's inside. It's a folded sheet of paper, and I wonder why he went to the trouble to put it in such a small box. Taking out the piece of paper, I find a reservation for a hotel and spa up in Napa.

"Wow," I exclaim, surprised. "This looks amazing. When do we go?"

"Tomorrow," he says softly, kissing along my jawline. "Do you like it? Greta suggested it, which means it's probably over-the-top nice. I even talked your father into letting us fly up there in his jet."

My eyes widen and my mouth pops open. He really put some serious thought into this, and I feel awful for not realizing what today meant to him. For not getting him anything to show him how much I love him.

"This is perfect," I say with a big smile I can't help, rolling over so I can snake my arms around his neck and kiss him. "You're perfect. Thank you, Jameson. This is just what I need. What we need. I can't wait to go."

He smiles that boyish smile and then leans in, kissing my lips, softly at first before deepening it. "Are you hungry?" he asks into my mouth. "Dinner should be ready."

I nod, rubbing our noses against each other's as I do. "Starving. What did you make me, oh romantic one?"

He chuckles into my mouth, nipping on my bottom lip. "A salad with all the things you like in it and lasagna because that's what I know how to make."

"Yum," I hum. "Let's go." I stand up. He rises after, taking my hand and intertwining our fingers, the last vestiges of the sun making the pink twilight that much prettier. Making this moment more special. "You're making me look like an awful girlfriend," I say, only half-kidding. Any further comment I had gets lodged in my throat when he opens the slider door for me, letting me enter first.

Candles. Oh my God, there are candles everywhere. Some in lanterns. Some on candle sticks. Some fat ones just set up on the table next to the bottle of champagne chilling in a bucket and two flutes. Multicolored rose petals are scattered everywhere. Across the table, the floor, the kitchen counter and beyond.

There are no overhead lights on. The entire room is glowing by candlelight with the sounds of the ocean behind us. It's the most beautiful, magical thing I've ever seen. My hand comes up to cover my mouth as tears threaten the backs of my eyes.

"Maybe that's because I'm hoping you'll be more than my girl-friend," he says, squeezing my hand and spinning me around just as he lowers himself onto one knee. And those tears that were threatening are now freely rolling down my face.

"Lyric, from the moment I first saw you over twenty years ago, I knew you were special. I think I must have loved you even way back then because when I look back on my life, I can't remember a time when I didn't love you. We've come so far this year. Experienced so many changes and grown so much as a couple. Where you go, I go. You're my tide. The glue that holds me together, and I can only hope that I'm that for you. I'll always be here for you. I'll always take care of you. And I'll love you until my last dying breath. It's only you, Lyric. Will you make me the luckiest man in the world and marry me?"

"Yes," I practically scream, but the sound gets muffled in my tears. "Yes," I say again, laughing with it this time. He stands up in an instant, enfolding me in his arms and lifting me off the ground as his mouth covers mine. "A million times, yes," I say into him. "I love you so much. But it's so much more than that, Jameson. It's the way you make butterflies erupt in my stomach every time you look at me. The way you make me feel like I'm home no matter where we are. The way you love me. I love the way you love, and that's exactly how I plan on loving you for the rest of our lives."

He kisses me like he's discovering my flavor in a whole new way. Like there is no more him or me, there is only us, and there is nothing that can divide us again. Nothing that can pull us apart. Jameson kisses me so hard I lose my breath. His tongue sweeps across mine one last time before he sets me down, taking my hand and sliding a large, emerald-cut diamond in a platinum setting onto my finger, both of us admiring the way it sparkles against the flicker of candlelight.

"I can't wait to marry you, Lee. I can't wait until your last name is my last name. Until I can call you my wife. I can't wait for all of it with you."

Thank you for reading Jameson and Lyric's story!
Want a glimpse of their future HEA?
**Keep reading HERE or check out my website
jsamanbooks.com!**

TURN the page for an exclusive look at the next book in the series, Love to Hate Her and dive into the world of the world's biggest rock band, Wild Minds.

Love to Hate Her

Viola

The air is hazy, thick with the cloying scent of weed as I meander my way through the throngs of people laughing, smoking, and generally having a great time. I don't belong here. At least that's how it feels. Especially since I have a sneaking suspicion what I'm about to discover.

"Hey, Vi," Henry, the bassist for the band, calls out to me with shock etched across his face as he grabs my arm and tugs me in for a bear hug. His tone is an infuriating concoction of surprise, delight, and panic. "What brings you out here?"

I'm tempted to laugh at that question, though it's far from funny. As such, it forces a frown instead of a smile. It really should be obvious. But maybe it's not anymore, and that only solidifies my resolve that I'm doing the right thing tonight.

Even if it sucks.

"I'm looking for Gus," I reply smoothly without even a hint of emotion, and his grin drops a notch.

Knowing that my boyfriend of four years is cheating on me should resemble something along the lines of being repeatedly stabbed in the back. Or heart. It should feel like death is imminent as the truth skewers my faith in men, my sense of self-worth, and my overall confidence into tiny bite-sized pieces of flesh. I should be a sniveling, slobbering mess of heartbreak. I should be nuclear-level pissed while simultaneously seeking and plotting a dramatic scene and meaningless revenge.

That's how it always goes for girls like me versus guys like Gus. And maybe I am just a touch of all those things. But right now, I just want to get this over with and go home.

"He's umm...," Henry's voice trails off as he makes a show of scanning the room as if he's genuinely trying to locate Gus amongst the revelry. My bet? He knows exactly where Gus is and is attempting to buy him and his current lady of the minute some time.

"It's cool," I say, plastering on a bright smile that I do not feel. "I'll find him."

Because when you've been friends with someone your entire life, in a relationship with them for the last four years, you don't expect them to betray you. You expect loyalty and honesty and respect. *You expect fucking respect, Gus!* Gus cheating and lying about it is none of those things.

"I can find him!" Henry jumps in quickly. "I'd probably have a better shot of locating him in here than you will. Ya know, cuz I'm taller so I can see around the crowds better. Do you want a drink or something? Why don't you go make yourself a drink while I look for him?"

I shake my head and step back when he moves to grasp my shoulder. "Don't cover for him, Henry. It just makes you a dick and him more of an ass."

Henry pivots to face me fully, a half-empty bottle of Cuervo in his hand, his eyes red-rimmed and glassy. He crumples, his shoulders sagging forward.

"I know. I'm sorry. But it's not what you think, Vi. It's not. It's just..." He waves his free hand around the room as if this should explain everything. Sex, drugs, and rock 'n' roll. This room is the horror show definition of that cliché.

I don't begrudge Gus or his bandmates success. I'm sublimely thrilled for them that their first album is taking off the way it is. It's been their dream—*our dream*—for as long as I've known them, and that's forever.

Which is why I should have ended it when Gus left for L.A., and I left for college.

I knew the temptations that were headed his way. I knew women would be throwing themselves at him and that I was going to be thousands of miles away living a different life.

Does it excuse Gus's actions? Hell no. Have I cheated on Gus once while in college? Absolutely not, and it isn't like I haven't had my own opportunities to do so.

But do I understand how this happened? Yeah. I do. I just held on too long.

"It was coming anyway," I tell Henry. "But it's nice to know he won't be lonely."

Yeah. That's sarcasm. And I can't help it, so I might as well allow the bitterness to make an entrance and take over the sadness that's been sitting in my stomach like a bad burger you can't digest. Especially as Gus has been adamantly denying his trysts, and Henry pretty much just confirmed them.

Henry's like a fish out of water, and I lean in and give him a hug. I always liked Henry.

"He's going to be so broken up about this, Vi. He loves you like crazy. Talks about you all the time."

I pull back, tilting my head and shrugging a shoulder. "That doesn't matter so much, though, does it? I'm at school, and he's out here with…" Now it's my turn to gaze about the room, my hand panning out to the side, reiterating my point. "Good luck with everything, Henry. I wish you all the success in the world. You guys deserve every good thing that's headed your way."

Henry scowls like I just ran over his dog as he shakes his head no at me. "You can't end it with him. You're a part of this. We wouldn't be here without you. We wouldn't be anything without you. You're like…," he scrunches up his nose as he thinks, "our fifth member. Our cheerleader."

"Maybe once," I concede, swallowing down the pain-laced nostalgia his words dredge up. The backs of my eyes burn, but I refuse to let any more tears fall over this. I cried myself out on the flight here, and now I'm done. "You guys don't need me anymore. You have plenty of other cheerleaders."

He opens his mouth to argue more before just as quickly closing it. "I'm sorry, Vi."

"I can't change it. It's done. Stay safe, okay? And be smart," I add.

"You too, babe. I'm gonna miss you."

This is the moment it hits me.

I'm not just saying goodbye to my relationship with Gus, but to my friendships with these guys. To late-night band practices and weekends spent down by the lake just hanging out. I'm saying goodbye to my entire childhood, knowing that we're all headed in different directions, and there is no middle ground with this. My throat constricts as I try to swallow, my insides twisting into knots.

Bolstering myself back up, I hold my head high.

I need to find Gus, and then I need to get out of here.

Wild Minds, the band that Gus is the second guitarist and backup singer for, opened for Cyber's Law tonight. *The* Cyber's Law. One of the hottest bands in the world. They're also on the same label that just signed Wild Minds. This show is a big deal. This contract an even bigger one.

This is their start.

They had given themselves two years to make it big. They needed less than one.

Heading toward the back of the room, I skirt around half-naked women dancing and people blowing lines of coke. It's dark in here. Most of the overhead lights are out, but the few that are on mix with the film of smoke, casting enough of a glow to see by way of shadows.

I bang into a table, apologizing to someone whose beer I spill when I catch movement out of the corner of my eye. Jasper, Gus's fraternal twin brother and the lead singer of the band, is tucked into an alcove, a redhead plastered against him as she sucks on his neck.

Where Gus is handsome, charming, and completely endearing, Jasper is the opposite.

He is sinfully gorgeous, no doubt about that, but he's distant, broody, artistic, and eternally happy to pass the limelight to an overeager Gus. Jasper was actually my first crush. Even my first kiss when we were fourteen. But that's where it ended. Since that day, and without explanation, I've hardly existed to him.

Sensing someone's watching, he pulls away from the girl on his neck, and our eyes meet in the miasma. His penetrating stare holds me annoyingly captive for a moment before he does a slow perusal of me. Unlike Henry, Jasper is not surprised to see me. In fact, his expression hardly registers any emotion at all. But the fire burning in his eyes tells a different story, and for reasons beyond my comprehension, I cannot tear myself away.

He tilts his head, a smirk curling up the corner of his lips, and I realize I've been standing here, staring at him with voyeuristic-quality engrossment for far too long.

But I don't know how to break this spell.

The smoldering blaze in his eyes is likely related to what the girl who was attached to his neck was doing to him. Yet somehow, it doesn't feel like that.

No, his focus is entirely on me.

And he's making sure I know it.

A rush of heat swirls across my skin, crawling up my face. I shake my head ever so slightly, stumbling back a step.

Noticing my inner turmoil, Jasper rights his body, forcing the girl away. She says something to him that he doesn't acknowledge or respond to. He runs a hand through his messy reddish-brown hair as he shifts, ready to come and speak to me when my field of vision is obscured.

Gus. I'd know him in my sleep.

My gaze drops, catching and sticking on his unzipped fly.

"You're here," he exclaims reverently, the thrill in his voice at seeing me unmistakable. I peek up and latch onto the fresh hickey on his neck. A hickey? Seriously? I didn't even know people still gave those. When I find his lazy gray eyes, I want to cry. Especially with the purple welt giving me the finger.

"I'm here."

He wraps me up in his arms, and I smell the woman who gave him that hickey. Her perfume possessively clings to his shirt, and I draw back, crinkling my nose in disgust.

"What's wrong, babe?" His thumb strokes my cheek. "Long flight?"

I step back, out of his grasp.

"Your fly is unzipped, and you have a hickey on your neck."

He blanches, his eyes dropping down to his groin while immediately zipping his family jewels back up. "I just took a leak."

I nod, but mostly because I'm not sure how much fight I have left in me. It *was* a long flight. And a long eight months before that. But still, it's one thing to know your boyfriend is cheating on you; it's another to see it in the flesh, literally.

"And the hickey?" I snap.

"Not what it looks like, Vi. I swear."

I reach up and cup his dark-blond stubbled jawline. My chest clenches. "Don't lie, Gus. It just ruins everything. I don't want to hate you, and if you lie to me now, I will."

He shakes his head violently against my hand, his expression pleading. "You're here, Vi. You're finally here. Nothing else matters."

"But it does. It all matters. The distance. The way our lives are diverging. I love you, Gus, but it's not like it used to be with us. None of it is." I swallow, my throat so tight it's hard to push the words out. "Let's end this now before it turns into bitterness and resentment."

"I could never resent you."

I inwardly sigh. He really doesn't get it. "But your penis might. You're fucking any woman who looks at you," I bite out. "Where does that leave me? How could you do that to me, Gus? To us? Do you have any idea how awful that feels?"

"I don't know. I didn't mean... You weren't here and I fucking missed you and I... I'm sorry. I'm so, so sorry."

"It doesn't matter anymore. It's over."

"You seriously flew out here to end it?" He's incredulous. And hurt. And I hate a hurt Gus. Even if we're not the stuff of happily ever afters, I do love this man. I'm just not so sure how in love with him I am anymore. He broke my heart. He broke my trust. And absence hasn't made my heart grow fonder. It's made it grow harder.

"Would you rather I ended it on the phone?" His face meets my neck, and my eyes fling open wide, only to find Jasper watching us from over Gus's shoulder. A curious observer, and my insides hurt all over again. His expression is a mask of apathy lined loosely with disdain. The way it's always been with me. All that earlier heat a thing of the past. I don't care either way.

"I don't want you to do it at all," Gus's voice is thick with regret as he holds me. "I love you, Vi. I love you so goddamn much. I just…"

"I know. I really do." I squeeze him back, feeling like I'm losing the only good part of my childhood in saying goodbye. "We're just in different spaces now, with different lives, and that's the way it's supposed to be."

He shakes his head against me, holding me so close and so tight, it's hard to breathe. He smells like that girl. But he smells like him underneath, and I cling to that last part because the scent of some unknown meaningless girl hurts too much. It rips me apart, knowing he did that to me.

To us.

I close my eyes for a moment and push that away. It's useless at this point, and I don't want to leave here more upset than I already am.

"Don't end it," he pleads, cupping my face and holding me the way he always has. "I can't lose you."

I lean up on my tiptoes and kiss his cheek. Tall bastard. "And I can't come in third. I handled second well enough, but not third."

"Third?"

"Music first. Other women second. Me third. It's done, Gus. No more lies or I'll hate you, and I'll hate myself."

257

"No," he forces out, but it's half-hearted. We're nineteen, and just too young. There isn't enough of the right type of love between us to fight harder for something we both know will never work. He doesn't want to be the bad guy. The cheating guy who pushes his long-time sweetheart-best-friend away. "You're breaking my heart." A tear leaks from my eye as I battle to stifle my sob. "I'm in love with you, and you're ending it." I blink back more tears, watching as he accepts what's happening. "I'm going to regret this," he states matter-of-factly. "Letting you go is going to be the regret of my life. Years from now, I'm going to hate myself for not making you stay."

But you're not fighting for me now.

"And that's why I have to go." I lean in and kiss him goodbye and then run like hell.

I make it outside, the heavy door slamming behind me. Warm, stale air brushes across my tacky skin, doing nothing to comfort or bring me clarity. I'm a mess of a woman as useless tears cling to my lashes.

"You're leaving already?" Jasper's voice catches me off guard, and I start. Why did he bother following me? "You just got here."

"Yes," I reply, twisting around to face the green eyes that have been fucking with my head since I caught them ten minutes ago. "You can't be surprised."

"He loves you. He's just lost in this life, ya know?" I shake my head at him. Jasper takes a long step in my direction, wanting to get closer and yet hesitant to. "So that's it? You just walk away from him?"

"I can't ignore the fact that he's been cheating on me."

"No. You can't. And I can't make excuses for it either."

"What do you want, Jasper? You can't honestly tell me you're disappointed to be rid of me."

"I see we're at the zero-fucks-left-to-give portion of the evening."

I continue to stare because that just about sums it up.

His eyes, filled with anger, indecision, and frustration, bounce all around, the street, the lights of the neighboring storefronts, the crowd still dispersing from the show, everywhere but at me. I can't stand this any longer, so I turn away and start to walk out into the Los Angeles night, away from the arena where Wild Minds–the band and the boys I've loved my whole life–just performed.

"It's yours," Jasper calls out, and I'm so confused by his hasty words that I freeze, turning back to him. His expression is completely exposed. Utterly vulnerable. And he's staring straight at me. Directly into my eyes in a way he hasn't dared since we were fourteen. My heart picks up a few extra beats, my breath held firmly in my chest. God, this man is so intense, I feel him in my fingernails.

"What is?" I finally ask when he doesn't follow that up.

"The album," he answers slowly, reluctantly, like it pains him to confess this, his darkest secret. "Every song on it is yours. All of them, I wrote about you."

I stand here, lost in space as I grasp just what he's saying. What it means, as random lyrics from random songs on their album flitter through my head. Song after song filled with the most achingly beautiful poetry.

"Jasper?" I whisper, my hand over my chest because I'm positive my heart never beat like this before.

But he is already at the door, having confessed his sins without waiting for absolution.

"Why did you tell me?" I yell after him, praying he'll stop. Needing him to explain this to me. *Why did you tell me, Jasper? Why did you pick this moment to ruin me?*

His hand rests on the frame of the now open door, his head bowed, his back to me. "Because I didn't think I'd ever get another chance, knowing I'll probably never see you again." He blows out a harsh breath. "But it doesn't change anything, Vi. Absolutely nothing. So you can move on without us and pretend like I never said a word."

And then the door slams shut behind him.

Jesus.

It takes me forever to move. To force myself to try and do just that. To try and forget his words and ignore the havoc they just created.

Knowing it's futile. Knowing those words will reside in me forever.

THE END

Want to know what happens next? Download Viola and Jasper's steamy forbidden romance, Love To Hate Her now! Free with Kindle Unlimited! You will also get more of Jameson and Lyric's story in this series!

End of Book Note

Hey everyone! This is the part where I get to talk to you all about this book. But before I can get to that, I have to thank a couple of people. Also, the incredible Connie Lafortune (author - check her out) was a beta. Oh, and of course my loving and supportive family. They rock!

Okay, people, so if you're a J. Saman fan, you might be scratching your heads. I mean, no crazy twist? No darkness or death? No love triangle? No obscure life situation that makes Jameson breaking up with Lyric understandable?

NO! This one came to me in a dream. No joke. I literally woke up one morning, grabbed my phone because it was the closest thing to me and started writing shit down. And then, like literally the next damn day, we left for freaking Disney Word. Meaning, I had zero time to write.That didn't stop me. I spent a few sleepless nights taking notes on my phone and writing down scenes, because I just had to get it out.

Anyhoo, this one turned out to be a traditional romance and I hope you still liked it. It might be a trope. It might follow formulary lines. But damn, I felt this story. I felt Lyric and Jameson. I wrote this story in 3 weeks. It flowed out of me and even though I kept

It flowed out of me and even though I kept second guessing my lack of twist or darkness, I stuck with it.

Because I came to a realization. Sometimes people genuinely fuck up! People make mistakes. People say the wrong thing. People let the love of their life go because we're all inherently stupid. So Jameson made an epic mistake. And it cost him years with Lyric. And then, maybe, Lyric gave in quickly. (I debated that one too).

But then, I put myself in her shoes. And I thought, if I really loved this guy, even after all these, even after he broke my heart, then would I really keep putting getting back together with him off if he was devoted and trying to show me just how much? Truth? I couldn't answer that. I seriously, could not. And I felt for Lyric. I felt her confusion and her struggle and her turmoil.

So I went with what felt right. Some of you might say that Lyric gave in too soon. But I'm prepared for that. Because love doesn't make sense. There is no perfect timeline for it. We can sit on the outside and look in and judge what we feel someone else should do, but in the real world, when we're engrossed in the emotion, it doesn't actually work like that. We follow our hearts and not logic. I think that's what I was trying to show. And I hope you forgave Jameson. I did. And then I didn't. And then I did, so...

Anyway, I hope you liked it. It was seriously a labor of passion and love. If you are a fan of mine, then you might have caught Gia Bianchi's (the midwife who delivered Cane and Greta's baby) cameo. You know I like to throw in characters from other books and that opportunity just felt too sweet to give up. I have another book coming out this fall sometime. Zero idea as to what date, but probably late September if I can get my stuff together, because that seems to be my schedule of things. If you keep reading, you'll get the first chapter. Starting very early next year, I'm going to be releasing two new series. I'm also going to be part of a big box set of contemporary romance. I'll be sure to let you know about everything. Especially if you're part of my newsletter.

Subscribe to my Newsletter- as mentioned above, you get a free book and my latest updates as well as promotions, freebies, etc. Find me on Facebook, Goodreads, Pinterest, Instagram and/or Twitter. I love talking with you. Oh, and please leave me a review!!

Made in the USA
Monee, IL
18 March 2025

14233471R00156